The Prophecy of the Kings

Book 1

Legacy of the Eldric

By David Burrows

The Prophecy of the Kings trilogy comprises
Book 1: Legacy of the Eldric
Book 2: Dragon Rider
Book 3: Shadow of the Demon

All rights reserved. No part of this publication may be reproduced, stored in a retrieval system, or transmitted in any form or by any means, electronic, mechanical or photocopying, recording or otherwise without the prior permission of the author.

This book is sold subject to the condition that it shall not, by the way of trade or otherwise, be lent, re-sold, hired out or otherwise circulated without the author's prior consent in any form of binding or cover other than that in which it is published and without a similar condition including this condition being imposed on the subsequent purchaser.

Third Edition
Copyright © David Burrows 2021
ISBN 978-0-9556760-5-5

Chapter 1
Escape

"Please, Emma," Kaplyn murmured, giving her his most charming smile, and using his softest tones. Emma pouted and Kaplyn felt that she was finally yielding. "You are very special to me and when I return…"

"And what will happen when you return? I am a serving maid. That is all. The best I can hope for is being your mistress," Emma snapped, flashing him an icy glare.

"You are special to me. You know that…" Kaplyn pleaded, coming closer and putting his hands on her shoulders, looking deep into her eyes. He smiled again, raising his eyebrows in a questioning manner.

Emma returned the smile and beneath his hands, he felt her soften.

"How long will you be gone?" she asked.

"Three weeks, perhaps four at the most," he replied. In truth, he had no idea. His plans were half formulated. Her face fell and she looked down.

"There is a fair at Perdrat. They will have archery and perhaps I can enter that. I need to go, Em," he said softly. "I'm stifling here; I hate it. I need an adventure before court life suffocates me."

Emma looked up and he could see the confusion in her eyes. "Most people can only dream of being in your position. How can you hate it so much?" she questioned.

"I just do," he replied "I have no freedom. I cannot go to the tavern with friends, get drunk or simply go on my own to the market. Bodyguards go with me everywhere. That's not a life."

"But you are a prince…"

"Some prince!" he interrupted. "I'm ninth in line to the throne and some of my own brothers and sisters barely recognise me. And father is threatening marriage to a princess. Thrace, of all places. He mentioned Gwen, but I wasn't paying much attention. I don't even know what she looks like and won't until it is too late."

Emma snorted, "You are twenty-one so I suppose marriage would be inevitable. Either way I will lose you, either to some misbegotten adventure or a rich strumpet from foreign lands."

"I need to escape. Please," he continued, "I am not asking a lot. Just distract the guard so that I can leave. Tonight, Sanfred is on duty. He is easily led so you should be fine."

"Not asking a lot? I know Sanfred. He'll have his hands all over me before I can say how the *Kalanth* are you?"

That was not quite what Kaplyn was hoping for. He just needed a distraction. To be fair he too knew Sanfred, and he knew that Sanfred fancied Emma. In terms of being easily distracted Sanfred was the prime choice. In his mind, it was tonight or never and, to escape, sacrifices were needed.

"Look, here's some gold," Kaplyn said taking out a purse with three sovereigns in that clinked encouragingly.

Emma's eyes widened as she felt the coins within. "I would help you even without a bribe," she said. "You know that."

"Of course I do," Kaplyn replied, taking her in his arms. The warmth of her body and scent of her hair almost made him reconsider the folly of his leaving, but then he was determined and gently he pushed her away.

"And when are you leaving?" Emma asked.

"Tonight," he replied, huskily.

Emma pulled back, staring at his face as though trying to commit every line to memory. "You *will* come back?" she asked.

"I will return with tales to make my brothers green with envy," Kaplyn grinned. He dreaded, however, what his father would say on his return and there was bound to be a punishment, but that was a problem for another day.

He went over to the bed and picked up his sword, buckling it about his waist. A saddlebag was next, filled with provisions for the road, and then four cloth sacks with lengths of twine followed. "I'm going to get Star," he said. "Go down to Sanfred shortly. Make sure he is *inside* the guardhouse, so he does not see me leave."

Kaplyn pulled on a grey woollen cloak, not particularly suited for an Allund prince, but one that might help him blend in with a crowd. Looking at himself in a mirror, he saw a young man in his early twenties, long dark hair partly obscuring a handsome face that often won the heart of a young woman. A scar running from his brow to his cheek made his face look more rugged. His brother, Tomlin who was four years older, had given it to him in a play fight that ended badly. Tomlin had sulked for weeks after their father had thrashed him.

Kaplyn had scrounged clothes so that he would blend in with the common folk. His linen shirt and wool trousers he had stolen from the laundry. He wore a leather jerkin, secretly bought at the market several weeks earlier. That had been an adventure all of its own. He had sneaked out of the palace one afternoon when the press of traffic leaving the palace grounds was at its heaviest. His riding boots were his own though and expensive, and these and his sword were the only items that might betray his privileged upbringing.

Kaplyn kissed Emma and, without a backward glance, left the plush rooms of his childhood, striding swiftly along the deserted corridors, thankful for the thick carpet that silenced his footfalls. Lanterns lit the brightly decorated corridors which, as a child, made playing when he should have been abed fun. Now, he cursed their light, preferring darkness to cover his escape.

Kaplyn's heart was hammering, but even still, he grinned broadly. He was doing it. He was escaping. Through silent corridors, he traced his way to an exit. After descending a tight spiral stair, he made it to the palace back door without meeting anyone. Pausing by the heavy oak door, he listened before opening it a crack. As the door swung silently inwards, the smell of the stables greeted him. He could not believe it was going so easily. The sounds of voices came to his ears, but the speakers were a long way off judging by the muffled tones.

Stepping out into the night, he was surprised by how mild it was. It was early spring, and the scent of blossom hung in the air, carrying with it an aspiration of better things to come. Quickening his pace, he hurried to the stables, striding into the deep shadow of the open door and grateful at least to be out of sight, albeit for a while. Horses fidgeted, heavy bodies thumped against wooden stalls, and hooves clattered on the stone floor. Kaplyn hurried to Star's stable, swinging open the wooden gate confining her. Star dipped her head in welcome.

On a peg, he took down his bow and a full quiver he left there for hunting trips. That was the only time he felt free. Stalking game in local woods was a favourite pastime. Farnham, the gamekeeper often invited him out to hunt pheasant and other game, depending on the time of year. Farnham was the closest Kaplyn had to a friend, and he was grateful for the lessons in tracking and general fieldcraft.

Next, he took the cloth sacks and tied one about each of Star's hooves. He had no idea how effective these would be at dampening any noise Star might make, but it was worth a try. Star nickered and, knowing her as he did, he sensed that she did not understand what was happening.

"Don't worry," he whispered stroking her warm flank. "Just a night ride. That's all."

He went to fetch a saddle and a blanket and then set about preparing Star for their journey, talking to her softly all the while. Once he had completed his preparations, he took her rein and led her from the stable. This was going to be the difficult part, he realised, leading Star across the cobbled roads to the small gate through the internal wall, protecting the palace and linking it to the town. To one side of the gate was a guard house and inside Sanfred would hopefully be paying Emma his undivided attention. Kaplyn felt a pang of jealousy. He genuinely cared for Emma. Once through the gate though, he was confident he would escape.

Even with the sack cloths, Star's hooves sounded loud to Kaplyn's fretful mind. He was thankful when he came in sight of the gate leading away from the palace, and he glanced warily at the small guard house to one side. No lights showed, and he blessed Emma for there was no sign of Sanfred. Hurriedly he led Star towards his goal, the pounding of his heart in his ears sounding loud enough to alert anyone in the vicinity. A few yards away, behind a door leading to the palace gardens, a dog started to bark.

Kaplyn quickened his pace, the dog's frantic barks ringing in his ears, but then he was alongside the gate. His skin prickled with excitement, and, at any moment, he feared a shout of discovery, but nothing happened. Then, all at once, he was through and before him a narrow road, flanked with tall rickety-looking buildings, led to the main city gates and freedom. The shops to either side had their shutters drawn but, even at this early hour there were lights shining from inside and the sounds of activity within.

A little farther on and he met the first people. Probably servants or staff going to bakeries or other employment to light fires. Some cast Kaplyn enquiring looks and he feared that his clothes blended less well with the common folk than he thought. It then dawned on him what the problem was. Star still had the sack cloths over her hooves. He stopped to remove them before continuing, but the din of her iron shod hooves on the cobbles echoed from the stone buildings, making him wince. Kaplyn retreated deeper into shadow in the lee of a large building, where he paused, waiting for the dawn and the opening of the city gates.

More people appeared and with them the occasional cart pulled by tired, dispirited looking horses. Soon, Kaplyn could see the faces of passers-by more clearly and glancing up he realised that the sky was less black. His moment had come. Kaplyn tagged behind a passing horse and cart. With his heart in his throat, he followed the flow of traffic to the gates where guards were only just swinging the gates open and waving traffic out. There was no attempt to stop anyone leaving, and Kaplyn simply rode through the opening as though he had every right to do so.

A short way from the city walls, he kicked Star into a trot, weaving between carts to get to the open road ahead. A smile creased his face, and he punched the air. "Yes!" he exalted, softly. He had escaped, but what future lay before him he did not know. This was the most significant adventure of his life. Finally, he was alone.

Chapter 2
Ambush

The cracking of dry branches snapped Lars from his melancholy. Daydreaming was dangerous, especially in a wood with night fast approaching. Lars' staff came up automatically and he turned to face the potential threat. A man crashed through the thick undergrowth; a cudgel raised in his right fist. His wild eyes screamed silent hatred as he bore down on the big man. Lars was a fighter, and his instinct took over. Other men might have blocked the cudgel's downward stroke, but Lars knew that time was crucial in a brawl. Without thinking, he lashed out with a straight-arm blow, aiming the staff's end at the man's throat, using the extended reach to his advantage.

The combination of the man's momentum and Lars' blow snapped his assailant's head back, jarring Lars' arm. His assailant's legs buckled, and he fell to the woodland floor, a scream impossible through his damaged throat. His eyes bulged and his hands went to his windpipe as he thrashed for air, grunting with the effort to breathe. Turning, Lars sought new enemies, and, to his chagrin, he saw several shapes moving through the trees, forming a ring of ragged-looking men around him. Seeing their comrade disabled so quickly the men were clearly cautious, advancing only slowly and trying to let others lead the attack, but greed and poverty drove them on.

"Surround him," one of the men shouted.

Lars cursed his earlier lapse of concentration. A foolish mistake he should never had made Slowly he turned, assessing the men before him, his staff held out, ready to counter an attack. They were a mixed bunch. Dirt made their appearance even more threatening. A smell of unwashed bodies assailed Lars. He knew that these were desperate men. Their clothes were torn and badly patched in places. All were armed with an assortment of cudgels, knives and two of them had swords.

"Move in together," the man who had spoken earlier demanded. He was clearly their leader. He pointed his sword towards Lars but did not advance himself. Lars kept turning, but no one moved. His eyes kept straying to the leader's sword, speckled with rust, the edge chipped and blunt. If the blade did not kill him, blood poisoning would. *Focus, watch their shoulders and eyes, not their weapons,* he thought.

The wounded man's thrashing became wilder. Others glanced down at him. His face had turned blue, and his tongue protruded as though seeking to absorb the air he so desperately needed. A few final kicks and then he was still, his body contorted in the final spasm.

"He's killed Ballan," one of the shorter men said unnecessarily. The others grumbled and then one man shouted a curse, leaping forward, his knife raised. Lars' back was to him, but hearing the shout and cracking of twigs, he spun around, sweeping the staff in an arc. The man ducked back as the staff whistled by his head, his eyes instantly turning from anger to fear. Lars stabbed down at him, but he was already scuttling back out of range.

"*He's one man*! Everyone, attack him!" their leader shouted.

"You've got a sword. You attack him," a man sneered.

Lars stared into the leader's eyes, daring him. He was as tall as Lars was, but lean. His nose must have been broken many times and so odd was the shape that it was barely recognisable. The leader waved at Lars with the sword's tip. "After three," he said. "One, two—*three!*" He screamed, lunging forward.

Lars threw the staff forward, allowing it to slip through his fingers until he judged the length right. He grabbed the staff before the end left his hand and punched at the leader. The staff jolted as it cracked into his face, but he was already turning, using all his strength he swung the staff in a wide circle. Lars was strong and he put all his effort into the blow. The wood whooshed through the air and his attackers rocked back on their heels, their eyes wide with fright as they were brought to a sudden halt.

The leader fell back, cursing and clutching his head in his free hand. When he removed his hand to inspect it for blood, there was a neat red circle on his brow where Lars' blow had connected.

"Anyone else who moves, dies," Lars announced. His heart hammered and he felt blood rush to his face. These men were bullies and, no doubt, cowards, but their numbers might overcome their fear.

He started turning again so he could see them all. "Kill him," a man wearing a fleece urged. He spat at Lars but made no move himself.

"He isn't worth it," another man said. He was fat and bald. One eye looked infected and was weeping, making it look like he was crying.

"He looks as poor as we do," the man with the fleece commented. "I doubt if he has any coin."

"We are not quitting *now!*" the leader said. "He killed Ballan!"

"What do you care? You hated him," the man with the weeping eye growled.

The leader smiled. Black gaps made his teeth seem more uneven. "Not until this fat pig is dead," he spat.

"We need a bow," one man said.

"Then go back to the camp and get one," the leader raged. The man did not need further urging, and ran off between the trees, disappearing in an instant in the growing gloom.

Lars muttered a prayer, "*Slathor*, give me strength!"

"What did he say?" one of his tormenters asked.

"How *the Kalanth* do I know!" the leader roared.

Lars realised he had to do something before the other man returned with a bow. Turning, he tried to decide which man might break if he charged him. He assessed each man in turn and soon found a candidate, a short man with wild dancing eyes and an ugly, uncaring face. His opponent held a sword awkwardly but if Lars had judged correctly, the sword would not matter. The man was also closest to the tree line, and if Lars could make it there then he could escape into the darkness.

His mind made up, Lars roared, leaping at the man, and swinging his staff. He had selected his target well, but, instead of fleeing, the man stood his ground, petrified by the suddenness of the larger man's attack. Lars swung his staff, its length keeping him from the other man's sword. The staff cracked against the other man's temple sending him flying. The blow was well timed, and its shock raced along Lars' arm.

Not stopping, Lars leapt over the body as two men sought to cut off his escape. Now that the action had started, adrenalin conquered the other men's fear. With shouts, they were all converging in on the big man. Lars flicked the staff out at the man on his right, missing his opponent who dodged to one side. It slowed him, but already the man to Lars' left was closing the gap.

"He's killed Arland!" Lars heard from behind him. "Take him alive!"

Something heavy slammed into Lars' back, catching him between the shoulder blades and knocking the breath from his body. Lars stumbled forward, his attack on the man to his left failing as his loss of balance threw off his aim. Lars gasped for air as the man to his left grabbed his staff but, rather than slow down, Lars let go, abandoning the weapon. The other man, not expecting to take the weapon so easily, lost his balance and fell heavily to the ground.

Someone from behind Lars tumbled into his legs, throwing Lars to the woodland carpet. Another man lashed out with his cudgel, striking Lars across the shoulders. He gritted his teeth and grabbed a handful of dirt in agony.

"I want him alive," the leader roared.

Twisting, Lars threw one man off him, but the others had caught up. Fear of their leader stopped their blows. Lars lashed out with his fist, catching one man under the chin, and throwing him backward. Someone grabbed his arm, and a man threw himself across his legs. Roaring his defiance, Lars threw out another punch. Then, Lars yelled as his hair was grabbed from behind, forcing his head back. A knife pricked his flesh, and a thin trickle of blood ran down his neck. Lars stilled.

"Don't move," the man with the knife threatened. His breath was foul and combined with the stink of his clothing was almost overpowering.

Cursing, the leader ran at Lars and booted him in the face. Lars rocked back on the ground while the men struggled to hold him down.

"You killed my brother," the leader screamed, kicking Lars in the ribs. "Tie his hands and feet. I will make you suffer," the leader continued, breathless with rage, his eyes bulging and spittle running down his chin.

The men obeyed and shortly Lars could not move. "Pick him up and carry him to the camp," the leader ordered.

It took three men to lift Lars, whilst two more picked up the body of the short man Lars had killed. Lars could see the bruise on his temple where he had crushed his skull.

Lars tried to escape, and his efforts caused the men carrying him to let go. He made it to his knees before the leader stood over him, his sword aimed at Lars' heart. "Tonight, you will die," he said. "Slowly—and before you die you will beg me for mercy, but do not expect to receive any."

Lars summoned all his strength, trying to break his bonds. He must not die. He had to find his wife and son. With a roar of rage, he threw every bit of his strength against his bonds. His muscles bunched and, for the briefest moment, he felt his bonds give.

The pommel of the leader's sword crashed against his temple, blackness engulfed him, and he knew no more.

Chapter 3
A Chance Encounter

Kaplyn reined Star to a halt, pulling gently on the reins. A distant scream some distance ahead echoed in his mind. What sort of animal could make such a noise? Breathlessly he waited for another sound, but none came. Even the woodland birds and animals fell silent at the inhuman cry.

Silently he cursed himself for being a fool. He should not have entered the wood. The path he was following had long since petered out and to make matters worse he hadn't a clue where he was. That was not quite true; he was in a wood somewhere between Dundalk, his home, and Pendrat, his destination. His earlier excitement had waned. His stomach growled and he shivered. He hated to admit it, but he was afraid, which was a new and unwelcome experience.

Never had he felt so alone. Always, there were people close by. Now his neighbours might be outlaws, krell or worse. As a child he had often heard tales of krell. No doubt, few people alive had ever seen one, but the tales alone were frightening enough. Monsters that haunted the night, killing people and drinking their blood. Or so he had been told. He glanced around, judging it too dark to ride safely, and perhaps his fear getting the better of him. Sighing, he dismounted before patting Star's flank.

"Good girl," he said, more to hear a voice rather than to calm her.

Wearily he took her rein and led her on, looking for somewhere safe to camp. The scream had unnerved him and, more than anything, he craved the company of people. He couldn't keep the tales from his childhood from his mind, of krell and other fell creatures that roamed the wild. He tried to dismiss them by reminding himself that these were fairy tales and nothing more, but a fear of the unknown kept returning to haunt him. The Krell Wars were real enough, but they were eons ago. Krell, if they still existed, inhabited only the wildest regions such as the mountains and forests of the world. The wood he was in was far too small and too near to the Allund capital. The king's troops regularly patrolled between the cities, the way was safe he tried to convince himself, or at least it ought to be...

Kaplyn stopped. The trees were merciless, growing close together, making him force a passage. His hands and face were scratched and sweat now made these sting. What had made him stop though was not the trees, but a faint glow ahead. He squinted, trying to reassure himself that there was indeed a light. He continued forward slowly when he heard voices. *Perhaps there was a clearing ahead. Charcoal workers*, he thought hopefully. He smelled the air but could only scent damp and decaying wood.

Loosely looping Star's rein over a branch, he unhooked his bow from the saddle and threw his quiver over his shoulder. He bent the bow to string it and once armed felt marginally better. Taking stock of his surroundings, he inched forward trying to make no noise. All around him was the faint rustling of branches and old leaves as the wind blew softly. Before too long he saw a line of trees and just beyond these, a small rise crowned with thick bushes. He became convinced that between the trees there was indeed a glow. Dropping to all fours, he crawled towards the bushes, parting branches to see through.

Before him, the ground dipped into a glade where a large fire cast enough light to see by. A man was pacing around the fire and four men were astride a fallen tree trunk whilst three others slouched on the ground. They gave the impression of men used to living rough, hardened by nights spent in the wild and, now he had seen them, there was no doubting that they were outlaws. Some wore leather tunics torn and stained with wear, while others had thick woollen cloaks whose colour had long since faded. Their weapons were crude, mainly cudgels or knives, although one wore a sword tucked through his belt. Only the pacing man wore both a sword and scabbard, probably taken as plunder.

The pacing man abruptly stood still and threw an arm out, indicating beyond the circle of light to the rear of the camp.

"Bring him here," he growled ominously. His voice carried easily to Kaplyn. "It's time to deal with the man who killed my brother."

Two men arose from the log and walked away from Kaplyn, disappearing amongst the trees. Kaplyn ducked lower, thinking that he must return to Star. Just as he was about to leave, the men returned, pushing another man roughly before them. He stumbled forward a few steps in a manner suggesting his hands were bound behind his back.

He was a big man, broad across the chest, with powerful shoulders. His hair and beard were blond, which was a surprise to Kaplyn for Allunds were brown-haired and Thracians marginally fairer.

At that moment, his captives were forcing him to his knees, kicking the back of his legs and pushing down on his shoulders. The prisoner resisted but their efforts were too much for him and he collapsed to his knees.

Striding towards the prisoner the leader raised his foot and slammed his heel into the prisoner's face. Toppling backwards, the big man managed to stop himself from falling. When he looked up his beard was flecked with blood.

"You will not have an easy death," the outlaw spat with undisguised hatred. "You killed two of *my* men. One was my brother—for that, you'll pay." He circled the prisoner before coming to a halt behind him. "The only thing is … I haven't decided how to kill you—*yet*."

"Let me finish him," one of the men sitting on the trunk offered, holding a long knife in his hand, his eyes shining with anticipation.

The leader shook his head. "He's mine. I want to see him squirm. Make sure that you hold him firmly." He waved his hand in the direction of two of his men. He then crossed to the fire as his men leapt to their feet to stand either side of the kneeling prisoner, each gripping a shoulder. The leader's dagger reflected the firelight as he drew it before plunging it into the fire.

"Let's see how strong he is without his eyes," he said through gritted teeth.

In his hiding place, Kaplyn tensed, and felt the colour drain from his face. Part of him wanted to leave and yet another part of him wanted to aid the prisoner—but what could he do? If the outlaws caught him, they would kill him. It was a dreadful dilemma, to stay and help or to leave, knowing that an innocent man might die because of that decision. Watching the outlaws torment the prisoner, anger blossomed in his chest and suddenly he knew what he had to do.

Crawling backwards, he sought deeper shadows before rubbing soil on his face to mask its whiteness, spitting on his fingers to soften the soil. Rising slowly, he stood braced against the trunk of a tree. His hunting bow, while not meant for battle, was a stout weapon. He placed two arrows point first into the ground by his side before nocking a third. Taking aim, he prayed to the Kalanth for an alternative.

The men either side of the prisoner struggled to hold him down as he fought against them. Removing the now glowing knife from the fire, their leader advanced, clearly enjoying himself as he brought his knife deliberately towards the other man's eyes.

Kaplyn struggled with his conscience until he could not afford to wait any longer. Drawing his bow a fraction more, he released the arrow. A scream of agony rang through the trees as the arrow hammered into the outlaw's shoulder. With a mingled wail of pain and rage, he dropped his knife.

In quick succession, Kaplyn loosed the other two arrows. He was good with a bow and could put ten arrows in flight in a count of sixty heartbeats. His aim, after the first arrow would not be good, but the effect was what he wanted.

One arrow hit the trunk the men were sitting on and the other flashed between two others. All eyes turned towards the trees, looking in Kaplyn's general direction but not at him. He kept still and it was soon clear from their bewildered looks that the outlaws could not see him. Silently he drew another arrow from his sheath and nocked it.

As though released from a spell, the men sitting on the fallen trunk flung themselves backward, behind the improvised barricade. The two men holding the prisoner let go as they, too, dived for cover behind the trunk.

"Who's out there?" one man cried out to his companions.

"Town guard?" came a muffled reply.

"Can't be," said another. "We're too far from the town. The guard would never come this far."

"King's troops then?" came back a timid reply.

"Quiet!" snapped the leader. "Cease wagging your tongues and use your bloody ears!" He alone was standing, clutching his wound; his face twisted in pain. After a moment, he seemed satisfied. "Get up," he ordered. When no one responded, he went over to the log and delivered a hefty kick to some poor unfortunate. A grunt followed.

"There's only one man, otherwise they would have attacked by now. Get out there and find whoever shot me!"

An outlaw timidly climbed to his feet. Kaplyn aimed and loosed another arrow that thudded into the trunk sufficiently close to send the man scurrying back for cover.

"He's a good shot," Kaplyn heard.

"I don't care," the outlaw chief screamed. "Get out there and bring me his head!" He delivered another kick, and Kaplyn heard a further grunt of pain.

Finally, one man dared to rise, either out of bravado or because of his leader's brutality. The man sprinted for the line of trees to Kaplyn's left. Kaplyn let fly an arrow, but his aim was poor, and the man escaped. Time was against him now with an outlaw amongst the trees. Again, he feared capture, but he could not leave the other man—not now.

Seeing their colleague's success and fearful of their leader's anger, two more men ran after the first. Events were now so out of control that Kaplyn had to shoot more accurately. The arrow hit one of the running men in the lower back, spilling him to the ground with a cry of pain. Briefly, the man struggled to crawl forward, but his strength left him, and he collapsed. The other man managed to reach the tree line where he disappeared.

Behind the log no one dared move, even their leader dropped behind cover, still berating the others for their cowardice. Forgotten and recognising an opportunity to escape, the prisoner climbed with difficulty to his feet and started to run towards the trees in the opposite direction taken by the two outlaws.

The outlaw leader, seeing his prisoner escaping, shouted out in rage. He stood up. A well-placed arrow barely missed his head, causing him to drop back with a yelp of agony as the barb already in his arm bit deeper.

Kaplyn shot two more shafts at the tree trunk in quick succession before scooping up his quiver of dwindling arrows. He ran through the thick vegetation, aiming in the general direction the prisoner had taken. He had little difficulty in finding him, following the sound of cracking twigs and the louder snap of branches.

Before Kaplyn could reach him, the large blond man stopped and turned to face him; his feet firmly planted and defiance in his eyes, even though his hands were bound.

"I'm a friend," Kaplyn said, skidding to a halt.

The big man relaxed. "Untie me," he replied, turning his back, and offering his bound wrists.

Kaplyn wanted to continue running and the delay made his heart hammer even faster. However, he slung his bow across his back and drew a dagger. As quickly as he could, he cut the bonds.

The big man rubbed at his chafed wrists. "Thanks," he whispered.

"Go!" Kaplyn urged. "They'll be after us."

They jogged deeper into the wood, but branches lashed their flesh, forcing them to walk. In the confusion, Kaplyn had no idea where Star was. He was considering whether he could find her when something caught his attention. He grabbed the other man's shoulder, forcing him to crouch. Not far away he heard someone crashing through the vegetation.

"They're over here," someone shouted.

Kaplyn kept a firm grip on the other man's shoulder.

"Stay still," Kaplyn whispered. At first, he thought the outlaws had discovered them, but the sound of their passage through the vegetation was fading. "Come on," Kaplyn whispered and led them away from the direction the outlaws had gone, taking care to keep noise to a minimum.

After a while, Kaplyn said softly, "That was close. We nearly stumbled into an outlaw. Something must have distracted him."

"Probably an animal," the other man suggested softly.

Kaplyn nodded, thinking about Star. "We need to keep walking. They'll still be looking for us."

In silence, they continued for the better part of the night, stopping occasionally to listen for signs of pursuit. After several stops, Kaplyn decided they were finally safe; he collapsed where he stood, breathing a loud sigh of relief.

"I'm shattered," the big man said, sitting down across from Kaplyn with his back against a trunk. Dark rings circled his eyes and he looked barely able to stand. "Name's Lars," he said, holding out his hand. Kaplyn shook it.

"Kaplyn," he returned.

"I'm grateful you came along when you did."

"What happened?" Kaplyn whispered.

Lars shook his head. "I was foolish enough to enter the wood, that's what happened! They must have seen me as an easy target, armed only with a walking staff. I put up a fight, but when the second man fell, their leader went wild, ordering me to be taken alive. Their numbers overwhelmed me."

The two men fell silent for a moment, each listening to the night noises, trying to discern if the outlaws were still following them. Above, an owl hooted and then there was silence.

"I've never seen anyone with blond hair before. Where are you from?"

"Gorlanth. It's far across the sea."

"I've never heard of it."

Lars nodded. "Few people have. Few Allunders even know land exists across the sea. A storm keeps all, but the bravest captains, close to the shore. Every day I pray to return home, to my wife and son."

Kaplyn saw the hurt reflected deep within his eyes. In respect for the other man's need for silence, he turned his thoughts to their predicament, estimating that about half the night remained. "We need to leave," he announced at last.

"Can't we rest here, for a while at least? It would be safer continuing in the morning when it's light."

Kaplyn was not so sure. The wood made him nervous, and he was keen to leave. He conceded, however, that it was more dangerous travelling in the dark.

"Very well, we'll stay here, but we need to take turns on guard."

Lars nodded and Kaplyn offered to stand the first watch. For a while he sat awake, listening to Lars' snoring which seemed loud enough to attract a host of outlaws let alone whatever creatures lurked in the wood. Kaplyn thought about his brothers and how they would manage this situation. Their memory made him smile. Karlan, the eldest brother, was pompous in the extreme. He would have ordered Lars to stand watch while he slept soundly. For a moment, Kaplyn felt a pang of jealousy towards Lars. Why should he sleep while Kaplyn was awake? Then he considered the experience Lars had just suffered and decided to let him rest.

His thoughts turned to Emma, and he felt a twinge of guilt. She and Sanfred might be in trouble by now. He would make amends upon his return he decided, but the guilt remained.

He regretted the loss of his belongings and especially Star, nevertheless he realised there was no going back. He had his purse and a few gold coins secreted into the lining of his leather jerkin, so he could afford to replace his losses. Then his mind turned to the man he had shot. Even though he was an outlaw, he hoped he had not killed him. It was an uncomfortable thought and one that would prey on his mind for some time.

After a while, when Kaplyn felt that he could not stay awake any longer, he shook Lars' shoulder. The big man stirred and looked up blearily. "Your turn to keep guard," Kaplyn said.

Lars grumbled, sat up and looked out into the darkness. Kaplyn waited to make sure his companion was taking his duty seriously, then laid down and instantly was asleep.

Chapter 4
Pendrat

"Are you still angry?" Lars asked.

"You *were* meant to stand guard," Kaplyn complained. After setting off, they had struggled through the wood until finally emerging from the trees at about mid-morning. Presently they were crossing an open field and their boots tugged as they tangled with the long grass.

"Nothing happened though," Lars answered. "It was wrong, but I was *really* tired."

Kaplyn regarded the other man. The night before he had cut an imposing figure, but the light of day told a different story. He was carrying too much weight and the colour of his nose suggested he was fond of ale. However, now he looked genuinely sorry, like a chastised puppy.

Kaplyn was not happy though. Something had awoken him. Something he had not recognised. He had sat bolt upright, his arms flaying at whatever had disturbed his sleep and he could not get the image out of his mind. A face had peered down at him, green glowing flesh and almond eyes with a tongue that had flickered across small, pointed teeth. Kaplyn was sure that the creature had touched his forehead. Then Kaplyn had yelled, waking Lars who had clearly been asleep the whole time.

By the time Kaplyn was on his feet with his sword in his hand, whatever had been near had gone. He had felt peculiar ever since, tainted as though touched by something evil. He rubbed at his forehead and then looked at his hand but there was nothing to see. He wiped his hand on his trousers. He did not mention his experience to Lars. He now felt foolish, having jumped at the shadows. Upon sighting the creature his immediate thought had been of krell, but now imps and demons plagued his mind. Fairy tales, he scolded himself angrily.

"I suppose we are both rested," Kaplyn grumbled, in answer to Lars' earlier question.

Behind them a rook cawed, causing Kaplyn to glance back. Something had disturbed it, and its flurry of wings carried easily on the still air. His face fell and he groaned.

"Don't they ever give up?" Kaplyn said.

Lars looked around. Kaplyn could not tell how many outlaws were following; they were still some distance. He broke into a run, urging Lars to keep up.

Think! What were their options? Ahead, there were a couple of copses, but hiding was a last resort. A rabbit scampered from a thicket, startling Kaplyn. It zigzagged in front of them before bolting into a gorse bush. Kaplyn kept running. Lars lolled along by his side; his face flushed.

Rounding one end of a copse, Kaplyn saw a stockade wall. "A farm," he gasped. "Keep running, it's not far. We'll make it before they catch us."

Kaplyn risked glancing back; five figures were following and the gap between them had shortened. As he ran, his sword slapped against his thigh, and he feared it would trip him. He held it still with one hand whilst he ran, his bow slung across his back.

Returning his attention to his front, he had a better view of the farm. The palisade comprised logs lashed together, while peeking over the wall, thatched roofs supported chimneys, venting grey smoke against a blue sky.

"Ho the farm!" Kaplyn shouted, waving his arm as he ran. "Ho!" he shouted louder, catching sight of a figure silhouetted on the wall. The pungent smell of livestock mixed with wood smoke filled the air.

Within bow range, Kaplyn came to a halt and shortly Lars staggered to a halt by his side, panting heavily, his hands on his knees as he gasped for air. Kaplyn glanced back, but there was no sign of their pursuers who must have hidden in one of the copses, probably waiting to see what happened next.

By now, there were several figures on the wall and to Kaplyn's consternation some were armed with bows. Two men approached through a gate, both carrying pitchforks. The taller of the two was the older, grey haired and with a rugged face no doubt acquired from long days spent in the fields. The other man, probably the first man's son judging by his age, was darker haired and broader across the shoulder. Neither man smiled as they came to a halt before them.

Kaplyn could not read their expressions. "I'm Kaplyn. We are lost and fleeing outlaws. Last night they captured my companion here, Lars, and I managed to free him." By his side, Lars was red faced and still breathing hard.

At the mention of outlaws, the grey-haired man's eyes sought the land behind them. "How many?" It was a demand rather than a question.

"Five," Kaplyn answered.

The other man snorted. "Cowards—the lot of them. They're content to waylay a lone man, but they'll never attack here, with so many."

"I may have killed one of them last night," Kaplyn answered truthfully. "And Lars killed the chieftain's brother. That makes them more dangerous."

The farmer's stoic look broke as he smiled. "Did you now? Killed some of them, did you? Good for you."

"I want to buy a horse, and food," Kaplyn asked, sensing they had the farmer on their side.

"I have a horse, but it's not for riding," the farmer answered.

"I can pay for it," Kaplyn took out his purse, counting out fifteen silver *calder*.

The other man's eyes widened. "You'd better see the animal before offering your money." He turned to his companion. "Kroner, go and fetch bread and cheese for these men. And fetch them a skin of wine while you're about it."

The farmer then led them through the gates where two other men and a handful of children and women stared at them wide-eyed.

"Go on," the farmer said to the children. "Stop gawping and get on with your chores."

"Will you be all right? I mean, with the outlaws out there?" Kaplyn asked.

The farmer smiled. "As I said, outlaws are cowardly creatures. Besides, there will be more men here by nightfall when they come off the fields. Thanks for the warning though."

"Here we are," the farmer said as they arrived before a tall barn. Inside, a very stocky plough horse snorted and turned its gaze towards them as they entered. As Kaplyn approached it gently butted his shoulder, seeking a titbit. "You'll have to ride bareback as there isn't a saddle. Not one that would fit, that is."

"You have no other?" Kaplyn asked. The farmer shook his head.

The animal had been well looked after and was clearly big enough to carry them both. Sighing, he decided it would have to do and he offered the farmer the coins. At that moment, Kroner returned with food wrapped in a large cloth and a skin of wine.

"Would you like to stay for a meal?" the farmer offered.

"Thanks for the offer, but no," Kaplyn replied. "I need to get to Pendrat. I'm hoping to take part in the games."

"Really?" the farmer said, sounding impressed. "Which sport are you entering?"

"Archery," Kaplyn said. The farmer looked at Lars.

"I'm heading to Pendrat as well. I'm hoping to make money in the wrestling."

"Well good luck to both of you. If you return this way, let me know how you got on. Now, Pendrat is some distance away and you may struggle to get there by tonight. If you prefer, you are welcome to stay here for the night," the farmer offered, but Kaplyn shook his head.

"The sooner the outlaws see us leave, the safer for you and your family. Can you direct us? I have no idea where we are."

"Fortunately, you are not far from the Pendrat road." The farmer led them outside where some more women had joined the men folk to see the strangers. "Go that way for a quarter mile and then you'll find the highway. Bear left and just keep riding. We'll watch your trail for a while and make sure that no one follows you."

Kaplyn and Lars thanked the two men. At the gate, Kaplyn mounted but Lars struggled, muttering all the while. After several attempts, he finally admitted that he had not ridden before. His face flushed red with embarrassment. Kaplyn dismounted, cupping his hands to help him and then Kaplyn mounted in front of Lars. They set off, waving to the farmer and his family as they left.

As they rode, Kaplyn kept looking back but after a while became confident that any pursuit was far behind. However, he hoped he hadn't visited ill on the farmers.

Gradually, the land became more wooded, and the trees made Kaplyn nervous; he had preferred the open countryside. Lars was gripping his waist so firmly that Kaplyn was having difficulty breathing.

"Tell me about your homeland," Kaplyn asked, seeking to set the other man at ease.

There was a short delay and gradually Lars' grip relaxed. The horse swayed as it walked but being such a broad animal, their seat was secure, even without a saddle.

"It's beautiful," the big man started wistfully. "Although the weather is more extreme than it is here. It is colder in the winter and the nights are longer. The summers are warm, though, and the spring is glorious when violets carpet the meadows. And the mountains…" His voice caught and Kaplyn glanced back. Lars' jaw was firmly set, and his eyes sparkled with unshed tears. Kaplyn looked to their front, embarrassed to have seen the other man's pain.

Lars did not seem to notice and continued his tale. "My people live in villages along the coast. Our homes surround a central long hall. In the winter nights, we tell stories and drink beer.

"I miss it," he sniffed loudly. "You'll have to forgive me; I left behind my wife and son and have no way to get back to them." After a pause, he continued. "What about yourself—where are you from and what do you do?"

The question caught Kaplyn by surprise. "I'm from Dundalk," he managed after what he hoped wasn't too long a pause. "I served in the palace guard for a couple of years but didn't get on with one of the Hest Commanders, so I decided to leave." It was a lie, but close enough to the truth to be plausible.

"What's a hest?"

Kaplyn glanced back. "It's a small unit of men in the army. Usually about ten men." At that moment, a bird took flight at the side of the path, startling the horse and Kaplyn. He hoped it wasn't a sign for the lie that he told.

"The palace guard?" Lars said, suitably impressed.

"It sounds better than it was," Kaplyn answered, dreading any further questions. Swiftly he changed the subject and for the rest of the day they chatted about Allund and its people. By early evening, the scenery had changed, becoming gently undulating as soft sunlight pleasantly warmed their faces.

Kaplyn urged their mount to greater haste as the sun started to sink below the surrounding hills, casting long shadows across the narrow path. He was fretful that they had not yet seen Pendrat. The wild, as they had already found to their cost, was a dangerous place and they had been lucky that they had encountered nothing worse than outlaws.

Just when he was about to give in and suggest stopping for the night, they crested a hill and at last, below them, was Pendrat. The path they were following ended at a rickety looking bridge, spanning a deep gorge. The other end of the bridge led to the main gates, which for the moment at least were open. Within the town, lamps were being lit and tiny flames sprang into being along the narrow streets as though by magic. Spurring their mount down the gentle incline, they hurried towards the town and safety.

The bridge's wooden planking clattered noisily as they crossed. Some sounded loose, much to Kaplyn's alarm. He looked over the side. The ravine fell away sharply towards a narrow, turgid stream whose waters frothed white against grey boulders. A stink of rotting vegetation wafted up, causing him to turn away. The sound of water was deafening as it crashed over rocks and boulders.

At the bridge's other end, two sentries stood idly, leaning against their spears. They stared up at the men as they rode by, humour sparkling in their eyes. Kaplyn feared that the guards might stop them, but then they were beneath the thick stone walls and in the town proper.

People thronged the main street but parted to let them pass, nudging partners or friends, smiling or laughing at the newcomers' misfortune to be riding double on an aged plough horse. Looking up to avoid their stares, Kaplyn saw bright banners suspended between the buildings.

A juggler was performing by the side of the street, keeping three balls spinning in the air. He shouted something to Kaplyn, who could not hear what he said, but it caused merriment to those surrounding the performer and they laughed gaily.

Kaplyn's gaze swept the crowd seeking the distinctive uniform of the palace guard and wondering whether they had already been here. There was no sign of them and so he aimed towards a large inn, nested between tall buildings, whose weather-stained beams sagged in the most alarming manner. A squeaking sign proclaimed it to be "The Thirst and Last." Kaplyn dismounted while Lars practically fell off as his legs buckled beneath him.

A scraggly youth emerged from an alley to one side of the inn. "Can I take your horse to the stable?" he offered, holding out a grubby hand.

"Aye, thanks," Kaplyn replied. "Here's a couple of copper *tell*. Take good care of him and make sure he is well fed and watered."

"Do you have any money?" Kaplyn asked turning to Lars.

"No. They took everything. I was going to enter the wrestling, although I was hoping to lose some weight beforehand." He patted his paunch. "It appears I've developed a taste for your countrymen's ale."

Kaplyn considered for a moment. Taking out his purse he took out several silver calder. "Here. Take these," he offered.

The other man shook his head. "I cannot," he said. "It's not right."

"Pay me back when you win," Kaplyn grinned, forcing the coins on the other man. "Now let's see if there are any rooms left."

Inside, the tavern was busy; the air was thick with smoke from clay pipes and a badly vented fire. Kaplyn paused uncertainly. He had never experienced anything like this before and turned to see what Lars made of it. The big man stood by his side, clearly at ease in the strange surroundings.

The smell was overpowering, a combined reek of spilt ale and months of accumulated cooking odours. He would have to get used to it, especially if he was claiming to be an ex-palace guard!

Kaplyn forced his way to the bar. Within moments, a sullen looking landlord appeared, wiping his hands on a greasy apron.

"What can I do for you, gents?" he shouted above the hubbub.

Kaplyn shouted a reply. "Two rooms for two nights … and supper."

The landlord eyed Kaplyn's clothes and his eyes narrowed. "That'll be four pieces of silver. Each. Pay for one night and the remainder when you leave."

Kaplyn started to rummage through his purse and the landlord's eyes nearly fell out of their sockets. Clearly, he had expected Kaplyn to barter at least.

"And six copper *tell* for the meal…each," he added.

Lars started to complain but Kaplyn mistook him. "It's all right, I'll pay."

"Up the top of the stairs at the back is one room and through that door is another," said the landlord, pocketing the money as swiftly as he could. "Go to the end of the corridor. It's the last one on the right."

"You paid too much," Lars advised as they started towards their rooms.

"The prices will be high because of the games," Kaplyn answered. In truth, he had no idea how much a room should cost. His purse was full but by Lars' look the landlord had cheated him. Frowning, he decided to be more careful in the future, not wanting to attract undue attention to himself. "Let's have a look at the rooms and meet up back here."

Leaving Lars, Kaplyn ducked through a door with a sign proclaiming *Duck or Grouse* above it. There was not enough room on the stair for two and he wondered what would happen if he met someone coming down. His boots thudded noisily on the steps as he climbed.

At the top of the stair, a door led into a small room barely large enough for the single bed and rickety table that supported a cracked washing bowl and pitcher. The roof was only inches above his head, and it sloped alarmingly over the bed, forcing him to crouch to reach it.

He hoped he wasn't disturbing someone below as the floorboards creaked ominously. Briefly, he wondered what was holding the place together as he sat down, testing the mattress. It was far too soft for his liking.

He went across to a small, cracked mirror hanging on the wall. He stared at his image for a while, checking his forehead. The memory of whatever had awoken him was fading but he still felt tainted. His skin looked unblemished and now, in the safety of the town, he dismissed the event as the over activity of a tired mind.

The room smelt musty. Opening the only window, he inhaled the fresh evening air. It carried a mixture of aromas—baking bread, stables, and other scents of a busy town. Even with its shortcomings, at least he felt safe.

Across the street, garlands decorated many of the windows, to ward against demons and other evil spirits. It appeared that the townsfolk also feared the spirit world and Kaplyn, after his night of being afraid, suddenly felt less foolish knowing others feared the dark. He left the room, hoping that the meal would be better than the accommodation.

Lars grinned up at him as he sat down. Kaplyn waved to the landlord for their meal, who in turn waved to a serving girl. She disappeared briefly before returning, holding aloft a heavily laden tray with practiced ease.

Smiling broadly, she set down two large wooden bowls containing a thick meaty stew and a plate piled high with large hunks of warm bread. When Kaplyn looked down at his plate he frowned. Potatoes and meat poked through a blanket of thick, brown gravy, looking very unappetising. Using a broad wooden spoon, he tasted a morsel. It was surprisingly tasty.

The serving girl returned with a large flagon of ale, and Lars looked guilty. "I hope you don't mind. I ordered earlier." Kaplyn nodded. He was not keen on beer and would have preferred wine. Looking around, ale seemed to be the drink of choice, so he remained silent.

"It's good to have company again, especially with fine ale on the table." Lars commented between mouthfuls.

"After last night, I'm just relieved to be within the town," Kaplyn answered. At that moment, a slurred and insolent voice at an adjacent table caught his attention.

"Aye, that's a fact!" A man hunched over a large but empty flagon of ale was saying. "Three wizards, and I spoke with them." Kaplyn's curiosity was aroused at the mention of wizards; in Allund wizards were rare.

In all, there were five men at the table, farmers judging by their appearance. He motioned Lars to silence as he eavesdropped on the conversation.

"Don't be daft, Gillan," retorted, speaking to another of the group. "There is no such thing as wizards, as we all know. If you ask me, you've been sitting here for too long and the beer has finally soaked your wits." The speaker was a small, but stout individual with a good-humoured face and smiling eyes. "Wizards are nothing more than a fairy tale and you have told enough of *those* in your time."

"How come I spoke to one then?" Gillan replied defensively, pushing himself forward to confront the other man. His face was round and fleshy, and his nose was red from years of hard drinking. His eyes seemed to be having difficulty focusing and he kept blinking at his antagonist.

"Are you causing trouble again Gillan?" the serving girl asked as she collected empty tankards from the table. The others about the table grinned while Gillan muttered angrily.

A hush had descended over the nearby tables as others listened in to the conversation.

"There were three of them," Gillan continued, determined not to lose face, and forgetting that he had already mentioned their number. "I saw them about half a mile from the town. One of them stopped to ask me the way here. It was he that said they were wizards, "Coming to entertain the good townsfolk.""

The others around the table smiled, enjoying Gillan's discomfort as he mimicked the wizard.

"Wizards?" Lars whispered to Kaplyn.

"Yes, I heard," Kaplyn said, slightly irritated. Then he decided he was being harsh. Leaning over he whispered to Lars, "Years ago, during the Krell Wars, wizards were supposed to have been common, but now they are rare. Some people still travel the land claiming to be wizards, although they are more usually just clever magicians, using sleight of hand to dupe their audience." Kaplyn turned his attention back to the speaker.

"And why shouldn't there be wizards?" one of Gillan's companions was saying, coming to the other man's rescue. He was a short, respectable looking fellow. The others in the group quietened to hear what he had to say. "Just because there are no wizards in Allund doesn't mean that there are none. And besides, look how many people are prepared to believe in other more fanciful notions such as demons; if they exist, then why not wizards?"

"Aye," a grey bearded man with large staring eyes interrupted. "That's a good point. Remember last year and old Fowler's farm!" Several nodded their agreement and, judging by their expressions, it was not a pleasant memory.

"That was never proven," replied his neighbour in a dismissive tone. "Surely you don't believe that Fowler was murdered by a demon. We're full-grown men, not daft children frightened of the dark." The man nodded towards Gillan who was too engrossed with his mug and its lack of content to take offence.

"Aye, maybe," his grey-bearded companion conceded. "But there is no denying that something strange happened that night. There are many prepared to believe that a demon took old Fowler. His wife was hysterical when we found her and her mind has since gone; she talks to no one now, save her dead husband." He sat back, balancing his mug in a casual manner on the edge of the table.

"I was one of the first to arrive at the farm," he continued softly. "That was just after his son rode into town, crying of murder. When we arrived at the farm, *by the Kalanth*, there was the most god-awful stench." He wrinkled his nose absent-mindedly with the memory. "It was unlike anything I had ever smelt before."

"If it was unlike anything you had smelt before then how do you know it was a demon?" Gillan retorted gruffly, clearly eager to get his own back now that no one was listening to him.

The other man's face was deadly earnest and his eyes blazed angrily. "You had to be there to understand, and then you wouldn't be so swift to disbelieve," he snapped

"Tell them about how you found old Fowler, Bram," another member of the group prompted. He looked a nervous individual; his face was white and his eyes wide with superstitious fear.

Bram grimaced. "It's a sight that will haunt me the rest of my days," he replied sadly, shaking his head as though to rid himself of the memory. "The look on old Fowler's face — such a fearful look that I am surprised I am still sane for having seen it. There was blood everywhere, and someone or something had ripped his heart from his chest."

"I have heard tell, that demons take the victim's heart for it contains their soul!" said another wisely

"That would explain the fearful expression on old Fowler's face," Bram agreed. "For when the old man died his final view was that of Hell itself." His statement left his audience in an uncomfortable silence.

"Old wives' tale!" a voice loudly proclaimed from behind the group. All eyes turned towards a tall, gregarious young man who gave them a mischievous lopsided grin as he casually leant against a chair; a large mug of ale held precariously in his fist.

"From what I hear, Fowler was an old man," the youth continued. "By all accounts he was as fat as one of his sows, and just as stupid." Taking a swallow of ale, he eyed the others through narrowed slits. "His time was due — nothing more, nothing less. And, if you want my opinion, it was nothing more mysterious than a heart attack that killed him," he said gesturing about the room with his mug and wetting several people with its contents. "And," he continued loudly, having seen the filthy looks he was receiving from those that he had soaked. "If I had died from heart failure, then no doubt *my* face would be twisted into an ugly grimace and there would be a horrible smell as well," he finished smugly.

Several laughed at this, although the laughter was somewhat forced for his story did not explain how Fowler's chest had become ripped open.

"Farlan, your face couldn't get any uglier!" A reveller shouted back. More laughter followed and this time it was heartier. It appeared that demons were for dark, unlit places and not for the brightly lit "Thirst and Last."

Kaplyn shivered, remembering last night's events. That experience had left its mark on him and perhaps for that reason he was more prepared to believe the story. Others too clearly believed it for Farlan was given more space. Even if you did not believe in demons, it appeared that it was not wise to tempt providence.

"Do you believe in demons?" Lars asked.

Kaplyn shrugged. "No, I suppose not," he decided eventually.

Lars shook his head. "My people believe in evil giants," he said. "We believe that one-day, at the end of the world, they will attack Fallor-Ell, the home of the gods. Since coming to this land, I have heard of little else other than demons."

Kaplyn nodded. "It's nothing more than folklore," he answered. "People believe in demons because our ancestors used to."

"There's logic in that," Lars replied. "But what do you think persuaded your ancestors to believe in demons?"

That was a profound question to which Kaplyn did not have an answer. In silence the two men ate, grateful at least for the company of others.

Chapter 5
The Spring Fair

The following morning, patches of light mist hugged the ground. The sky itself was cloudless and the sun felt pleasantly warm on Kaplyn's back as they made their way towards the competition arenas. By his side, Lars groaned loudly, putting his hand to his forehead.

"What's the matter?" Kaplyn asked. He could guess but was feeling devilish.

"Too much ale," Lars moaned. He looked pale and his eyes were red rimmed. Kaplyn shook his head, grinning.

They came to a large field filled with tents whose apexes sported bright coloured pennants. Even though it was early, a buzz of voices, occasionally interrupted by shouts of exultation from spectators, filled the air.

Kaplyn was nervous, but the archery was not until later. He considered himself a good shot and fancied his chances of winning. In the meantime, he followed Lars to the wrestling arena. A long-faced official with pious eyes took Lars' entry fee, which he tossed with a loud clatter into a metal pot beneath the table by his side. Lars offered Kaplyn a brave smile as he went to join the other contestants to await their bouts.

A barrel-chested referee with wild, unkempt hair, and an even wilder look in his eyes bullied the men into a line.

"Stand straight," he grouched, standing before the men like a drill instructor. "When I touch your shoulder, and say a number, then remember it. One's will fight two's."

He walked down the line touching each man's shoulder and saying either one or two. "Right, pair up. There are five arenas. Off you go and good luck."

The men turned, looking somewhat bemused until other referees took charge, leading the way to the arenas.

Kaplyn followed Lars and five other men. Their referee started the fight and, much to Kaplyn's surprise, Lars managed to win the first two bouts without any problems. He was surprisingly agile and clearly knew some clever holds. The third fight proved more difficult. Lars' opponent was about his size, but it soon became clear that he knew little about wrestling and was simply using his weight and height. Lars finished the fight with a double arm lock that, no matter how hard he squirmed, his opponent could not break. He yelped for a submission and the referee signalled that the fight was over.

There followed a short break while Lars awaited his next challenger who, as yet, had not finished his fight in one of the other arenas. Lars sat on the grass, taking time to recover. Then a tall gangly individual swaggered into the ring, oozing an air of confidence. Looking down his long nose at Lars, his lip curled in a sneer. Most contestants wore similar apparel, vests and tight trousers, so their opponents did not have anything to grip. Lars' vest did nothing to conceal his over large paunch.

The fight started and Lars circled his opponent who abruptly leapt towards the bigger man and delivered a hefty blow to Lars' chin before skipping back. The crack from the contact was audible and a roar went up from the crowd. Someone jostled Kaplyn and he nearly lost his balance, having to grab the rope separating contestants and spectators, for support. Kaplyn glanced over his shoulder and gagged on the smell of stale breath.

"Sorry," grinned a man leaning on his shoulder and almost immediately Kaplyn was shoved again as the man became excited a second time. "Go on, Remus. Hit the lump of lard."

Lars was holding his chin and was glaring furiously at his opponent who was circling, trying to get behind him.

"Hit him again, Remus," shouted the man behind Kaplyn.

Without warning, the lighter man stepped in, delivered a blow to Lars' chin with his fist and stepped nimbly back. Lars turned to catch him, but the other man kicked out against Lars' knee and again spun away.

Lars seemed to be moving very slowly against the lighter man and Kaplyn thought he could not last much longer. Already his nose was bleeding, and he had a distinct limp. His opponent was clearly enjoying himself and he skipped back and forth in front of Lars.

"That's my boy," shouted the chap behind Kaplyn, and others in the crowd shouted encouragement. The jostling and the loud voice in his ear was annoying Kaplyn. Pushing back against the supporter he cast him a withering look that seemed to do the trick. The other man raised his hands apologetically and stepped back a few inches.

Focussing once more on the arena, twice more Lars' opponent lashed out, each time his fist catching Lars in the face. Lars almost looked to be standing still by comparison to the other man's speed. Then suddenly, with no warning, Lars had caught his opponent's arm, spun, and ducked under the arm, turning it harshly up the other man's back. His opponent's face dropped, and he tried to stand on tiptoes, but Lars forced the arm higher until Kaplyn fancied he heard the joint pop.

"Ouch," shouted the man behind Kaplyn. "That must have hurt."

Kaplyn afforded himself a smile at the other man's misfortune as the referee leapt in to stop the fight. Lars' rival dropped like a sack of potatoes and rolled on the ground clutching his arm. The referee raised Lars' arm, signalling that he had won.

Amazingly, the next bout was the final. Kaplyn pushed his way through a sizeable crowd, apologising as he went for treading on toes or having to be too forceful to gain passage. The nearest betting tout was a short, bad-tempered looking individual with a large hook shaped nose.

"Five silver *calder* on Lars to win," Kaplyn shouted above the din. The tout snatched the money, which swiftly disappeared into a large pocket. He scribbled something on a slip of paper and thrust it into Kaplyn's hand. He was already serving the next person and Kaplyn pushed his way from the queue while trying to decipher the unintelligible script on the discoloured paper.

When Kaplyn arrived back at the arena Lars was standing by the ropes, doubled over with his hands on his knees. His face was pale, and his knees were shaking. "Too much beer, Kaplyn." Loudly, he belched and grinned. "He looks a bit more of a challenge," Lars said nodding to the opposite side of the arena where a broad-chested man glared disdainfully back. He was of equal size to Lars, with upper arms almost as thick as his thighs. His nose looked like it had been used to straighten a wall.

The referee who had initially paired the fighters came into the ring and, in anticipation, the crowd fell silent.

"In the final…" the referee bellowed. "On my right-hand side, needing no introduction, Darl from Pendrat,"

"Darl for champion," someone shouted.

"We're with you, big man," shouted another.

"And on my left, is Lars," the referee continued above other shouts of support for Darl. "As you can see Lars is not from Allund, but we don't want to hold that against him."

"Break his leg, Darl" someone shouted.

Kaplyn grimaced. By the sounds of the support, Lars was in trouble whether he won or lost.

"Let's have a clean fight. Start!" said the referee and dozens of voices shouted encouragement.

Warily Lars circled his opponent.

"Come on big man," taunted Darl. He waved a hand beckoning Lars and trying to encourage the other man to attack.

Lars shook his head. Kaplyn wondered if he was still trying to recover his breath.

A flicker in Darl's shoulders caused Lars to step aside, but the Allunder did not attack. He merely sneered at the other man's caution.

Then, with a loud bellow, Darl ran at Lars, catching his outstretched arms and forcing them back. The two men stood, toe to toe, each pushing with all his might. Lars ducked and twisted at the same time, crossing Darl's wrists as he did so.

The Allunder also twisted, trying to prevent his elbow from locking, and at the same time, he brought his booted foot down hard on the side of Lars' knee. Lars instinctively buckled, releasing his armlock and saving his knee from serious damage. Kaplyn grimaced, but Lars swiftly recovered as he swung his elbow up hard, catching the other man under the chin, forcing him back. As Darl retreated, blood sprang from the corner of his mouth, and he scowled angrily at Lars for the affront.

"Finish him, Darl!" someone in the crowd urged. The big man took this as his cue and launched himself at Lars a second time.

The collision nearly knocked Lars from his feet. He grabbed Darl's arms, preventing him from encircling his waist.

To the crowd the fight looked like a stalemate as the two men strained. Slowly, however Lars forced Darl's arms back and the Allunder realised that he was in trouble. In desperation, he dropped to one knee and pivoted, throwing Lars' body weight over his shoulder.

He tried to catch Lars off balance, but Lars allowed himself to fall forward, maintaining a firm grip on the other man's wrist. With a fluid grace, he somersaulted across the other man's shoulder, wrenching his opponent's arm as he landed.

Darl cried out in pain and nursed the injured limb. Lars rolled away from his opponent and quickly rose to a crouch, waiting for Darl's counterattack. The other man was still recovering and seeing Lars waiting for him seemed only to infuriate him further.

Screaming with rage he ran at his opponent and kicked high, aiming at Lars' head, but Lars neatly caught his heel and ducked under the ill-timed blow. He in turn kicked out at Darl's standing leg while retaining his grip on the other, causing the big man to go down in an untidy heap with Lars on top of him.

Lars was panting from the exertion and did not look like a champion wrestler. "*Karlam*, aid me!" he bellowed.

Darl however was face down and couldn't see the look of pain the exertion cost Lars. Kaplyn grimaced; Lars was winning but marginally.

Straining, Lars forced Darl's left leg behind his right knee and then folded his right leg, trapping his left. Darl screamed.

"I submit!" he bellowed.

The referee leapt in and slapped Lars on the shoulder. "Fight's over. Let go! *Now!* Before you break his leg."

The crowd howled.

"Fix," someone shouted. "Darl, you've cost me a week's wages!" cried another.

Kaplyn did not wait to congratulate Lars but sought out the tout he had seen earlier, before the other man could escape. Kaplyn grinned, enjoying the tout's discomfort as he claimed his winnings.

"Not sure I should pay out," the tout muttered.

"Why?" Kaplyn growled.

The other man grimaced. "Well, that Lars was not from these parts. He could be professional."

"You were happy to take my money, so pay up," Kaplyn countered, giving the tout an ominous look. It worked; the tout counted out a handful of silver *calder*. Counting it, Kaplyn made his way through the crowd towards Lars who was still sitting on the ground, gasping.

Kaplyn smiled down. "Well done! It was a good fight," he acknowledged, crouching down.

Lars nodded but said nothing between loud gasps for air. Kaplyn waited patiently for the big man to recover.

"*By Slathor!* That was hell," he managed finally, groaning as he did so and gripping the grass in pain.

Kaplyn grinned at his discomfort. "Who is Slathor?" he asked.

Lars forced a smile. "He is one of my gods. We have many."

"And Karlam?"

"God of war," Lars managed.

When Lars was finally ready, Kaplyn helped him to his feet.

"If I had known that you Allunds liked to fight, I'd have found another country to be shipwrecked in. Five fights! It's too much, there has to be an easier way to earn a living."

Lars shook his head as he started slowly towards the referee who was coming towards the pair with the big man's winnings. "How much did you bet on yourself?" Kaplyn asked.

Lars paled, shaking his head. "I didn't save enough; the ale was too good. Still, I'll be able to sleep content tonight as at least now I can afford a room and lodgings," he said holding the prize purse, clearly enjoying the weight of the coin.

Kaplyn led them towards the archery range. There were more people now and the pavilions created funnel points, squeezing folk together. Someone bumped into Kaplyn and inadvertently his gaze fell upon a small, grey haired old woman standing a few yards away. Claws, disfigured by arthritis, clutched a shawl yellowed with age about her throat. She glared about the crowd, looking down a long thin nose speckled in warts.

When her gaze met his, her thin lips parted, her eyes widened and to Kaplyn the world seemed to slow. He tried to look away, but the damage was done.

Her arm came up and she pointed at him. He tried to step backwards but the press of bodies trapped him. At first, he assumed she had recognised him and would alert the palace guard when they came this way, but that was unlikely he realised almost as soon as the thought popped into his head. Lars stood by his side and behind them voices murmured.

"Old Kate's going to make a prediction," Kaplyn heard someone say.

As if on cue the old woman spoke in a low gravelly voice, while still pointing directly at Kaplyn. "I *see* you." Her gaze seemed to penetrate Kaplyn's very soul.

People stopped to listen and Kaplyn found himself at the centre of a ring of people. A hush fell upon the crowd.

"You would destroy us all!" she muttered, shaking her head. "The prophecy haunts you; beware lest you set in motion events that cannot be stopped. The Eldric are lost, never to be found."

"I see also the ghost by your side. Oh, he is not there yet—but he will be! I know his shape and his desire, and the gleam in his eye. Death he will bring to us all. You would summon dragons: a living plague to ravage the world."

Around Kaplyn the crowd murmured, and people cast him troubled looks.

"Superstition," Kaplyn said, albeit softly. He was shaking and his brain refused to function.

"Kate often sees things," a man behind Kaplyn said.

"Aye," said another. "Like the flood last year when the cattle drowned."

"*Superstition* is it!" Kate answered. "One day you will see the man I speak of. Think then upon my words. Beware the dragons and befriend them to your cost."

Kaplyn turned his back on the woman and forced himself into the crowd. Kate had fallen silent, and it was clear that there was no more entertainment, so the mob parted to let him past. Some people followed as though expecting Kate's premonition to come true immediately. Kaplyn looked over his shoulder; fortunately, Kate wasn't there.

The thought of the archery competition was furthermost from Kaplyn's mind and instead he sought a quiet place behind a large tent where he sat down upon the ground. Lars joined him. Several people that had followed looked on from a distance but soon lost interest and went on their way.

"What was that about?" Lars asked.

"An old fraud, trying to enhance her reputation as a witch!" Kaplyn suggested, trembling, and clearly shaken by the event.

"Dragons, though," Lars said.

"There are *no* dragons. She was deranged, probably *mad*," he complained.

Lars looked unconvinced. "Who are the Eldric?"

"Who *were* the Eldric," Kaplyn corrected. "They came over the sea several hundred years ago. For a while they brought peace and even stopped some of the wars."

"How did they accomplish that?" Lars asked.

"I can see that I need to explain some of our history," Kaplyn looked up to the sky. His heart was slowing and talking was helping to calm him.

"Trosgarth and Aldrace are nations to the north of Thrace. In the past, they were constantly waging war with just about everyone. That was a time of petty kingdoms. When the Eldric arrived, they were much more advanced than we were; both culturally and militarily. They landed here in Allund," Kaplyn laughed. "That nearly started a war, but common sense prevailed, and it was a good thing too. The balance of power shifted in favour of the Southern Kingdoms. Then I suppose that people became more interested in trade than fighting."

"What happened next?" Lars asked.

"Peace lasted for many years, but always Trosgarth resented the Eldric whose weapons were far superior to anyone else's; some were even supposed to have been magical. The peace ended when an Eldric Lord called Drachar sided with Trosgarth. Why he chose to do so, no one knows. The Eldric were reputedly powerful sorcerers and Drachar the most powerful of all. He was able to summon the most potent demons."

A roar from a nearby crowd interrupted Kaplyn. Overhead a few birds raced from the din, their black forms in stark contrast to the white clouds that now filled the sky.

"Do you want to find the archery?" Lars asked.

Kaplyn shook his head. "Not now. It's probably too late judging by the noise from the crowd. I'm happy to sit here for a while."

"What happened to Drachar?" Lars asked. His eyes were wide. "Did he summon demons?"

Again, Kaplyn nodded. "There was a war later called the Krell Wars."

"I've heard of krell. But what are they?"

"I don't know. I've never seen one, but they are meant to be half-demon, half-human. Drachar united the krell tribes and I think that was why Trosgarth sided with him. The battle of DrummondCal decided the war. The Eldric, leading an army from the Southern Kingdoms, defeated Drachar, using sorcerers and summoning demons of their own. It was a devastating battle by all accounts.

"Drachar was killed but some say that his ghost was too powerful to be banished and it remained, seeking to rise again in the distant future."

"And that's the basis of the Prophecy the old woman spoke of?"

"Yes."

Lars shifted uncomfortably and his frown suggested he wanted to ask more.

"Let's find some food," Kaplyn suggested.

"My treat," Lars beamed back, patting his bulging purse. "What about the Prophecy first though?"

Kaplyn smiled. "The Prophecy is rather cryptic so don't expect to understand it." Kaplyn searched his memory before reciting it.

> *"When Tallin's Crown once more does shine,*
> *Drachar's shade will rise sublime,*
> *Three Princes Royal through time to sleep,*
> *An appointment with destiny —three Kings to keep,*
> *Trosgarth's arm across the land will reach,*
> *Of war and famine —- his army to teach,*
> *And one will stand to oppose his throne,*
> *A King resurrected in his mountain home,*
> *Of air, fire and water — he will be born,*
> *To aid the people — when all else is forlorn."*

"I see what you mean about being cryptic. Any ideas what *Tallin's Crown* is?"

Kaplyn shook his head. "No idea."

"And the Eldric? What became of them?"

Kaplyn frowned, the other man was insatiable, but his curiosity was understandable. The Eldric had always fascinated Kaplyn. "No one knows. There are only ruins where their cities once stood. There are Eldric artefacts around, cooking utensils, the occasional sword and such, so there is no doubt they existed. But what became of them? It's said they disappeared after the Krell Wars."

"*Disappeared*," Lars snorted. "An *entire race*! How can that be?"

"I know it sounds ludicrous," Kaplyn continued. "And there are many rumours about their disappearance. People talk about seeing Eldric ghosts on pilgrimages to this place and that."

"The old woman mentioned a ghost."

"Aye, some people believe in a shaol, or a guardian spirit. They are supposed to watch over us, protecting and guiding us. I'm not sure if that is what she meant, but personally I still think she was deranged."

"She was certainly spooky. Her eyes were strange, I can't describe them. They seemed to stare inside you if you know what I mean."

Kaplyn shuddered. He did know what Lars meant. "Come, let's get some food," he said rising.

Lars continued to question Kaplyn as they walked. "What do *you* think became of the Eldric?"

They crossed a relatively crowd-free area, aiming towards a tent from which came the smell of barbecued meat. Kaplyn's mouth watered. "I think they were ashamed of the destruction caused by one of their own kind. Thousands perished in the Krell Wars and to make matters worse it is said that a demon takes a person's soul when they die."

Lars grimaced. "That's horrible. But where did the Eldric go?"

"I've no idea," Kaplyn replied. They entered the tent and joined a queue of people. At the front, a diminutive plump woman was serving what looked like pork on a large slice of bread. Lars fell silent for a while. The two men arrived at the head of the queue and good to his word Lars paid.

They ate as they meandered between the tents. Kaplyn recognised a pennant flying over one particularly large tent. "Look, that's where the karlot competition is being held; with any luck, I may salvage something from today." Fate so far had been unkind to Kaplyn, having lost his horse and nearly killed by outlaws. Things had to improve. Together the two men made their way over to the tent as Kaplyn explained that karlot was a board game. Once at the tent, Kaplyn gave the official his name and paid his entry fee.

Kaplyn played and won four games of karlot and quickly, much to his surprise, found himself in the final. In this round, a thin faced Hullender, whose eyes sparkled in anticipation, faced him.

Kaplyn guessed he was a merchant, judging by the rich cut of his clothing and numerous gold rings, which he twisted nervously. A hush descended over the watching crowd as they waited.

Kaplyn won the toss to start. Throughout the previous games, he had adopted standard openings. Now, facing his opponent in the final game, something prompted him to change tact. His opponent looked confused as Kaplyn slid the krell piece, in front of his kara-stone, forward two squares. Since there was a time limit, he had to counter quickly and Kaplyn recognised his move as the dristal's gambit.

The pieces on the board represented mythical creatures and the dristal was a large bird of prey, which dwarves had ridden into battle in the final days of the

Krell Wars. The move opened the opponent's defence by attacking the chanth, a demon of considerable power. Kaplyn ignored the threat and continued to build up an attack on his adversary's sorcerer. In the ensuing moves Kaplyn managed to keep one piece ahead of his rival. When an opening presented itself, he confidently took his challenger's dwarf chieftain.

The Hullender, sensing victory slipping from his grasp, altered the pattern of play. Kaplyn found the sudden attack across the front of the board difficult to counter, but fortune was with him. The Hullender had left his kara-stone vulnerable and swiftly Kaplyn took the piece with a krell. He sat back in relief while a look of pain crossed the Hullender's face as he realised his fatal mistake. Finally, he smiled, admitting defeat, and offering Kaplyn his hand. Kaplyn had won and his recompense was a far heavier purse than when he had arrived.

Chapter 6
Vastra

Kaplyn met with Lars later that evening in the tavern. They ordered meals and a large flagon of ale with two mugs. Lars initially looked green at the sight of the ale, but his colour soon returned after his first draft.

"Your health," he said, belching loudly, and placing his mug firmly on the table.

Kaplyn looked startled. Half of its content was gone "Your health," he replied, raising his mug, and taking a cautious sip. It was a strong brew.

"At least I'm better at wrestling than sailing," Lars commented. His voice betrayed the hurt that he was obviously feeling.

"How did you become shipwrecked?" Kaplyn asked, sensing the other man wanted to talk.

Lars took another swallow of ale to wet his tongue. "Our voyage was between villages for trade," he said depositing the heavy flagon on the tabletop. "My father was the Glan-Can, which is chieftain, of our people. I was travelling with the crew to negotiate in the trade of our cargo."

"Glan-Can—is that like a prince?" Kaplyn asked.

"I'd never thought of it like that, but I suppose you are correct. We don't have kingdoms and my father's land was quite extensive."

Kaplyn hid a smile behind his hand; the coincidence that both he and Lars were royalty was too much.

"Anyway, the distance was not great, barely a few miles along the coast and we had done this trip dozens of times before. It was usually a safe enough journey for we sailed in sight of the coast, so there was little chance of becoming lost." He took a deeper drink of ale and Kaplyn waited patiently for the big man to continue. Lars put his mug down and wiped his beard, signalling to the landlord for more.

"This time though a strong wind followed us, and it soon became a storm, forcing us farther out to sea." His eyes looked distant and Kaplyn realised that the tale was painful. "The storm seemed to have a mind of its own and whichever way we turned it followed. Never had I seen such waves. They towered over us, drenching the planking, and sweeping two men overboard. Then, as suddenly as it had started, it ceased.

"It was unnatural. Behind us was a wall of black clouds, reaching high into the heavens. From within this, we could hear the loud booming of waves as they danced to the storm's frenzied tune. And yet, about us, the sea was as calm as a village pond."

The landlord appeared through the crowd and set a fresh flagon down, slopping the contents messily on the table. As swiftly as he came, he went, leaving Lars to continue his story. Kaplyn topped up their mugs.

"Suddenly a shape surfaced yards from the gunwale. What manner of sea beast it was I did not know but it was a fearful sight. Its head towered over us on a long thin neck, and I will never forget the fear I experienced as its eyes watched us, running about the deck like headless chickens."

"Slowly the monster dipped gently beneath the sea, as if its curiosity was satisfied and it was off to find its supper. The crew breathed a sigh of relief, hoping beyond hope that it had swum away and left us in peace. Quickly we ran to put up the sails and escape before the storm engulfed us. We were too late though; the sea erupted as the beast reared high out of the water, landing with a crash on the gunwale." Lars brought a giant hand down hard on the tabletop with a loud slap as if simulating the sea monster's attack. Several of the tavern's occupants jumped with shock and turned around to see what the commotion was.

Lars ignored them and continued with his story. "The wooden timbers cracked like dry twigs and the sheer weight of the creature capsized us. I dived over the rails just as the ship went down. When I surfaced, I could hear the others screaming in terror, as the beast hunted them down. Then the gale hit once more.

"I grabbed on to wreckage and clung on for all I was worth, calling to Harlathan, the god of the sea, to save me. It was a fearful ride; giant waves tossed me like a leaf in a storm," Lars paused to take a drink.

"Go on. What happened next?" Kaplyn asked, enthralled.

"I don't know how long the storm lasted, but later the sea jettisoned me onto a sandy beach. For hours I lay there, trying to convince my stomach that the world was finally still.

"Since then, I've been wandering around doing odd jobs, trying to get by," he looked thoughtful. "That would be nearly a year ago. I miss my wife and son, but deep down I know I'll never see them again."

Kaplyn wanted to offer him a token of comfort, but words were not enough. He needn't have worried though; Lars took a long draught of ale and grinned at the now empty glass. "Come." he said. "Our purses are full, and the evening is young. Landlord!" he shouted above the noise of the crowd. "Where is that man?"

Kaplyn looked at his own ale and grimaced. At that moment he felt, rather than saw, a shadow fall over them. Swiftly he looked up and was startled to see a man standing by his side, looking down at him. The stranger must have been light-footed to get so close without Kaplyn realising.

"May I join you?" he asked, waving a hand towards the spare seat beside them.

The stranger's face was long and thin and his features fine, reminding Kaplyn of an alabaster sculpture that he had once seen. His hair was oily, raven black and cut short, accentuating a high forehead. A brooding countenance marred what some folk might otherwise have considered good looks. Even his clothes were sombre, although his fleece-lined doublet and short riding cloak looked expensive. Kaplyn doubted that he lacked money.

"I am Vastra," he said in a way that seemed to imply it was of some importance. "And I have a proposition for you."

Kaplyn looked to Lars, but he merely shrugged.

"Take a seat," Kaplyn finally offered, nodding towards the empty chair.

Vastra lowered himself as though standing was wearisome. "I'm looking for hired help. I seek an artefact and need an escort and then help in its recovery," Vastra continued.

"Recover or steal?" Lars asked.

"The work is honest. I assure you," Vastra replied tersely.

Lars looked puzzled. "Why choose us?" It was the question uppermost in Kaplyn's mind.

"I saw you both competing in the games. You both won events and I think you would be well suited to the task I have in mind," Vastra replied.

"Where are you going and what do you seek?" Kaplyn asked.

"I am travelling to Tanel," he announced boldly.

"Tanel? It's an Eldric city. It is nothing more than ruins."

Vastra nodded, "It is I am a scholar and have been led to believe that there may be something of interest there."

Kaplyn was curious. "And what might that be?"

"Once you have decided whether to accompany me, I shall tell you more."

Kaplyn was thinking of returning home, maybe by a roundabout route to visit an old friend. Tanel was not too far out of his way though and it might prove to be an interesting diversion. Company would also be welcome on the long ride. He was uncertain, however, and did not want to commit himself until he knew more.

"You will be well paid," Vastra assured them, seeing their reluctance. "Ten *calder* to escort me to Tanel and two gold pieces if you are successful in retrieving the object."

Kaplyn was impressed; it was a considerable sum. "Tomorrow," he announced finally, having decided to be cautious. "We will decide then. Meet us first thing in the morning and we will let you know our decision."

A smile touched Vastra's lips, and he bowed fractionally before rising from the table and leaving through the press of bodies.

"A strange man," Lars commented watching Vastra's retreating form.

Kaplyn shivered, surprised by the effect the stranger appeared to have on him; it was as if his soul had touched something dark.

Kaplyn awoke early, cold and disorientated by his strange surroundings. The last thing he remembered was opening the window to let in the fresh night air, which had been foolhardy for his blanket had fallen off in the night, leaving him shivering. Lars was a bad influence, and he tried to remember how much he had drunk before retiring.

Deciding it was best not dwelling on the matter he hurriedly arose causing his head to spin. Blinking in confusion, he waited for a moment for his head to clear. With a sinking heart, he realised that the clothes, strewn in disarray around the room, were not how he had left them the previous night.

His brow beetled as he looked about at the mess and a sickening realisation dawned. Someone had robbed him. He grabbed his clothes, searching them. His money and all his winnings were gone. In despair, he sat forlornly on his small bed.

His sword still rested close to his bed where he had left it and that was a blessing at least. It alone was worth a considerable sum, and he would have been devastated to return home without it. He cursed under his breath and then more loudly, jumping to his feet and grabbing his shirt. Throwing it on, the threads cracked. He would find the landlord and give him a piece of his mind. Never before had he been robbed, and someone had to be held to account.

Descending the tight stairs, he pulled his jerkin on, noting the torn lining where he had hidden the coins in case of emergency. Again, he cursed. Shouting for the landlord he stormed into the tavern. The proprietor appeared almost at once, bumping into a chair in his haste.

"I have been robbed!" Kaplyn stated bitterly. "Someone has taken my money," he continued.

The landlord looked bewildered, "Slow down, sir. Sit, and tell me what has happened."

Kaplyn ignored him. "Somebody came into my room late last night and stole my money, including my winnings."

The other man looked nonplussed; he held out his arms in a helpless manner and started to stammer a response. "Are you certain? Could you have misplaced your purse?" he asked defensively.

Kaplyn scowled. "The money has gone!"

The landlord stroked his chubby chin nervously. "How are you going to pay your bill?" he asked suspiciously.

"I have paid already," Kaplyn replied.

"But your friend ran up a hefty bill last night on food and ale," the landlord returned.

Kaplyn was stunned. "How dare you! A thief robbed me while under the protection of your roof. There is no lock on my bedroom door, and you do not even employ a night watchman."

"This is a simple establishment sir," The landlord countered. "We cannot afford such precautions. Besides, no one has ever been robbed here before."

Kaplyn realised that they were not alone; a figure was sitting in an alcove, partially hidden by the shadows. He recognised Vastra who leaned forward with an amused expression.

A sudden commotion caused Kaplyn to turn as Lars stormed into the room, wearing a look of thunder. His face was red with suppressed rage. "My money has gone," he stated bluntly. Kaplyn could see the pain reflected in his eyes; his winnings had meant a great deal to him.

Kaplyn turned to the landlord who was now pale and sweating profusely.

"You will have to pay your bill immediately!" he insisted. His eyes kept darting towards the door as though he was hoping for the intervention of the town guard.

"We have no money! It's all been taken!" Kaplyn hissed.

"Then you'll have to pay with something else," the landlord continued hopefully, his eyes straying to Kaplyn's sword.

Seeing the direction of his gaze Kaplyn felt his anger rising. However, Vastra interrupted before he could reply. "I might be able to help," he suggested softly, and the group's attention focused on him. "How much do these gentlemen owe?"

This was obviously much more promising, and the landlord brightened visibly. "Four *calder* and twelve *tell*," he declared after a pause and much hand wringing.

Vastra opened his purse and placed coins on the table, which the landlord scooped up, muttering his thanks before darting away.

"There was no need to pay him," Kaplyn argued, turning to confront Vastra. "It's partly his fault the burglar got into my room."

"Did they take everything?" Vastra asked.

"Yes!" Kaplyn replied thinking about the hidden coins.

"It would appear that we are in your debt," Lars stated through gritted teeth.

"I'll replace your money and add to it if you will accompany me. The offer I made last night still stands."

"I will go, if what you want is reasonable," Lars sounded defeated.

Kaplyn was in a quandary. Never before had he been penniless, and he was still coming to terms with the situation. "Tell us what you want," he said, realising he had no option. In his place, his brothers would have laughed and walked away, but Kaplyn's conscience would not let him do that.

"Sit down," Vastra invited. They complied, although Kaplyn disliked someone telling him what to do.

"I am a sorcerer," Vastra confided in them, much to their surprise. "There is an artefact in Tanel which I wish to find."

"A wizard?" Kaplyn asked uncertainly.

"A sorcerer," Vastra corrected. Something in his tone suggested that the difference was important.

"I have seen many magicians in the past," Kaplyn replied, in no mood to pander to Vastra's ego. "Can you prove that you are what you claim?"

"I do not perform tricks, if that is what you are asking," Vastra said with menace in his voice. His eyes glittered with suppressed rage. "You will be paid for your work," he reminded them. The mention of money also reminded them of their debt.

"Tanel is a ruin!" Kaplyn continued, taken aback by Vastra's anger. "There is nothing there, except stones."

"Then you will be well paid just to escort me," Vastra replied sighing. "It is little more than a few days ride, and then you will be rich."

"What is it you seek?" Kaplyn asked.

"It's a gold pendant about the size of my hand," Vastra said. "On one side is a map and on the other Eldric writing."

"How much is it worth?" Lars asked.

"It is priceless," Vastra said simply, although his eyes gleamed as he spoke. "Of course, it is only of value to the right person, and I am offering you a rich reward for your help," he continued, making it clear that it was worthless to anyone else but him; clearly, his trust only went so far.

"Why is it that no one else is seeking it, if it is so valuable?" Kaplyn asked suspiciously.

"Only a few people can unlock its whereabouts and, even if its location were known, its recovery would be difficult." Vastra paused as if considering how much to tell them. "There is an element of risk," he continued. "I have watched you both during the games and you seem to be capable men."

There was a moment's silence. "How do we know that you have the money?" Kaplyn asked.

Vastra unhooked a pouch from within the folds of his jacket; it was evidently full and clearly heavy. Vastra opened it and removed twenty silver *calder* and four gold coins. The purse remained bulging. Lars cast Kaplyn a glance at the sight of such wealth.

"Be warned," Vastra said suddenly, returning the coins to the purse. "I am quite capable of defending myself." The purse quickly disappeared within his jacket. "I only warn you in case you decide that you like the look of my purse rather than the work I offer."

"I am no *thief*, if that is what you are inferring!" Kaplyn snapped irritably.

"If you are an honest man, then there is no insult intended."

Vastra's apology, thin though, it was mollified Kaplyn.

"I'll meet you outside as soon as you are ready. I have supplies and horses," Vastra said, rising.

"It looks as though our fortunes have changed once again," Lars commented.

"Aye, but perhaps not for the better," Kaplyn replied.

"Is it possible that Vastra had something to do with the theft?"

Kaplyn had not considered that possibility and frowned deeply. "No. I am assuming the thief climbed through the window. Otherwise, he would have to have gone through the tavern and that is busy most the night, judging by the din. If that was the route the thief took, Vastra doesn't look capable and besides, I doubt he is *that* desperate to hire our help; there are plenty of others around." Kaplyn was seething but he was also intrigued to be going to Tanel.

"Come," he said. "We'd better not keep him waiting. I need to fetch my bow. I'll see you outside shortly."

True to his word Vastra was waiting outside. The boy, from the night they had arrived, was saddling three horses. Lars cast Kaplyn a sideways glance and grimaced at the prospect of more riding.

Vastra handed Lars a heavy double-handed sword. The big man eyed it suspiciously.

"There are many dangers on the road," Vastra explained. "I look to you two for my protection."

Lars buckled the sword about his broad waist but no matter how he tried to adjust it he looked ill-suited to it. "I would have preferred an axe," he grumbled. Vastra ignored him and mounted.

Lars and Kaplyn also mounted and together the three men rode from the safety of the town. Once more the wild was calling, but as to their future…? Kaplyn was now at the mercy of someone else and he didn't like it at all.

Chapter 7
Shelter for the Night

They rode for the rest of the day. It was a pleasant journey, at least for Kaplyn. Lars complained bitterly, sitting astride his horse as though expecting to fall off with every step.

Gradually evening claimed the land and shadows grew longer. Kaplyn felt anxious but did not know why. There were no signs of dwellings, and he certainly didn't want to spend a night outdoors. However, this was not the source of his growing discomfort.

Abruptly a lark flew overhead calling shrilly. The horses startled and crabbed across the path. Then Kaplyn understood what was worrying him. His horse was nervous, and he was sensing that.

He glanced at the other two men and saw discomfort reflected on both their faces. "Do you feel it?" he asked.

"What?" Lars answered, although Kaplyn heard the strain in his voice.

"Kaplyn's correct, there is something not right this evening. We'd better hurry and hope to find shelter," Vastra answered. He spurred his mount on and they followed as best they could. Kaplyn grabbed Lars' reins and urged his own mount to canter. Glancing back, Lars was bouncing in his seat in an alarming manner, gritting his teeth in pain.

Cresting a rise, they finally saw a small settlement, although still some distance ahead. It was nothing more than several long low wooden buildings surrounded by a stout palisade, probably a farm Kaplyn realised.

By now the heavens were a mixture of fiery reds and burnished golds as the sun sank below the horizon, illuminating the underside of clouds, gathering in the darkening sky. By the time they reached the farm, apart from the skeletal silhouettes of trees, Kaplyn could barely see. He hoped the occupants would not refuse them entry for arriving so late. They halted a respectable distance from the palisade. A thick briar bush grew in profusion around its base, adding to the defences. The smell of wood smoke and cooking wafted towards them and Kaplyn's stomach growled in anticipation.

"Hello, the farm," Kaplyn called, and in silence they waited for a reply.

A torch became visible between the posts, followed by voices. They watched the partially obscured flame dance as if by magic toward the wall, finally coming to a halt on top of the palisade.

In the torchlight, a dark-haired man with a thick, unkempt beard peered at them. His face stood out in stark contrast to the surrounding night as he raised his torch aloft. By his side several other figures joined him, many armed with longbows.

"We are seeking shelter for the night," Kaplyn called up.

The first figure raised his torch, looking at them between the posts as though having some difficulty in seeing them.

"How many are you?" he asked in a deep voice.

"Three," Kaplyn replied.

"Three?" the fellow questioned. "Come forward into the light so we can see you."

The man cursed the darkness as they walked their mounts forward until they were looking up at the farmer. His grey beard marked him older than Kaplyn had first thought.

"You're travelling late!" the farmer accused.

"We are returning from Pendrat and the games. This is the first farm we have seen this evening," Kaplyn explained.

"The games?"

Kaplyn had deliberately mentioned them, hoping their account of the games would be recompense for their food and lodgings.

"Take a torch," the farmer said, waiting for Kaplyn to come forward before dropping one to his outstretched hand. "Place it twenty paces back along the path." It was a wise precaution intended to see if anyone else lurked behind.

Kaplyn complied and returned to the other two as the gates swung inwards. Inside, a dozen men carrying an assortment of weapons and farm implements surrounded them. Behind them, the gate thumped closed.

"You will have to excuse our precautions," the farmer said coming down a short flight of steps leading from the wall. "There's been talk of outlaws hereabouts."

"You have our thanks, it's a dark night and we are very glad to find shelter," Kaplyn said.

"You're welcome to spend the night in my house," the farmer replied. "Ralph, my youngest, will see to your horses."

A strapping man in his early twenties stepped forward and took their reins before leading the animals away.

The other farmers returned to their own homes, leaving the three travellers to follow the farmer who introduced himself as Callan; the seven men accompanying him were his sons and Callan introduced each in turn.

Callan's house was a long single storey timber building, crowned with a thick thatched roof. A tall stone chimney rose into the night sky, venting the cooking fires. The windows were small and thick; coarse materials covered the openings, keeping out the evening chill.

They ducked beneath a low door and stepped down into the room. The floor inside was lower than outside giving the room additional height, much to Lars' obvious relief.

Kaplyn entered last to discover a long table dominating the room. About it several women and numerous children were sitting, watching them with awe. The table was heavily laden with bowls of steaming food and a delicious aroma filled the room. Lars brightened at the sight of the food and his eyes widened further when he saw a large flagon of ale in prime position at the table's centre.

Kaplyn felt he should nudge the bigger man to make him behave.

At that moment, extra chairs appeared followed by a round of introductions. In turn, Kaplyn introduced his group as the farmer's wife served the food. Callan asked where they were from. Kaplyn repeated the lie that he was formerly from Dundalk, and he had worked in the palace guard. Questions rained down on him about the King and the royal family. As a simple soldier, he knew he should know very little about them and he found the questions awkward.

He was glad when the focus of attention turned to Lars. The tale of his shipwreck overawed them and next, Kaplyn and Lars spoke about the games.

One of the farmer's daughters kept looking at Kaplyn and he tried to look elsewhere, only to find his attention wandering back to her good looks. To his embarrassment, he found that she was still watching him. Cheeks reddening, he hurriedly looked away. She was about his age and very pretty. Unfortunately, he could not remember her name amongst the rush of so many.

He suddenly realised that Callan was talking to them. Feeling foolish he listened to what he was saying.

"What about your quiet companion, did he also compete in the games?" Callan was asking.

Vastra shook his head, feigning not to reply.

Not wishing to offend their host Kaplyn spoke on his behalf. "Our companion is a wizard," he declared, hoping to lighten Vastra's mood. Instead, he received a withering look and too late he realised his error.

The farmer's eyes widened. "A wizard?"

Vastra cast Kaplyn a sideways look. There followed an embarrassing silence before Vastra spoke. "Perhaps there is some tasks that I could help you with?" he offered, half-heartedly.

The farmer's eyes brightened considerably. "Aye, that there is. If we could be the first to get our crop to market, we would get a higher price," he stated hopefully; Vastra nodded.

"I have a bull which has not yet sired an heir," Callan continued as though he could not believe his luck.

Vastra's nod this time was barely perceptible, his eyes locked on Kaplyn's as though daring him to let the farmer continue. Under Vastra's glare, Kaplyn felt a cold shiver run down his spine.

"Well, it's getting late," Kaplyn interrupted, taking the hint. "We've been travelling since dawn and if you don't mind, we had better get some sleep."

"I'm sorry," Callan replied. "I had no idea time had passed so quickly; it is rare that we have visitors. We don't have any spare beds, but you are more than welcome to sleep in Ralph's room. He can move in with one of his brothers."

Kaplyn thanked Callan who stood up to escort them to their room. The family bid them goodnight and Kaplyn passed close to the girl whose good looks had attracted his eye. She smiled sweetly at him, and he left the room with the imprint of her face and the scent of her hair indelibly stamped into his mind.

Ralph's room was tiny, and a single pallet lay on the floor. Vastra immediately claimed it. For a moment, Kaplyn wanted to order him off the pallet, but he controlled his anger, settling instead with a dark look, which Vastra simply ignored. Muttering, Kaplyn removed his belt and sword, which he dropped on the floorboards with a thud before sitting to remove his boots. He lay down, trying to get comfortable.

Not being very tired he listened for a while to the noises of Callan's family moving about the other rooms. For a while he lay awake hoping that Callan's daughter might come to the room and together, they could go somewhere private. The thought made it harder to sleep, but shortly not even thinking about her could keep him awake and he drifted into a silent slumber.

Soon, the only noises about the farm were the chirruping of crickets and the occasional bleat from restless sheep housed within the stockade for the night. A lone sentry patrolled the tall stockade wall, taking measured strides along the narrow wooden walkway while waiting patiently for the rays of the sun to pronounce the dawn.

Kaplyn awoke abruptly, immediately at a loss as to where he was. He became aware of raised voices outside followed by a brief glow that danced across the ceiling. The plaster was old and crumbling and had formed odd lifelike shapes. He realised that somebody had carried a torch by the window. Now it was dark—completely dark.

"Where am I?" he croaked, sitting up.

Lars muttered something unintelligible and sat up, knuckling sleep from his eyes.

"See to the sheep and make sure they're secure," someone said in a muffled voice.

"Right you are. You fetch my bow and I'll meet you around the front," came the reply.

Kaplyn remembered then the farm and Callan. "Lars, something's going on. Where are my boots?" He groped round with his hands. Lars opened the door allowing a soft light, cast by the dying embers from the fire in the other room, to filter through.

"Are we getting up?" Lars asked, yawning, and stretching. "It must be about midnight."

"You two can get up," said Vastra from the bed. "But don't expect me to." He turned over and pulled the blanket over his head.

Kaplyn glanced at Lars who shrugged. Kaplyn grinned; the more he knew about Vastra the less he liked him.

Outside, Kaplyn nearly bumped into a knot of people standing by the door. Other farmers surrounded Callan and his sons. Some were holding torches while others armed themselves with bows and arrows, much to Kaplyn's consternation. Somewhere beyond the stockade an eerie howl filled the air. Immediately another howl followed, but closer.

"Wolves," Callan explained looking towards the distant sound.

Kaplyn frowned. "Why are you concerned? The stockade will keep them out surely?"

"This howling has been going on for some while and the volume suggests an uncommonly large pack. We're manning the walls as a precaution." Callan replied, stringing his longbow, placing one end against his foot and bending it using both hands. His wife handed him a quiver of arrows. "Thanks," he acknowledged.

Kaplyn thought he sounded nervous. "Where are our horses? I have a bow."

"I'll fetch it," Ralph volunteered from behind his father.

"I'll come with you and get my sword," Lars said. Both men left and returned shortly. Ralph handed Kaplyn his bow and a quiver of arrows.

"OK, if we're all ready? Let's go then," Callan said.

Kaplyn stumbled in the dark. About him the farm was a riot of different noises; sheep were bleating, dogs were barking, and loud thuds came from the stables as the horses bumped against the wooden walls. Thunder crashed close by, and abruptly the noise from the animals escalated.

When they mounted the palisade steps, the wolves' howling increased. Around Kaplyn, men muttered angrily.

"What are wolves doing down here this time of the year?" one fellow asked no one in particular. He held his torch over the stockade wall, trying to increase the range of its glow. All at once a grey shape slipped into view.

"Bloody animal," one man shouted above the general din. He rapidly bent his bow and nocked an arrow, but the wolf was gone.

"Some of you hold the torches out," Callan suggested. "Get some boys up here," he called over his shoulder. "Give them torches."

Shortly some youths arrived. One lad passed by Kaplyn. He looked about twelve. His eyes darted about the adults and when someone handed him a torch he jumped in alarm. "Hold it out over the stockade," the man proffering the torch said. "Hold it high, so that the archers can see."

The lad nodded and stood beside Kaplyn. Kaplyn felt sorry for him. It was dark and cold, and the boy had probably just left the comfort of his bed.

"A chilly night," he offered, and the boy nodded, seeming incapable of speech.

"It'll be all right," Kaplyn tried to reassure him.

By now a pool of light illuminated a short distance from the stockade wall.

"Over there!" One man yelled. Immediately several arrows flew to the spot. However, the wolf had slipped back into the shadows.

"Damn, not even close," someone muttered.

"Another one!" Bows bent and arrows flew. Angry curses followed the wolf as it escaped.

Three more shapes ran from the darkness, sprinting for the palisade. From their position on top of the stockade, the farmers only caught glimpses of the wolves. Several bows sang and arrows struck the dirt about the racing forms. No wolves were hit, and they were soon lost from view beneath them, hidden by the thick briar hedge.

"Blast and damn—missed." One chap cursed. "They're too fast."

The men leant over trying to see the wolves, but the palisade itself made it difficult to look down and the briar hedge concealed them. Below, they heard the frantic scratching of claws on wood.

"What the hell is going on?" Kaplyn heard. "Wolves don't attack farms."

"Tell them that," someone answered.

"They're demon lead," shouted another.

"Hold your tongue," Callan called. "I'll have no such talk, especially in front of the youngsters."

Several more shapes bolted from the darkness and scores of arrows thumped into the ground around the racing forms. Voices shouted warnings to others to prepare, but the wolves were difficult targets. With growing confidence, more ran from the darkness, racing towards the wall. Abruptly yelps filled the night air as arrows finally found targets.

"We would do better if we had something to stand on, so we could shoot down over the palisade, Callan," Kaplyn suggested.

The farmer nodded and shouted down to his wife to get as many people as she could to find boxes and stools.

"And boiling water," Kaplyn called as an afterthought. "Where is Vastra?" Kaplyn muttered under his breath.

Lars shook his head. 'Probably still in bed!"

Women arrived, each carrying a stool or box that the men used to step up to shoot down upon the briar. Cauldrons filled with boiling water followed and farmers tipped these over the wall and onto the briar. Several wolves broke cover and arrows swiftly brought these down.

Still more wolves came. The wolves' recklessness alarmed Kaplyn; even though bodies littered the ground, newly arriving wolves seemed undeterred. To make matters worse, the sound of splintering wood suggested some were close to breaking through.

Within the compound young children screamed hysterically. Most of their parents were busy on the wall and the few that remained within the compound struggled to keep control.

"I'm no help here," Lars said. "I'll go below."

Kaplyn barely nodded as he released another arrow, sending a shape stumbling head over heels. He glanced over his shoulder. The pandemonium below startled him; people were scurrying back and forth and smaller children were huddled together, crying.

Abruptly a scream rent the night air.

A wolf loped around the corner of a building, followed heartbeats later by a second. Both paused, teeth bared. Kaplyn saw a small boy standing alone, howling with fear. The wolves started to lope towards him, swiftly gathering speed.

"Lars!" Kaplyn screamed, pointing. "The boy!"

Lars had reached the bottom of the stairs and he turned and saw where

Kaplyn was pointing. Bellowing, he sought to distract the animals as he sprinted towards the boy, his sword raised.

Fortunately, Lars arrived first; bowling the boy out of the way his sword fell, cleaving the skull of the nearest wolf, which was in mid-leap. Even at a distance, Kaplyn heard the thud of the sword's contact. The wolf collapsed in a growing pool of blood just as the second wolf leapt at Lars who was struggling to free his sword from the downed wolf's skull.

"Look out!" Kaplyn yelled.

The wolf hit Lars, tumbling them both to the ground. For a moment neither moved; then Lars pushed the body off and stood up. An arrow protruded from the beast's side. Farther along the wall towards Kaplyn, Ralph lifted his bow and Lars acknowledged his help with a wave.

A woman ran to the boy, scooping him up and sprinting to a nearby building. Seeing this, men started to forsake the walls to protect their families.

Then a new and more terrifying howl carried on the still night air, freezing Kaplyn's blood. This was different to the other howls, like that of a wolf, yet much more powerful—a portent of evil.

Callan turned to Kaplyn. "What *in the name of the Kalanth* was that?"

"*Werewolf!*" one of the men close to Kaplyn muttered. Others agreed and a murmur went around the defenders.

Kaplyn turned and found Vastra standing there. Overcoming his shock he asked, "A werewolf? Is that possible?"

Vastra shrugged. "I've never heard of werewolves except in tales."

"If you are a *wizard* then you should help!" Kaplyn said. His patience of the other man was wearing dangerously thin.

Vastra scowled. "I'm a *sorcerer*, not a wizard. Whether I help or not is my decision, not yours. However, I *have* decided to help. Look to the torches, what do you see?"

Kaplyn frowned. "I don't understand"

"What colour are the flames of the torches closest to us?"

"Blue."

"And flames burn blue in the presence of a demon," Vastra returned.

"*A demon?* You are kidding?"

"Not a demon fully manifested in this world, but I suspect a wolf has been possessed. It's probably trying to seek a human host."

Kaplyn couldn't believe what he was hearing. Vastra shook his head as though he knew it was a waste of time trying to explain.

"Give me one of your arrows," Vastra said.

Kaplyn complied and using the tip of a small knife, Vastra scratched a rune on the arrowhead. Kaplyn frowned and the frown deepened when Vastra spat on it.

"The rune needs a water-elemental, otherwise it is just scratches on metal," Vastra explained. "If it is a demon, then the rune will cause it greater harm than the arrow ever could. Look to your front. Don't be alarmed for I will conjure a light. It won't last long so you will have to be quick to spot the possessed wolf."

Kaplyn turned to face the night, certain that Vastra was mad.

Vastra muttered something and at once a bright light flared, illuminating the ground before them, causing Kaplyn to jump in shock even though he had been warned. The glare made him squint while his mind reeled with the knowledge that he had just witnessed real magic.

To his front was a sea of writhing bodies. Hundreds of wolves filled his view. Round marble eyes stared back, reflecting the light, making the animals seem hellish.

"Look! There! Near the back of the pack!" Vastra said.

Kaplyn did not know what to look for and then all at once he did. One wolf reared up amongst the bodies. It was unnatural. It tried to stand on hind legs as though human. Kaplyn drew back his bow, sighted and let loose the arrow without pausing.

By his side Vastra muttered something unintelligible, causing the arrow to flare in its flight like a shooting star. A deep-throated cry filled the air as the wolf reared backwards, falling amongst the others.

Abruptly the light failed, and night returned Kaplyn retained an image of the wolf in his mind and the look of baleful hatred on its face horrified him. Never had he encountered such a thing. He now had an inkling why his people were so superstitious. If Vastra was correct and this was a *possession*, then what would a full-fledged demon be like?

All around Kaplyn was a stunned silence; abruptly the wolves in the briar hedge broke cover, running away from the farm. Howls filled the air, but these seemed more normal and there was even a note of fear.

Kaplyn turned to talk to Vastra, but he was gone; it was almost as if he had never been there. Kaplyn shivered. Soon he was alone and there was no sense remaining. Within the stockade the people remained busy and Kaplyn avoided them as he made his way back to his room. Vastra was either asleep or feigning it and Kaplyn was too stunned to seek answers, or even to wait for Lars. All at once he felt a dreadful lethargy. Throwing himself onto the floor and kicking off his boots, he was asleep in seconds.

The morning came much too quickly. Sunlight streamed through the chinks in the fabric covering the window. Kaplyn and Lars awoke to find Vastra lying on the pallet, staring at the ceiling. Together the three men rose and returned to the main hall where they found Callan and his wife waiting to serve them breakfast.

"Thank you for last night," Callan said. "We killed upwards of thirty wolves. I had my men burn the bodies in case the sheep get wind of their stench."

"Did they find anything unusual?" Kaplyn asked, sitting down.

Callan shook his head and laughed, "You mean the mutterings about a werewolf? I think we let our imagination get the better of us. Your friend's light scared them off though. That was a fine piece of magic if I may say so."

"Is that what happened? I wondered why the wolves turned tail if you'll pardon the pun," Lars said. "They ran off because of the light? Well, I suppose that makes sense. It scared me half to death. You should warn someone before doing that, Vastra."

Kaplyn convinced himself that he was being silly; it was a wolf he had killed and nothing more. He helped himself to bread, which he buttered and smothered in honey. He caught Vastra eyeing him, but the other man looked away. Kaplyn felt foolish all at once. Had Vastra been teasing him about a possession?

"It's a strange portent though, the wolves attacking last night, especially coming so soon after the krell raid on Burland farm," Callan said.

Kaplyn was shocked. "I hadn't heard about any krell raids."

"Where have you been?" Callan asked. "Krell have been raiding the borders for several years now, and they are becoming bolder. Burland was a good day's march from the mountains and their route must have taken them close to Kinlin castle. They killed or captured everyone, and only three men survived. They were in the fields and returned to find no one left, other than charred corpses."

"I'm sorry," Kaplyn said, genuinely disturbed. "The news had not reached Dundalk."

Callan nodded. "The survivors live with us now and we are stronger for it. By the time the King's troops arrived the krell were long gone, but to give the Hest Commander his due, he followed them as far as he dared. The mountains are a dangerous place, and I cannot say I blame him for quitting. Perhaps if we were richer then the King would choose to protect us better."

Kaplyn frowned, fighting an inner rage. He did not like to hear accusations against his father, especially ones suggesting his people were being left defenceless. He vowed to speak with him upon his return.

Callan toyed with his food. "You would be welcome to stay with us," he said. "We could use your bow arm and your friend's strength." Callan smiled at Lars and then timidly looked at Vastra. "I admit that a wizard would be more than useful. What do you say?" he asked.

The offer touched Kaplyn. "I'm sorry," he replied, not wanting to hurt Callan's feelings. "Your offer is tempting, but unfortunately we have other commitments."

Callan smiled. "Never mind. You did us a good service last night. If you are ever in the area and need a place to rest, then you would be more than welcome to stay with us." Callan suddenly brightened. "Now, if the offer still holds, then we would appreciate your friend's help with the corn, and there is my bull."

At the edge of a large field a small crowd gathered, waiting to see Vastra cast his spell. Rumour had swiftly spread that Vastra was responsible for the light the night before and, anyone that wasn't otherwise busy, crowded around, eager to see magic performed.

Vastra glowered at Kaplyn before crouching down to study the tiny green shoots poking above the rich soil. Kaplyn smiled. That he had riled Vastra was a small victory. He grinned across at Lars, but the big man was intent on Vastra who was experimentally rubbing soil between his fingers. He looked satisfied and started to trace a rune in the dry soil, muttering a few words as he did so. The crowd edged forward, trying to hear better and many looked disappointed as though they had expected the shoots to leap from the soil to a brazen fanfare.

Vastra merely arose and the crowd reverently parted to let him pass as he started towards the stockade.

"Is that it?" Callan asked uncertainly, watching Vastra's retreating form.

Kaplyn nodded, not knowing what to say; last night was the first time he had seen magic performed and he, too, was not sure of what to expect. The farmer beamed as together they followed the reticent sorcerer back to the stockade and his prize bull where a similar spell was to be cast. Afterwards the crowd dispersed happily believing that the bull would now sire many heirs.

While they returned to Callan's house, Vastra remained silent, ignoring Callan's thanks. Kaplyn could not understand his behaviour, after all the farmers had been more than courteous. Even though it was simple fare, it was all they had to offer. At the house Ralph, holding their horses, awaited them. Some children came to watch them go and Kaplyn noticed the girl from the previous night, standing behind the small figures. He smiled awkwardly, pleased by her attention but feeling guilty about the thoughts he had harboured towards her the night before.

Once more Callan thanked them for their help, reminding them again that they were welcome to stay. Kaplyn looked at the girl and quickly returned his attention back to Callan and once more he rejected his well-meant offer. A memory of Emma declaring that she was only a maid sprang to mind. What would his father think if he knew he was eyeing up a farmer's daughter? Kaplyn thanked Callan for his hospitality and together the three men mounted. As they set off Kaplyn glanced back, and the girl waved to him. Smiling broadly Kaplyn returned her wave, all thoughts of his earlier guilt banished as he grinned broadly. It was going to be a beautiful day.

Kaplyn's mood changed as they rode. He kept thinking about Vastra's ill temper when dealing with Callan. A short way later and he could contain himself no longer. "Why were you rude to the farmers, Vastra?"

"Because they are clods," Vastra sneered. "They do nothing more than dig in the dirt, hoping for better days."

The outburst surprised Kaplyn and he signalled to Lars to keep him from voicing his own anger. For a while they rode in silence. Kaplyn frowned as he considered what might have upset the sour wizard. He was losing patience with the other man and was debating whether to leave him and to head for home. Emma would be pleased to see him, and his brothers would be green with envy when he told them about his recent adventures. Initially, he had felt obliged to accompany Vastra, after he had paid for his lodgings, but now he felt that debt was paid, especially after helping to defend the farm against the wolves.

Just as Kaplyn was about to say something, Vastra broke the silence and this time Kaplyn detected a note of sadness. "I was brought up on such a farm with my mother. I never knew my father and, until recently, I did not know who he was. Can you imagine a small boy growing up in such a close-knit community without a father? Bastard they called me." His face flushed red, and his eyebrows beetled.

"I was later told that my father was a traveller who stayed the night, requesting lodgings — as we just did. He was with a group of men. Rich men at that, possibly even nobles — or so many thought. The sight of their wealth no doubt turned my mother's head. I questioned others in the village and one man claimed to have seen a crest on their saddles. He drew it in the dirt, and I copied it. Later I discovered it was the royal crest, no less!"

Kaplyn's heart lurched; he had a terrible premonition of what was to come. A crow rose from the bushes to their side and cawed shrilly into the air as though voicing its own anger.

Vastra's eyes blazed with suppressed rage. His eyes flickered briefly to the crow as he composed himself before continuing. "Some years later I found out who my father was."

He seemed to be waiting for them to ask whom, but neither did.

"It was the king!" Vastra announced.

Kaplyn's breath caught, and he stared at Vastra, not wanting to hear any more.

"The king was in his early forties then, but there was no mistake," Vastra continued.

Kaplyn was stunned. His heart was beating furiously, and he felt his face redden. "You cannot be sure it was the king," he stated firmly.

"Oh, but I *am*," Vastra sneered. "Much later my mother, amongst others, described him to me and I have since seen him with my own eyes. There is no mistake.

"Also, do not forget, I am a *wizard*," he spat the last word as if it was a rotten taste in his mouth. He glared angrily at Kaplyn. "I have ways of finding out the truth — ways that you could not imagine."

Kaplyn could not believe it and he wanted to protest.

"That is not a reason to hate the farmers," Lars interrupted. "They work hard. You saw their homes. They have so little and yet they were willing to share their provisions with us."

"They are happy to live their lives as slaves and have neither the intelligence nor wit to seek a better life!" Vastra snapped.

"You were lucky to be able to escape such a life, and you should not begrudge the farmers theirs. Not everyone is capable of magic!" Lars replied.

Vastra looked furious. However, he bit his lip and refrained from a retort.

Kaplyn also remained silent—his feelings in turmoil. He had kept his origins a secret from the other two men and now, more than ever, he must guard that secret. His gaze kept going to Vastra and he realised that, if he spoke the truth, then they were half-brothers. He *couldn't* believe him, nor the coincidence that had brought them together. He was perplexed but reasoned that he had better stay with Vastra—if only to keep an eye on him.

Was Vastra a threat to his father? The venom in Vastra's voice suggested he was, and a premonition of fear sent a shudder down Kaplyn's spine.

Chapter 8
Dark Thoughts

They camped by a shallow stream that gurgled merrily over pebbles. It was a pleasant site, but Vastra chose to sit apart. Kaplyn and Lars cooked a meal and called Vastra over as soon as it was ready. Stiffly he arose as though his joints pained him, and he came across to sit beside them, accepting a plateful of a thick stew without uttering a word of thanks.

Kaplyn sought to engage him in conversation, trying to keep his own feelings in check. "You mentioned a difference between sorcerers and wizards. What is it?"

Vastra searched Kaplyn's expression as though judging whether he was mocking him. Finally, he set his plate down and started to speak.

"When I was young, about six or seven years old, an old man took me under his wing. He must have seen the other boys bullying me or perhaps he was lonely and sought company. Whatever the reason, he suggested that I help him, and become his apprentice. He was the town's wizard. Wizards are the Akrane in the Eldric tongue. He was held in high regard by the farmers but being a wizard, his power was limited." Vastra looked at Kaplyn.

"Go on," Kaplyn urged.

"Well, he could do magic, but it was a mean sort of magic. Simple things like predicting when it would rain, encouraging seeds to germinate and such like"

"That sounds like useful magic to me," Lars interrupted.

Vastra ignored him. "He taught me to read and write. I remember being terribly excited. He had a small library and I enjoyed reading above all else. After about a year he showed me his spell book. Then, it seemed a marvel but now I know it was very minor magic. He explained that a wizard was like a receptacle within which magic could be harnessed. All Akrane wizards were like that, and the greater the wizard the deeper the capacity for magic."

Vastra paused. He toyed with a stick, absently doodling in the soil by his feet. "He taught me to draw the symbols from his book. Runes they were, and the more intricate the rune the more powerful the spell. I learnt swiftly, memorising each symbol, even though I did not yet understand them."

"Once I had mastered the runes he taught me their names, making me repeat them over and over. Only then did he take me to one side to try a spell. I traced the rune and spoke the name. We both waited. It was a simple spell to light a fire. However, nothing happened. I was devastated and I tried repeatedly to cast the spell. The old man knew long before I would admit defeat that I didn't have the capacity to be a wizard." The stick Vastra was toying with snapped as he pressed it into the ground.

"While I was training, the other boys feared me; lest I learn some great magic. After my failure, they tormented me more than ever."

Vastra looked Kaplyn in the eyes. "You asked what the difference was between a wizard and a sorcerer; then I will tell you. The old man had other books and one told of the Eldric sorcerers—Narlassar they named themselves. Sorcerers use the spirit world for their spells and that is *far* more powerful than the Akrane magic, for it is boundless."

Kaplyn wanted him to stop but the tale captivated him. The Eldric intrigued him, and he hungered to know more. "What happened?" he asked.

"I hid a book about the Eldric in my bedroom. There were runes in it that seemed to speak to me, and I felt that I knew some of their names. I traced one in the soil using a stylus and said the name aloud. Nothing happened so I spoke the name again, repeating it in different ways. After many attempts a flame flared into being, spinning in front of me as though in a dance. I was amazed. It was a fire elemental, and it was beautiful, like a tiny figure within an orange flame. It disappeared after a while and so I cast another rune and spoke that. It was a water elemental and that too danced around my room until fading."

"I found that while an elemental was present, I could cast some of the spells that the old man had taught me. I was using *his* magic, but through the spirit world."

"When the old man found out, he was furious—and afraid. He refused to speak to me, but I was not bothered for I had my magic and next time the others bullied me I summoned a fire elemental. It worked a treat, burning the bully's hair and scalp, too, before disappearing. After that no one picked on me again and I was finally treated with respect."

Kaplyn was stunned. He could imagine the farmers leaving Vastra alone, but not out of respect. They would have been terrified.

Lars, too, looked taken aback.

By now it was dusk and only a few birds were singing. Kaplyn could hardly believe that, only last night, wolves had attacked and here was Vastra, scaring them half to death with ghost stories. Kaplyn grimaced.

As though prompted by his thoughts a lone wolf howled in the distance and Kaplyn jumped before looking over his shoulder.

Vastra sneered. "You are afraid," he laughed. "I tell you stories about elementals, and it scares you. There are forces in the world far more terrifying than wolves or elementals."

"What do you mean?" Lars asked.

"Demons," Vastra said.

"And you know about them?" Kaplyn asked.

Vastra remained silent but held his gaze.

Kaplyn grew annoyed. "I have heard that wizards are every bit as powerful as sorcerers."

Vastra snorted. "Perhaps if a wizard had a kara-stone, but not otherwise."

"What is a kara-stone?" Lars asked.

"A kara-stone is used for storing magic," Vastra continued. "Some think that a kara-stone is what remains when a wizard dies. There are other theories, but there is no doubt that the stones are rare. With one, a wizard can increase his powers and, some say, become as strong as a Narlassar sorcerer, but frankly I don't believe that!"

"What do the stones look like?" Lars asked.

"I don't know. I've never seen one, although I believe they are simply stones to look at."

They fell silent and then Vastra rose. "I'm going to turn in," he said.

"What about a guard?" Kaplyn said. "You'll have to take turn at sentry."

Vastra sneered down at him. "I am not afraid of the night." He turned, seeking a comfortable spot to lay his blanket.

"I don't trust him," Lars whispered.

The other man's honesty relieved Kaplyn. "I agree. But I have reason to stay with him for a while at least."

Kaplyn didn't want to explain that Vastra was a threat to his father, not without giving away his own identity.

"We need to take turns on guard," Kaplyn said. "I'll take the first watch."

Lars nodded and laid his blanket by the fire.

Kaplyn looked out into the growing night. Vastra was becoming more and more of an enigma. Fate had brought them together and Kaplyn knew he should keep Vastra close. He was very afraid of the consequences otherwise.

Later the next morning, as they rode, the scenery changed and they found themselves on the edge of a flat plain, stretching far into the distance. Ahead, low hills interrupted the skyline and Vastra explained that Tanel lay at their base. Herds of wild deer fed upon lush grass, moving away each time the riders drew even remotely close. Finally, they could see the ruins of Tanel ahead and, in anticipation, they increased their pace.

Kaplyn was very disappointed. As he had predicted it was nothing more than ruins. A few buildings partially survived, but these were husks without even roofs. At some time in the past the city walls must have collapsed, and people had probably scavenged the stones for their homes, judging by how few remained.

They paused at the city's boundary. Vastra was still moody, and their arrival had done little to cheer him. "Come," he said simply, turning his back to the city.

Riding a few hundred yards Vastra dismounted, bidding them do likewise. Lars tethered the horses to a nearby tree and joined them, looking back at the remains. Vastra walked forward, taking a pouch from his belt before squatting on the ground. Kaplyn was surprised to see the bag only contained sand, which Vastra used to trace an intricate design on the ground. The rune was very complex and Kaplyn and Lars watched in silence.

Once satisfied, Vastra started to speak arcane words that slipped from Kaplyn's mind immediately after hearing them. As before at the farm, nothing appeared to happen, but then the air shimmered and, all at once, the ruins were gone — in their place was a city; no longer the crumbling remains that had marked the site previously, but a whole city; a city of tall, bright spires and high solid walls.

Both Kaplyn and Lars stepped back in fear.

"How is this possible?" Kaplyn asked, truly in awe of Vastra.

'This city exists in another time," he said, smiling with pride. "The Eldric did this to safeguard their home."

Kaplyn and Lars could not take their eyes from the walls. A faint circle of light shimmered between them and the city, as though they were seeing it through a giant lens.

Kaplyn had the distinct impression that the city was still a long way off, even though it appeared to be only a few hundred yards away. There were two walls encircling it, and within they could see spires and rooftops. The inner wall towered protectively above the outer wall and together they wove an intricate pattern around the circumference. Bridges, guarded by tall watchtowers, linked the walls at intervals and a tall tower rose at the city's heart, a silver pennant flying bravely from its peak.

"Are you sure it's uninhabited?" Lars asked. Kaplyn agreed; he could easily imagine people watching them from the narrow windows.

Vastra pointed to the central tower. "That tower is where you will find the pendant. There is an element of risk, and I don't know what you'll find inside. No doubt the buildings will be old and may even be unstable. Remember that the pendant has a map on one side and Eldric writing on the other."

Kaplyn felt breathless with the prospect of exploring and wanted to start immediately.

"We should rest before entering," Lars suggested, seeing Kaplyn's look of eagerness. "It would be wise to be refreshed before starting."

"Very wise," Vastra answered. "Tonight, I will keep watch."

Kaplyn looked at Vastra uncertainly, remembering his refusal to stand guard on previous occasions.

"Have no fear," Vastra said. "I will stand guard. Lars is correct; you need to be rested before entering. Tomorrow will be the greatest moment of your lives."

Kaplyn looked at the city with a mixture of fear and anticipation. *What could go wrong?* he thought. After all, the city *is* deserted.

A silver pennant flew over the central tower, a last defiant symbol of the greatest nation to populate the land; and yet all that now remained was an empty city; only a sanctuary for the ghosts of the forgotten past. By now, the sun was sinking quickly, and the shadows were lengthening like giant snakes as darkness crept from the hollows in its eternal struggle to lay claim to the land.

In the distance, a wolf howled welcoming once more the coming night, causing a shiver of trepidation to flutter down Kaplyn's spine.

When morning came, Kaplyn awoke feeling greatly refreshed even though he had woken in the middle of the night. He had been gratified to find Vastra pacing the camp's perimeter. At least, on this occasion, he had kept his word.

Kaplyn rose and went over to Lars to wake him. The other man grumbled before sitting up, rubbing his eyes and blinking at the Eldric city as though he had forgotten about the previous day's events. Vastra had already prepared breakfast and together they ate in silence.

Kaplyn enjoyed the quiet. He was afraid but did not want to admit it. He took in his surroundings. It was early, the sun had barely risen and only a faint glow lit the horizon. Clouds dominated the sky, but patches of blue suggested it might clear later. The air smelt wonderfully fresh, carrying with it the gentle scents of spring. In all likelihood, it was going to be a beautiful day. Nonetheless, he could not still the hammering of his heart and the trembling of his hands.

All too soon the moment came to leave. Taking his bow, Kaplyn stood by the camp's perimeter, looking towards the great walls. Lars joined him and glancing at the other man he saw the fear in his eyes. Kaplyn smiled to himself, recognising his own inner turmoil. At that moment, a golden dawn framed the city whilst around them birds twittered, welcoming the birth of a new day. Kaplyn's smile turned into a grin at the prospect of an adventure.

"Come on," he said, slapping Lars lightly on the shoulder. The other man smiled back.

"Aye, if we leave now, we can be back for lunch!"

"Is that all you think about, food?"

"Don't forget the beer," Lars replied, grinning broadly.

Vastra was ready with ropes and grappling hooks. In high spirits, they walked towards the halo of light and the city beyond. The two men paused in front of the shimmering air.

"I don't suppose there is any point in waiting?" Lars asked.

Kaplyn shook his head. Together they stepped forward and immediately Kaplyn felt as though his muscles were leaden. It was almost impossible to move, and he really had to struggle to make progress, as though walking through deep treacle.

Kaplyn tried to look at Lars, but even that was hard work.

"Keep going," Kaplyn urged as he struggled on, and then all at once, as quickly as the strange feeling had come, it left as though a giant invisible hand had released him.

"What, *by all the gods*, was that?" Lars proclaimed. "Vastra could have warned us. I thought we had triggered a trap!"

Kaplyn looked back. The halo of light was behind them, and they could see Vastra beyond, although he was strangely still.

"I have no idea what it was. It doesn't seem to have been a trap; after all nothing happened," Kaplyn replied.

Now they were through the halo he could see the city more clearly. Up close, signs of weathering made the stonework seem less mystical.

"Come on, let's see if we can enter," Kaplyn said.

They aimed towards a large, double gate, flanked by tall watchtowers. The timbers were thick and durable; each plank was twice the height of Lars. The big man strained against the portal, but it remained shut.

"It seems the Eldric didn't want anyone to enter," Lars conceded.

Kaplyn looked around. "It would take at least a day to walk the perimeter and, even then, we might not find another entrance unlocked. Can you throw a rope over the outer wall?"

Lars nodded. To Kaplyn's amusement it took several tries but eventually a grappling hook sailed over the wall and a rope dangled from the battlement. Lars gave it a tug to check it was secure.

"After you," Lars offered.

Kaplyn looked up and, taking the rope in both hands, started to climb, using his feet to walk up the wall. It was a difficult climb but after a while, they were finally standing on the battlements of the outer wall.

"Now where?" Lars asked. "The towers?"

It did seem the next logical step. The towers guarded a bridge connecting the inner and outer wall.

"We can but try," Kaplyn replied, knowing it was too easy and there was bound to be a complication. Access to the bridge was through the tower and a door blocked their path. Kaplyn tried the handle.

"Thought so. It's locked."

"Another rope up to the next level," Lars suggested.

Kaplyn looked over the battlements. It was a considerable distance to the inner wall, which was quite a lot higher than their present position.

"Can you do it?" Kaplyn asked.

Lars grinned and set about repeating the earlier task of throwing a grappling hook over the inner wall. Again, it took several attempts, but the big man's strength was equal to the task.

"Well done," Kaplyn praised him when he finally succeeded. Lars drew in the slack and then tied their end of the rope around one of the crenelations on the outer wall. The rope was at an angle from the outer wall to the inner and Kaplyn didn't like the idea of climbing it at all.

"This climb is going to be much harder than the last one," Lars said.

Kaplyn nodded. "And I don't much like heights," he admitted.

"Neither do I," Lars said.

"I'll go first," Kaplyn offered.

The hard part was starting. Kaplyn found the trick was to hook his heels over the rope and to pull and slide his way up the rope. Halfway up, he made the mistake of looking down, causing his head to spin. The inner wall was much higher than the outer, so they were already high up.

By mid-morning, they were finally standing on the battlements of the inner wall. Both men were breathing hard and sweating freely.

"That's some view," Lars said, looking into the city.

Kaplyn nodded. Broad streets radiated from the city's heart like the spokes of a massive wheel. Tall trees and grassy verges lined the streets, and to their amazement the trees were in blossom and a gentle fragrance filled the air.

The tower, marking their destination, drew Kaplyn's attention. It arose ominously above the surrounding buildings, a giant obelisk pointing accusingly to the heavens and the gods beyond.

"I don't like this place, I feel as though we're being watched," Lars said.

Kaplyn tore his gaze away from the city and nodded. "I agree. It's a strange place. Let's get on with this, the sooner we leave the better."

They followed the narrow walkway atop the battlements for a short way and came to a tower. Kaplyn tried the handle, and, to his satisfaction, it opened. They entered the cool dark interior. Stone stairs spiralled down into the depths below and Kaplyn began to feel giddy as they descended the tight and seemingly endless spiral.

At a run, he came out into the open where he found himself looking along one of the broad streets. Kaplyn was in awe as they walked down the street. The houses to either side were stone-built, with no sagging beams in sight.

"Do you think we should look inside?" Kaplyn ventured, wanting to explore.

"No!" Lars countered, almost before Kaplyn had finished speaking. "Vastra warned us that it might be dangerous. Let's not chance our luck."

"You're right," Kaplyn agreed, albeit reluctantly. He could barely take his eyes from the buildings and felt drawn to them like a moth to the flame. "What a pity. We could be passing a fortune."

All too soon, they were standing in the tower's shadow, looking up in awe at its size. Kaplyn climbed broad stone steps leading to a set of wooden doors. He tried the handles, but the door refused to open. A circuit of the tower proved fruitless, and they found themselves standing before the steps once more.

"How do we get in?" Lars asked doubtfully. "I mean, we can hardly break the doors down — can we?"

Kaplyn shook his head. His gaze kept returning to a small window set ten feet above the ground. After a moment, he realised why it had caught his attention and a broad smile crossed his face.

"That window's open," he said, pointing.

Lars groaned; its shadow revealed that it was only just ajar. Grinning, he stood beneath the window with his back to the wall and cupped his hands. Kaplyn placed a booted foot in Lars' hands and the other man hoisted him up.

Kaplyn reached the sill and pulled himself up, using his toes to push himself up the wall. He sat there so that he could work the window open wider.

Gradually his eyes to adjusted to the darkness within. The room was large but sparsely furnished. He could see a few wooden chairs and a small round table, covered in a thick layer of dust. Tapestries, bleached with age, decorated the walls.

He wanted to enter.

"Lars, wait for me. I'll open the doors to let you in," he instructed. With that he jumped through the opening to the floor, barely a few feet below. Almost as soon as he did, he felt a terrible premonition. Then the light failed, plunging him into a despairing night.

    Kaplyn fell. Not the short distance he had anticipated, but an eternity. Blackness engulfed him and he knew no more.

Chapter 9
Alone

"Wake up!" demanded the voice.

Kaplyn didn't want to; the pain was too great. He remembered falling, reaching out to grab hold of anything to stop his fall—his heart lurching, his arms flailing, air rushing past his ears, complete and utter darkness and then … nothing.

This wasn't a dream. His head, legs and back all hurt. A moan escaped his lips; raising his hand, he felt a lump on his temple. His eyes were open, yet he couldn't see. Panic escalated and he fought against it, trying to remain calm, breathing deeply.

Groaning, he tried to rise but agony caused him to flop back.

"Help," he croaked. Even to his own ears his voice seemed frail. "Help," he tried again, louder. Silence, not even a bird or the sound of wind. "Is anyone there? Lars, can you hear me?"

To distract himself he went through a mantra, flexing his fingers, his wrists, his elbows, checking for damage. There were no breaks, but each twinge suggested plenty of bruises.

Something was digging into his back. Sitting up resulted in beads of sweat forming on his brow. Releasing a breath, he groaned. Momentarily his head swam, and he waited for the nausea to subside. Behind him, he discovered shards of wood. One long length had twine attached; his bow he realised. It was broken. He cursed; it was a good bow, a gift from a friend.

Grimacing, he arose to a crouch, tangling himself in a scabbard hanging from his belt. He sucked air into his lungs and the fresh wave of pain caused him to wince. He drew the sword, checking that the blade was whole. He drew his knife and felt it. That, too, was undamaged.

An elusive glow caught his attention and he turned, trying to find it. Gradually it grew in intensity, like the coming of the dawn. Nonetheless, it took a while for his eyes to focus. A large, grey object surrounded him, probably a wall. Something was dreadfully wrong though; with that premonition, he looked down.

Lurching to one side, a cry escaped his lips; he dropped his knife, which clanked noisily. Throwing out his hands his fingers cracked against a solid surface, causing him to yelp.

It was impossible. It did not make sense.

He was crouching apparently on thin air; beneath him was a terrifying drop. He stared into the depth in disbelief before shutting his eyes.

Refusing to look down he opened his eyes and cast around for something that *might* make sense. His vision was better. He was within a building of sorts, and a circular stone-built wall was about twenty feet from him. Higher up, the wall disappeared into shadows.

"*Kalanth, save me*," he murmured. Keeping his head held high he groped for his knife. Finding it, he sheathed it before twisting around to take stock of his situation.

Relief flooded through him; there was an open doorway framed in the wall about three times his body length from his position. Beyond the doorway was a solid looking floor and beyond that a wall. He wanted to run towards it and the safety that beckoned.

"Be calm," he murmured, slowing his breathing. He risked looking down. Giddiness threatened. He swayed and fell, slamming his hand against the invisible surface. He exhaled slowly, trying to stave off vertigo.

Lowering himself to his knees, he slid his hands experimentally forward, but they slipped over an unseen edge. Air whooshed from his lungs as he slammed into the invisible barrier. He swore, but common sense made him lie still. He dare not move, not without knowing how far the platform extended. His arms were completely over the edge. Extending his reach there was no sign of anything below. If he had run to the door, as he first wanted, he would have fallen, and he could only guess how far that was.

Sweat trickled down his brow and stung his eyes. Blinking, he felt to his left and found a similar drop; to his right however the path continued. It was not very wide; he had been lucky not to fall off when he had first lost his balance. To his irritation, the path led him away from the doorway and he had no option but to follow on his hands and knees. The path took a few more turns, but then headed once more towards the doorway.

With only a few yards to go, a clang sounded from above. It was distinctly something large and metallic striking stone. An eerie shriek followed, echoing from the shadows above, causing him to jump. He concentrated hard on the door ahead, too afraid to look up. The distance was too far to jump, and he struggled to recall the last few turns. Was there a pattern?

His mind blanked as a louder scream reached him.

Involuntarily, he looked up just as a black shape detached itself from the shadow. Giant wings beat the air clumsily as though the beast was unused to flight; each stroke sounding like the snap of a ship's sail in a storm.

Scrambling forward his hands searched for a path and for a moment he made progress, but once again the floor disappeared under his fingers and again, he fell flat. Another scream sounded and the flapping of wings seemed right above him.

The opening was barely the length of his body away. Scuttling into a crouch he hurled himself at the doorway. His injuries flared afresh, tearing a cry from his lips. He tumbled into the wall, winding himself. A dry flapping sounded behind him. Fighting for breath, he grabbed his dagger, turned and thrust it before him.

The creature flew hard at the doorway causing him to recoil, crying aloud, but the wall at his back blocked his way. It screamed in frustration. Fortunately for Kaplyn it was too large to fly through the doorway. However, it refused to leave, and its wings beat frantically, keeping it near its prey.

It extended a leg, trying to land. With a shout, he thrust at it with his knife, causing it to retreat. Its head cocked to one side and malevolent eyes locked on his, as though willing him to come out. The head was that of a man; long, greasy hair was plastered against an emaciated skull and its oily skin barely reflected what little light there was.

"Kalanth protect me!" he screamed.

The beast's forehead wrinkled. It emitted another ear-splitting scream of rage, revealing rows of razor-sharp teeth. Dropping his knife, he covered his ears.

"Come to me, human," it said thickly.

Flight seemed impossible; he dare not turn away less it attack. He remembered his knife and grabbed it.

The creature hung there for several heartbeats. It was losing height and Kaplyn realised it was tiring.

"Curse you!" it shrieked. "Damn you to hell." With a flurry of wings, it disappeared into the shadows. "*Curse you*!" it screamed finally, and a hundred voices echoed back from the distant recesses of the tower.

Choking, he cast about for a safe escape. The tunnel ended by the doorway but to his left it continued. Scrambling to his feet and keeping his back to the wall, he staggered away from the room with the beast.

Alternately running and stumbling he fled. The tunnel widened, turning sharply to his left and, with relief, he lost sight of the doorway behind.

Sheathing his dagger, he drew his sword. He wouldn't be able to wield it in the confined space, but its extra reach gave him confidence. He continued, glancing over his shoulder every few steps lest the creature followed.

Legs aching, he decided to rest and flopped down on the stone. The lump on his temple was painful to touch and he wondered whether he was concussed. Nothing seemed real. The beast and a room without a floor were unbelievable.

Was this Hell? Was he dead?

A sob escaped him. He arose too quickly, and pain lanced through his legs and ribs; his vision swam, forcing him to remain motionless until the feeling of weakness passed. Determination forced him onwards.

There was no change to the surroundings for some time, then something ahead caused him to pause. It was a light, but it wasn't daylight, this was too blue. A memory triggered: flames burned blue in a demon's presence. Did demons exist?

Very slowly he continued, his sword outstretched for protection. Gradually, the light grew and with it came a rushing sound. Then the reason for the light became evident. Blue flames leapt out of the floor and into the ceiling, completely blocking the tunnel. His heart sank. He couldn't go back and now the way forward was blocked!

Throwing himself down, fresh stabs of agony made him cry out. He slammed a fist into the tunnel wall and grimaced with pain. He thought about Emma, the first time in quite some while but the face of Callan's daughter came unbidden to his mind. He dwelt on her soft features for a while before realising something was wrong.

"What the…? That doesn't make sense."

Only then did he realise there was no heat coming from the flames. Frowning, he tentatively probed the stone floor ahead, finding that it, too, was cold. With a muttered oath, he thrust himself away from the wall and walked forward, his hands outstretched. His frown deepened; there was simply no heat.

Walking to the edge of the flames he thrust a hand forward, quickly snatching it back, testing the heat.

Nothing.

No heat. No burns.

He thrust his hand into the flames more slowly and for several seconds kept it there feeling nothing but a blast of air. Knowing that a delay might weaken his resolve he stepped into the flames.

The rushing air threatened to lift him from his feet. He exulted. His skin felt alive and vibrant as though the flames were purging his body; his ribs felt mended, and the bruises gone. Feeling his temple even the lump was gone.

Striding into the flame's embrace his ears rang with the rush of air. Breathing deeply his lungs tingled and he felt lightheaded. As he walked, the flames seemed to continue forever and the further he went the more confused his senses became. Suddenly he was no longer sure of the right direction; was he even going in a straight line, and he might even now be in a room, rather than a corridor?

A flicker of orange caused him to gasp. Orange flames he understood; they meant heat. Picking up his pace he loped through the conflagration. His skin felt hot, then smouldering. He was burning. Covering his head with his arms he screamed aloud, racing forward.

Without warning, he was in a corridor, free of the surrounding flames.

Yelping in agony he continued to run, throwing his sword in front of him before struggling from his jerkin. Tearing it off he threw it after his sword. Shielding his head with his arms he kicked the jacket and sword ahead.

When the heat was more bearable, he slowed and, looking back, saw that fierce orange flames barred the way. Even at this distance, the heat was intense.

He could not believe he had just come from that. Bending, he retrieved his smouldering jacket, but the sword was still too hot and so he used his jacket sleeve to pick it up.

Shaking his head, despair washed over him and, staggering, he turned to continue his nightmare journey. He had not gone far when gradually the light faded and within a dozen more paces it became black as night. The darkness was terrifying. He held his sword out protectively, using the blade to feel his way ahead. Without warning, it struck something hard, jarring his arm.

With his free hand, he felt wooden planks and traced the outline of a door. His fingers sought the handle. He pushed the door open to reveal an immense cavern, stretching across a lake. It was light enough to see, although there was no obvious source of illumination and then he realised the rock walls were glowing.

The size of the lake astounded him; the opposite shore was lost in the distance. Immediately to his front was a small sandy beach and at its edge, water lapped, looking cold and deep.

"Now what do I do?" he muttered angrily, sitting down, and glaring into the distance. There was clearly no way around the lake; wet, glistening rock walls plunged into the water to either side of the beach.

Go back? He thought. *No, that would be suicide. The flames had been real and besides there was that creature.*

Continuing forward seemed the only option. Angrily he removed his boots and jacket, making these into a bundle. He slung his sword across his back using his belt as a baldric and stepped into the water, cursing roundly at the cold. For some way, the water only came to his calves. Just as he thought he might not need to swim, the ground shelved and, in less than a pace, the water came to his chest. Gasping, he threw his bundle ahead and started to swim vigorously.

"I'm going to survive!" he hissed. His thoughts went to Lars. Suddenly he was afraid that the big man might have followed him. The thought that Lars, too, might fall into this trap spurred Kaplyn on.

As though mocking his determination a distant splash caused him to start. With his own splashing, he was initially uncertain of what he had heard, but the thought was enough. The gods alone knew what lurked in the lake. He foolishly tried to swim higher, keeping as much of his body out of the water as possible. Very quickly his legs became leaden, and he had to swim more evenly.

Just when he felt he could go no further, a dank moss-stained wall materialised from the gloom ahead. Glancing over his shoulder, all he could see was blackness. His teeth chattering, he increased the urgency of his stroke, praying he was going the right way.

A small beach appeared at the foot of the wall, looking very like the one he had left. His heart sank, but at least he would be out of the water. Putting his feet down, water closed over his head; it was deeper than he had expected. He struggled to the surface, coughing, and retching and grabbing his bundle.

He forced himself on and all too slowly the beach drew closer. He risked putting his feet down and this time was rewarded with soft sand beneath his feet. Rising, he waded to the beach, throwing himself onto the dry ground.

"*Thank the Kalanth*," he spluttered.

Trembling, he rose to a sitting position, looking back at the still waters. The beach was different to the one he had set off from; this one was wider and there were more rocks. Relief flooded through him that he had crossed the lake, but was he any better off?

A faint sound came from somewhere across the lake and for a second his heart stopped. Holding his breath, he strained to hear any further noise. A swirl of water a few feet from the shore caused him to jump. A shiny black shape broke the surface, glided along for a few yards before lunging once more into the depths. He kept his gaze fixed on that point as he scrambled away from the water's edge.

The ripples lapped the beach. Whatever he had seen had been real. He could not move and continued staring out into the lake with cold water dribbling from his wet hair into his eyes. Where was he? He had to know.

Rousing himself from his stupor, he turned away from the beach. A tunnel beckoned immediately behind him, but before entering, he dressed and, to his disgust, his wet clothes clung unpleasantly to his body.

A few yards into the tunnel hope came flooding back; this passageway sloped upwards. The incline increased and heartened that he might escape this hellhole he quickened his pace. However, after a while the slope became impossible. He kept sliding back and his calves were aching. Then he nearly fell, and it was all he could do to remain standing, his hands flat on to the wall to prevent himself slipping back. Somehow, the slope had become severe both before and behind him. He doubted that he could go on and yet it did not make sense that the slope could be so steep. Angrily he drew his dagger. Stabbing a crack between the stones in the floor he tried to climb, but the slope seemed to be getting worse.

At least he had a purchase, but he could not stay there forever. He had to try to reason out the situation. Was the tower somehow feeding on his fears? He remembered the flying creature from the first room and realised he had been in a similarly bizarre situation when that had appeared. The thought spurred him on. Wedging himself tightly into the corner, between the wall and floor, he attacked the mortar between two of the stone blocks immediately to his front.

It was an act of desperation, but as he dug, the mortar became softer and fell away easily until he had cleared most of it from around one of the blocks. He had initially contemplated making handholds to help him climb but realised that he might be able to remove one of the blocks and gain access to whatever lay beyond.

A deep groan resonated about him. The intensity and suddenness caused him to slip, and he scraped his knuckles against the stone in his efforts to stop himself. From the gloom below, a figure materialized. In mounting panic Kaplyn once more attacked the block but could not get a firm grip. Pushing the tip of his dagger between the stones he tried to lever one of them out, but his knife jammed.

The figure was close enough to see tattered clothing hanging from burned and grazed flesh. The creature, for he could not bring himself to believe this was a man, carried a sword that, either due to a trick of the light or sorcery, seemed to glow eerily, illuminating the tunnel walls.

It paused sniffing the air, then went into a crouch. Suddenly it leapt closer, emitting a deep snarl.

Kaplyn twisted the dagger, but the blade snapped with a loud and sickening click. Rather than try to lever the stone out he pushed hard. To his surprise, it slid effortlessly inwards.

As though sensing his escape, the creature screamed and leapt the intervening distance, its sword raised to strike.

Kaplyn pulled with all his strength on the stone on the right-hand side of the opening. It came away with a crash, smashing onto the floor. He kicked it, propelling it down the slope.

The creature collided with the stone, which slammed into its shins, shattering them. It fell and then it and the stone accelerated down the tunnel, the creature's screams continuing until abruptly there was silence.

Kaplyn closed his eyes and finally took a breath. He peered through the hole into a room; it was an armoury judging by the assortment of weapons stacked in disorganised piles.

He scrambled through the opening, and found his way blocked as his sword caught on the rough edges. Untangling himself, his wet clothes clung uncomfortably to his flesh causing him to shiver. When he was finally through, his attention went immediately to a dais in the room's centre. Someone had placed a sword and scabbard upon it. The other weapons within the room paled into insignificance by comparison.

The pommel was a semicircle of steel inset with a clear pale blue gem, and the blade was a dull jet-black that seemed to trap the very light. Drawing nearer he became aware of fine gossamer runes inlaid into the sable metal. He recognised the script as Eldric but could not read that language. A voice came from behind him, causing him to jump and bang his knee painfully against the dais.

"Do not touch it!" the voice said.

Kaplyn grabbed the sword and spun around, the point of the weapon levelled against whatever new devilry the tower had conjured. A figure stood unmoving within the shadows like a granite statue, but there the resemblance ended for he could see by the eyes that it was a living being. Why, though, had he not noticed him earlier? The figure detached itself from the shadows and came forward.

He was an old man, leaning heavily upon a wooden staff as though bearing the weight of the world's woes on his shoulders. Every few steps his staff swept the ground before his feet. His eyes were milky white and Kaplyn realised he was blind.

"Too late, I suppose," the newcomer admonished gesturing toward the blade, a disarming smile creasing his face. "Put the sword down. I mean you no harm."

Kaplyn refused to move.

"Perhaps though you are right to take the weapon," he continued, matter-of-factly. "It's Eldric made, and it served its previous master well."

Kaplyn was confused. Was he blind? His milky white eyes clearly marked him as unsighted and yet he spoke as though he could see. At the mention of the sword, Kaplyn abruptly became aware of it. Its balance was perfect, but it felt odd in some way; almost as though it were alive. He recalled how quickly it had come to his hand. For a heartbeat, he considered dropping it, but instead gripped the hilt more fiercely.

The old man's attention was fully upon him, stunning him with the intensity of his gaze.

"Lower the sword," the other man said softly. "As you can see, I am unarmed."

Kaplyn kept the weapon raised, taking a step backwards. "I don't trust anything here," he answered, trying to keep calm.

The other man smiled. "And very sensible too. However, I mean you no harm. Now put your sword down so that we can talk."

Kaplyn found himself lowering the weapon even though his instinct was to keep it levelled.

The other man sighed and turned away. He raised a hand and seemed to feel the air above the weapons as though sensing them.

"Where am I?" Kaplyn asked.

"Tanel. It is an Eldric city."

"I know I am in Tanel, but this tower seems so unreal," Kaplyn said.

"You are in but one tower within Tanel. The tower is real, and not a figment of your imagination. The city beyond, in its day, was the finest in the land. It is deserted now, but you will find that out, no doubt."

The old man seemed to dismiss Kaplyn, and his attention turned to an untidy stack of weapons. Axes, Kaplyn realised, looking closer.

"The dwarves would be interested in these," the old man said. "Although what they truly seek is not here. I feel sorry for the dwarves, very sorry indeed. Already their ordeal has begun, and I fear that they will suffer greatly in the coming years."

"Who are you?" Kaplyn asked.

The old man turned to face him, smiling absently. "Ah, I was forgetting. Old men tend to ramble, or so people tell me. Now, where were we?" He paused, lost in thought. Kaplyn was about to ask him again who he was when the old man became alert all at once.

"That's right. We cannot have this." Before Kaplyn could react, the other man leant forward, and his fingers gently brushed his forehead. His speed surprised Kaplyn who jumped back, raising his sword protectively between them.

"It's all right," the other man assured him. "You carried the mark of a demon upon you," he said, wiping his hand on his robes as though they were contaminated.

"D…demons don't exist," Kaplyn stuttered.

"Oh, but be assured that they do."

Kaplyn shook his head, finally convinced that the other man was mad. "Do you live here?" he asked.

The old man looked about the armoury with a trace of a smile on his lips. "No, and certainly not in an armoury. Once, long ago, many lived here — but the Krell Wars put an end to that; now only ghosts inhabit Tanel."

"Perhaps you should find the Eldric, and the city will awaken to the sounds of happy voices." He stopped his pacing and looked up expectantly, but Kaplyn was at a loss for words.

The other man's look of hope faded. "It seems only fair to remind you of why you are here then. You are searching for a pendant. You will recognise it when you find it. Continue your quest through this tower and you will succeed. Do not fail though, the tower is unforgiving, and you may end up becoming part of what you see."

"What am I seeing?" Kaplyn asked glancing around the room. "Is this place real?"

"Yes, it is real, though it exists in another plane to your own world. Long ago the Eldric, in their wisdom, decided to hide their cities for they could not bring themselves to destroy that which love had built."

"Where are they now?" Kaplyn asked. He found himself distracted for the briefest moment.

"Gone," came the reply, his voice sounding incredibly sad. When Kaplyn looked up the other man was no longer there. He was shocked and searched the room in confusion, but he was alone.

He went to the door to see if the old man had departed that way. The door was ajar and through the crack he could see a stout wooden table blocking the way. It looked heavy. Putting his shoulder to the door, he heaved and was rewarded with a loud rasping sound as the table moved.

Stepping through, he found himself in a room, empty apart from furniture thickly coated in centuries of dust. It was much larger than the armoury and was the first room to show signs of inhabitation; old ornate tapestries hung at odd angles upon the walls.

He decided to re-enter the armoury and explore the stacked weapons, thinking that perhaps the pendant was amongst them. The armoury was a boy's dream, masses of weapons of every kind. Most of them showed signs of rust, and that somehow made the Eldric seem less god-like. He paused by the axes, stooping to pick one up, knowing that Lars would appreciate such a weapon. The one he selected was large and double bladed with a smooth ebony shaft. Fine Eldric lettering decorated the handle, but again he could not decipher this.

Finding a stack of bows he removed the twine from one, using this to make a loop by which he could carry the axe. He took a bow to replace the one he had broken earlier. The twine was too old to use but perhaps he could replace it later. He ran a thumb along the bow, marvelling at how smooth it was. It was a laminate construction; a combination of wood and bone, shorter than other bows he was used to and much more curved. He went back to the dais and took the scabbard, having decided to keep the Eldric sword that he kept drawn as a precaution. He tucked the scabbard into his belt.

He needed arrows and a quick search found several full quivers buried beneath a pile of rotting tapestries. He selected one, which he slung across his shoulder alongside the axe before allowing the tapestries to fall back into place. Lastly, he replaced his broken knife. He spent a short while longer exploring the room, but there was no sign of a pendant and so he decided to revisit the next room.

The adjacent room, apart from the door behind him, had no other obvious exit. A stout wooden chest dominated the corner, and he ransacked the drawers, but discovered only tableware. Not really knowing where else to look, he slowly made another tour of the room. One of the tapestries caught his eye. It was of a dragon flying over a grassy knoll. The dragon was exquisite. It had a graceful swan-like neck, and its wings were like ship's sails in the wind, trapping as much air as possible, holding it mid-flight.

Cautiously he lifted the tapestry's edge with his blade. The ancient cloth shed dust, making him cough as he brushed it from his eyes, waiting for the air to clear. Behind the tapestry was a door and, remembering the previous traps, he checked carefully around the frame before trying the handle.

The hinges groaned as the door swung inwards, causing Kaplyn anxiety in case anything living was beyond; however, the adjoining room was devoid of life. It was similar in size to the one that he was in, but the outer wall curved gradually reminding him that he was within a circular tower. Skirting a wooden table surrounded by ornately carved high-backed chairs, he crossed the room heading towards another door.

He stepped through the doorway, gripping his new sword for comfort and, at last, a shaft of sunlight from a small window lifted his spirits. Dust motes floated in the air, shining like tiny angels. He guessed this was where the guests retired after dining. A display of weapons dominated one wall while tapestries covered the remainder. A glass chandelier hung from the ceiling, casting small rainbows against the walls.

A flash of gold made him look twice. In the centre of the room was a desk and upon it was the object that had caught his attention and with mounting hope he crossed the room. It was a pendant with a thick gold chain. Sweeping it up it easily filled his palm. It was heavy. On one side, there was a map and on the other writing, again in a fine Eldric script.

Instantly he recognised the map as being of his homeland, Allund. He also recognised the Pen-Am-Pelleas, mountain range between Allund and Thrace. He couldn't read the Eldric writing though.

Not wanting to delay any further, he looped the chain about his neck, tucking the pendant into his shirt before turning to leave.

He had a shock as he walked through the next door. Lars was sitting on a window ledge at about chest height from the floor. It was clear that he was about to enter and now his concentration was wholly on the short drop to the floor below. What was bizarre though was that there was a hole in the floor just below the window and the other man seemed oblivious to it.

"Stop!" Kaplyn cried.

Lars visibly jumped and when he looked up a broad grin lit up his face.

"Kaplyn," he said. "Where, by *Slathor*, have you been?" He shifted his weight as though about to jump down from the window ledge.

"Stop," Kaplyn repeated but more gently. "Do not move. Stay where you are," he warned, quickly crossing the distance between them. The other man looked back uncertainly but clambered back onto the ledge.

"Where have you been?" Lars repeated. "You've been ages. I thought you were lost."

"It's a long story. I will tell you later but for now I have a terrible urge to be out of the city before sunset." However, the hole beneath the window and the shadows within held his attention.

"What are you staring at?" the other man asked.

"That hole in the floor," he said waving his arm in the general direction.

"What hole?"

Kaplyn was shaken. "You mean that you can't see it?" He picked up a nearby chair and walking over to the hole he held the chair over it before letting go. As Kaplyn expected the chair fell through the hole, but he didn't hear it landing.

The other man nearly fell off the window ledge with shock. "What the…? What happened to the chair?"

"I take it that's the window I entered?" Kaplyn asked. The other man nodded.

"Come, let's get out of here," Kaplyn urged. Skirting the hole in the floor, he pulled himself onto the window ledge. He paused letting the fresh breeze caress his skin. He took in the scene before him. A cobbled street separated the tower from tall brick buildings opposite. Without waiting he jumped down and, with a thud, Lars landed by his side.

Kaplyn removed the axe he was carrying and gave it to Lars, grinning. "You can get rid of that sword now."

The man took the weapon and his eyes shone as he examined it. After a moment, he slung it over his shoulder before dropping his sword with a clang. "Thanks. But did you find the pendant?"

Kaplyn nodded.

"What, *by Slathor*, took you so long? I was frantic with worry. It's really spooky being in the city on your own."

Kaplyn laughed, "You should worry. Wait until you hear what happened to me, and what nearly happened to you if you had jumped through that hole back there."

Lars paled.

"Come on," Kaplyn urged, and he started to jog, back the way they had come. Shortly, they arrived at the city walls and swiftly they ducked through the opening where stairs led them back up to the battlements. Climbing the stairs, they soon arrived at a door leading out to the battlements. The sun was setting, and the horizon was a mixture of fiery oranges and reds. Low gentle hills extended beyond the city and the landscape was dotted with copses. A warm breeze carried with it the fragrance of spring, lifting Kaplyn's sprits.

Looking back inside the city, Kaplyn's gaze fell on the tower. From this view, it did not look dangerous, but Kaplyn now knew its secret.

"We need to descend the rope," Lars reminded him. Kaplyn grimaced. The rope was attached to the graplin hook Lars had thrown earlier. It didn't look too secure, so Kaplyn anchored the graplin hook in the corner of the crenelation giving it a better purchase. The rope extended at an angle down to the outer city wall where it was tied around another crenelation. Kaplyn pulled on the rope, satisfied that it was secure.

Kaplyn went first and, sitting on the battlement, he grasped the rope. With some difficulty he leant forward, hooked an ankle over the rope, and then swung the other leg over. Hand over hand he descended, letting the rope slide beneath his ankles. It was a quick descent and they soon found themselves standing on the outer wall. The other rope they had climbed earlier let them descend to the ground and they soon found themselves outside the city.

"Wait a moment," Kaplyn said.

He removed his jacket and wrapped the new sword and scabbard in it. For some reason, he was reluctant to let Vastra see the weapon.

"Ok. Let's go," he said.

Lars led them away from the wall. Ahead, Kaplyn could see their horses and near to them a lone figure sitting on the ground. They were still some distance, but they were surprisingly still. Kaplyn then noticed the large circle of air shimmering before them in the failing light. The campsite beyond was like looking through a telescope.

As before, as soon as Kaplyn stepped into the circle he could barely move as though his muscles were frozen. Panicking he struggled harder. Abruptly he was through and all at once Lars was by his side.

"I hate that," Kaplyn said. "It really feels as though you are stuck."

"Yes, I know what you mean," Lars answered breathlessly and eyes wide with fright.

Together, they walked towards the camp. Kaplyn realised then that all around him were the sounds of life. Birds were singing and insects droning. In the barrier, everything had been silent. He shivered and glanced back at the Eldric city. He had escaped, but at what cost?

Chapter 10
The Journey to Kinlin Castle

Vastra was sitting by the fire and as soon as he saw them, he sprang up, coming forward to meet them.

"I don't trust him," Lars said in a whisper.

"Me neither," Kaplyn whispered back. Lars' admission was a relief as Kaplyn was uncertain about Vastra and hearing Lars' concern was helpful.

Vastra's eyes reflected his excitement as he came closer.

"The pendant — do you have it?"

Kaplyn nodded.

"Give it to me!" Vastra demanded, extending a thin arm, his fingers shaking with excitement.

All at once, Kaplyn was unwilling to give the pendant up, especially after all he had been through.

Vastra's smile vanished and his eyes blazed. "Give me the pendant!" he repeated taking a menacing step forward.

His action made Kaplyn even more reluctant to hand it over. By his side Lars cast him an anxious look.

Vastra scowled and then his frown softened. "Of course, your gold!" he reached into his robes and removed the heavy purse. "As promised, two gold pieces each and the silver *calder*," he fished out four gold coins and a veritable pile of silver. He looked up, but Kaplyn did not offer up the pendant.

"I'll double it," Vastra continued. "It's more than a fair price."

"We could have died in there!" Kaplyn accused.

Vastra's look was one of thunder. "You agreed!" he hissed. "Look!" He tipped the contents of the small bag onto the ground. Bright gold coins bounced on the soft grass before coming to rest. It was a small fortune. "Here is all the gold; now give me the pendant."

Kaplyn shook his head.

"It's worthless to you," Vastra said in disbelief. "What is wrong with you?"

Kaplyn remained defiant and after a while a smile touched Vastra's thin lips, and his manner became politer. "Perhaps I have been hasty. Your adventure has probably taxed you. Come, sit by the fire, and relax. Tell me what happened. We will discuss the pendant afterwards." He bent down and recovered the fallen coins.

Vastra led them to the fire. The aroma of cooking filled the air. Kaplyn's mouth watered, he was famished. A stew simmered in a metal pot that sat in the embers at the edge of the fire. Stirring the contents with a ladle Vastra dished a portion out to each in turn, filling small bowls and handing them both a hunk of bread.

Kaplyn recounted his tale as they ate; however, he omitted telling them about the Eldric sword and the old man. For what reason, he was not sure.

Throughout the story Vastra often interrupted, seeking clarification. When Kaplyn had finished speaking, even Vastra looked pale. "I had no idea that it would be so difficult," he said. "But you did well to recover the pendant." Lost in concentration he toyed with his food with his spoon.

"I've had a thought," Lars announced.

"Don't strain yourself," Vastra muttered.

Lars frowned but continued. "Some parts of Kaplyn's tale remind me of the Prophecy he told me about."

"Prophecy?" Kaplyn asked.

"You know, Tallin's Crown and all that…."

Kaplyn shook his head, "I don't understand?"

Lars continued. "There was a part in the Prophecy about someone being born of air, fire and water."

By their side, Vastra sucked in his breath.

"Your journey through the tower reminds me of that. You could argue that you were born from air, fire and water."

Kaplyn smiled. "That's rather fanciful," he said thoughtfully and even Lars went quiet as though the statement was rather lame.

Vastra though seemed agitated. "Who are you?" he asked looking at Kaplyn.

"Kaplyn," he shrugged."

"Are you concealing something from me?" Vastra demanded.

Kaplyn shook his head, but he was uncomfortable that Vastra was staring at him so intently. "I am not hiding anything," he insisted.

At that moment, some instinct made Kaplyn draw back from Vastra but not quickly enough. Vastra's hand lashed out and grabbed his wrist. Pain shot through Kaplyn, and he cried out. Vastra barked some meaningless words and abruptly blackness engulfed Kaplyn.

Kaplyn passed out but only for a few heartbeats. Vastra snatched back his hand from Kaplyn's wrist as though burnt.

"What just happened?" Lars demanded.

"I'm not sure," Kaplyn replied, but then realised he might indeed know. "I think that Vastra just cast a spell."

Vastra shook his head, but then seemed to reconsider. "I tried to read your mind."

"What? How dare you!" Kaplyn shouted. He felt his face grow hot and knew that he was turning crimson. "But your spell failed?" Kaplyn continued.

Vastra's eyes smouldered with suppressed fury.

"Why did it fail?" Kaplyn demanded.

"The pendant," Lars suggested. "The Eldric were powerful sorcerers, or so you told me."

"Is that true? Did the pendant protect me?" Kaplyn asked.

Vastra gave Lars a look of hatred. "Yes."

"How?"

Vastra massaged his hand. "It nulls magic. I should have suspected that."

"You mean that while I wear it, magic won't work against me?"

Vastra nodded. Kaplyn could see how much that admission pained him.

"Why do you want the pendant?" Kaplyn asked.

"It's a map to help find the Eldric," Vastra replied.

"That doesn't make sense," Lars interrupted. "Kaplyn told me the Eldric disappeared long ago."

"True. However, the pendant describes the last journey of one of their explorers. If I can, I intend retracing his steps."

"I want to go with you," Kaplyn said. A strong urge had suddenly come over him that this was important. Something that the old man had said had convinced him. It was a niggle he couldn't quite explain.

Vastra flashed them both an angry look. "Very well! You may accompany me, but *first* give me the pendant."

"No," Kaplyn insisted. "I will carry it. You may read it of course, but I will carry it."

"You don't know how to use it!"

"Use it?" Kaplyn asked

"You cannot read Eldric, so it's of no use to you," Vastra continued.

"As I said," Kaplyn continued. "I will let you read it, but I will bear it."

Vastra's eyes rolled heavenward. "Very well," he snapped. "Keep it if you must. But I hope, for your sake, it is not cursed," he added. With that he arose and stormed away.

At the mention of a curse Kaplyn saw fear reflected in Lars' eyes.

"*By Slathor*, you should be careful," Lars warned. "He is a bitter man and would make a terrible enemy."

Kaplyn nodded. "I agree, but I have done you a disservice; you deserve the gold."

Lars merely shrugged and shook his head, stroking his beard. "Gold is of no use to me. My heart's desire would be to return to my homeland, but money will not achieve that. There isn't a ship in the land willing to cross the sea." A wry smile crossed his face. "Perhaps it is fated that I should accompany you. My gods decide our fate— whether for good or ill, it would mean little to them. Besides, from what I hear about these demons and krell I think you will need a strong arm by your side."

Kaplyn grinned and offered his hand in friendship. Lars nearly crushed his fingers in a vice-like grip.

"I'd better hide this," Kaplyn said, rising and picking up his folded jacket with the sword still concealed inside. He crossed to the horses and the small pile of luggage. Vastra was not in sight, so he swapped the sword from his jacket to a blanket, which he hid amongst his belongings. He took a moment to find spare twine for his new bow.

"It seems that the Eldric knew how to make weapons," Lars acknowledged, coming over to join Kaplyn. He was admiring his axe.

"May I see them?" Vastra asked.

Kaplyn jumped and wondered where Vastra had come from. By his side, Lars cast him an anxious look. Kaplyn looked at Vastra but saw no malice there. He must have calmed down, he handed him the bow. When Vastra had looked at that Lars handed him the axe.

"They are definitely Eldric made," Vastra said eventually. "You took a risk in taking them."

"Why?" Kaplyn asked.

Together they returned to the fire and sat down. Vastra picked up his bowl and toyed with the remaining food with his spoon. "Some weapons were custom made. To anyone else but their owner, and perhaps their heirs, they would be a curse."

He looked up at the other two men. "Oh, I was not joking about a curse. There are such things you know. These two weapons seem all right though; the writing on the axe is merely a good luck charm."

Lars and Kaplyn exchanged glances. Lars was probably thinking about the hidden sword.

"Now it is your turn to tell us about the pendant," Kaplyn said, trying not to sound concerned. He did not believe in curses but then again, a week ago, he had not believed in wizards either. "What is it and how will it help us to find the Eldric?"

At the "us" Vastra looked at Lars and scowled. He put his bowl down and picking up a twig he poked into the ash at the fire's edge. "The remainder of the quest will be hazardous," he said, ignoring the question and staring instead into the heat of the flames.

Kaplyn wondered whether Vastra was deliberately trying to frighten them into giving up the pendant. He found himself inadvertently feeling the talisman beneath his shirt.

"You would do well to take the gold and leave it at that," Vastra continued.

Kaplyn smiled. "You will need our help. As you say it will be a dangerous journey, especially alone."

Vastra became sullen and looked as though he was going to argue, but he merely shrugged. "Let me see it," he asked.

Kaplyn withdrew it from within his shirt and held it for Lars and Vastra to see, making it clear that he was not going to let go.

He showed them the map first. A path led from Tanel through a forest and then to a mountain range where a spot was marked between two peaks. The shape of the land and the mountain range made it unmistakably Allund. Kaplyn turned the pendant over and Vastra's lips worked as he silently read the fine gossamer writing.

"It appears that if we are to learn what became of the Eldric then we must travel to the Pen-Am-Pelleas Mountains," Vastra said. He sat back but did not venture anything else. He looked pensive.

Kaplyn frowned for he had deduced as much himself from the map. "What does the writing say?" he asked.

"It's merely a description of the map," Vastra said. He emptied some herbs into a cup and took a pan of boiling water from the fire to fill the cup.

Kaplyn replaced the pendant in his shirt, eyeing Vastra warily as the other man blew upon his steaming cup. It was clearly pointless trying to get him to speak further, so he decided to retire for the night.

Kaplyn went to his possessions and took out a blanket, which he spread on the ground. He distrusted Vastra and, although he was tired, he lay awake for some time listening to the night noises. He held the pendant beneath his shirt, half expecting trickery from the reticent wizard. Eventually he fell asleep. Soon dreams engulfed him and, for the first time in some while, he slept fitfully.

Kaplyn awoke to clouds and patchy sunlight. Immediately his hand went to the pendant. Momentarily he had feared that Vastra had stolen it, but to his relief it was still there.

All around him birds tweeted tunefully, but Kaplyn failed to hear them. His mind was reviewing the terrible events of the previous day. A tremor ran down his body, probably due to the cold. Something Lars said about the Prophecy niggled, but he could not fathom it; then the thought was gone.

Stiffly he raised himself onto his arm, relieving the ache in his back from sleeping on the hard ground, and he looked out across the large open expanse. The city was gone and all that remained were ruins. Part of him was relieved.

Vastra was standing at the edge of the camp, looking out across Tanel, while Lars was trying to rekindle the fire. Lars grinned broadly. "You're awake at last," he said.

"How long have I slept?" Kaplyn asked. His throat felt parched and even to his own ears his voice sounded croaky.

"All night and most of the morning," Lars replied.

Vastra walked over and peered down at Kaplyn. His eyes were narrow and Kaplyn shivered, this time not because of the cold.

"We need to leave once we've eaten," Vastra announced, turning around, and returning to the fire where he set about preparing breakfast.

"He's a moody one," Lars said. "We'll need to watch him," he added in a whisper.

"I intend to," Kaplyn replied, and together they went to join Vastra. Hurriedly they prepared and ate a frugal meal since they were eager to be on their way in advance of the rain that threatened.

As soon as they were mounted, the skies opened. A torrent of freezing cold rain fell, drenching the three men who sat miserably hunched over their horses as they rode across the large open plain. All about them, the rain formed a grey mist, blurring the landscape. Their horses struggled as the ground became wet and spongy.

Kaplyn was cold, wet, and miserable. Just as he was about to suggest they look for shelter, the rain ceased.

Soon the clouds dispersed, leaving a clear blue sky at least as far as the horizon where clouds gathered menacingly. Their mood lifted as their clothes gradually dried in the warm sunshine. In the distance, a rainbow appeared, stretching high into the sky, its summit lost from view in the blue heavens.

"My people have a story about rainbows. They say that at the end of a rainbow a dwarf sits forging jewellery fit for a princess," Kaplyn said. "The dwarf offered to marry a princess, but she spurned him and, in a fit of anger, he persuaded his people to wage war against her people. Unfortunately, in the war the princess was killed and in anguish the dwarf killed himself. His punishment in the afterlife is to make jewellery to please her."

Lars smiled. "In my land a rainbow is a staircase to the heavens for Sarl, the god of rain. He carries a great ash bow and silver arrows in his quiver. The arrows light up the sky when he hunts. You can hear his growl when he misses; he is a poor hunter and his aim is poor," Lars concluded with a grin.

Kaplyn laughed and he even thought he saw Vastra smile briefly, although he urged his horse ahead as though unwilling to share their mood.

"Sarl?' Kaplyn repeated the name, enjoying its sound. "That seems an appropriate name for a poor marksman. I should lend him my bow and then perhaps his aim would improve."

"You should not mock the gods lest they take you up on your offer," Lars countered, although his eyes sparkled with merriment. "Besides, if his aim improves, we would be in trouble."

They rode in silence before Kaplyn spoke. "These gods of yours, where are they now?" he asked.

Lars looked about him and he became serious as his eyes searched the heavens. "They're all around," he whispered softly. "If you listen you can hear their voices on the wind. They plot our trials to strengthen us for the future, testing us with blizzards, gales, famine and drought, amongst other hardships."

Kaplyn frowned, "Aren't gods supposed to be kind and gentle?"

Lars shook his head, rubbing his beard. "Let me tell you what my people believe and then you may judge for yourself. Fallor-Ell is their home and that is where our souls go when we die. It is said to be a beautiful and tranquil place.

"The gods treat us well, almost like gods ourselves. We laugh at our hardships, seeing the necessity of the cruelty thrust upon us, so we have strength and resolve for the coming battle. Food within Fallor-Ell is plentiful, and game willingly surrenders to our knives for it is an honour to be eaten by the god's guests. Wines and beers flow freely in giant rivers where great buckets hang by the banks so we may drink our fill."

Kaplyn grinned at the image, which seemed an appropriate reward for the big man's soul.

Lars smiled back but became serious again as he continued. "It is foretold that one day, at the end of time, the evil giants will gather the fell creatures of the world, and together they will attack Fallor-Ell, seeking to overthrow the gods. When this happens, only the spirits of the bravest mortals will fight alongside the gods. That is why they test us, to strengthen us."

They rode in silence for a moment before Lars asked. "What about your people? Do they believe in gods?"

Kaplyn shook his head; his long hair blew in the wind and covered his eyes for an instant. "I don't, but others do. Farmers often pray to the Kalanth, the Old Ones, for a good crop or fine weather."

"What are the Kalanth?" Lars asked. "I've heard them mentioned before."

"They are demigods who are said to have walked the earth many years ago," Kaplyn replied. "They were tasked by the Creator to prepare the world and to banish evil in preparation for the coming of man. There are still many shrines to the Kalanth; at hallowed sites such as a hollow or a dale where it is believed that an Old One once lived. Some farmers still leave gifts for the gods at these sites."

"Gifts?"

"Yes. Nothing much, just food or wine. It is not a surprise though that the offerings disappear. There are many vagabonds who dare the wild, living solitary lives away from civilisation."

"Have you ever seen one of these sites?"

Kaplyn nodded. "Yes, there was such a place close to Dundalk where I lived. It was a small wood, on an uneven hillock, where a stream had carved its passage over the years. I have to admit it was an odd place," he reflected. Until then he had not thought about it much even though he had often gone there, seeking solitude away from the tedium of court. "It was very beautiful, and peaceful.

"I suppose that it was the Eldric who stopped us believing in the gods," he continued more thoughtfully. "They would have seemed very wise with their magic and their learning. They probably laughed at our superstitious fears. Over the years their culture mixed with ours and their understanding of science taught us to be less fearful of the dark. They explained many mysteries that for centuries had held our people in superstitious thraldom."

"They must have been a great people indeed to explain all the wonders of the world," Lars stated sadly.

Kaplyn realised he was being foolish, for there was still much that they did not know. The world was a big place and they had barely explored their own borders, let alone those beyond. "Perhaps we are not as wise as we would like to believe," he conceded.

Later that morning Kaplyn looked towards the distant mountains, crowned with wreaths of sombre clouds. Kaplyn expected their journey would take many days yet.

He was deliberately taking their route close to an old friend's home, and he was anticipating the visit, remembering with fondness the hours spent with Hallar, his closest childhood friend.

He watched the landscape change around them while they rode. At first the grass was a rich deep green, and the ground soft, but later the scenery became undulating and on the top of each hillock was a crown of tall oak trees. Gorse and bracken grew in profusion around the stony trail, and rabbits often scampered across the path a few yards ahead of their plodding mounts, swiftly disappearing amongst the thick vegetation.

They continued across lush countryside for two days, occasionally meeting sheepherders tending their flock or farmers tilling the fields, and these folks greeted them with open curiosity. The farm folk were eager to exchange food for a chance to discuss news from afar. They were all too glad of the company and a chance to break their lonely vigils.

Vastra hung back during these encounters, looking anxious to be on his way. He was aloof and distant, and his eyes often strayed towards their distant goal as though willing them to be upon the road again.

When they woke on the third morning from Tanel the mountains were more prominent, but still some distance away. The day started dreary and damp, the sky turned leaden and low clouds touched the treetops with soft misty fingers. The rain, when it came, was a downpour and, once more, the riders were very quickly soaked and miserable.

They were camped by the banks of a stream that offered little protection from the chill wind, when Kaplyn suggested finding shelter. He told them he knew somewhere they could get hot food and shelter, and a chance to dry their clothes. It was only a short detour, he explained. Vastra insisted on continuing, saying time was too short for detours. Kaplyn was growing impatient. They were close to his friend's home, and they could reach it by mid-morning.

After arguing in the wet for some time, Kaplyn finally told Vastra that he and Lars were leaving to seek shelter. Vastra visibly fumed as they started to pack. He had no choice and, muttering, he put away his own belongings. As though making a point though he rode behind them and Kaplyn could almost feel his hateful glare on his back.

Feeling guilty, Kaplyn tried to draw him into their conversation; he had to look over his shoulder and shout above the noise of the rain and wind, but his only reply was a menacing silence and, finally, he admitted defeat. Wearily they rode into the lashing rain with heads bowed.

Kaplyn reined his horse to a stop at a fork in the road. Silhouetted against the dreary sky, a small castle was perched defiantly upon a rocky hill. Kaplyn grinned at the familiar sight. The keep's copper roofs had long since turned green, and they added a splash of colour to the otherwise monotonous stone.

By his side, Vastra cast him a questioning look.

"Someone who lives here owes me a favour," Kaplyn said. "I stopped a thief from taking his purse. He turned out to be a baron … that is the man I saved was a baron, not the thief," Kaplyn continued. "He said if I was ever nearby then I was welcome to call in."

"Quite right," Lars answered. "You probably saved him a tidy sum and his dignity, no doubt."

Kaplyn was relieved that Lars at least had accepted his tale and ignoring Vastra he spurred his horse towards the castle and the open gates that beckoned.

Chapter 11
An Old Friend

Two sentries armed with long pikes stopped them at the castle gates.

"What's your business?" the older of the two men asked. Both seemed surly at having to leave the comfort of the guardhouse. Rain cascaded from their helms and into their eyes, causing them to blink as they looked up at the riders. The sound of the rain, drumming on the nearby roofs, made Kaplyn eager to gain sanctuary and his temper was mounting the longer he was kept from being dry.

"I'm an acquaintance of the baron and would like to speak with him," he answered, trying to keep his voice calm.

For a moment, neither guard spoke. Kaplyn realised he must look like a beggar in his mud-splattered clothes.

"Give me your name and I'll ask if he will see you," the guard offered after a pause.

"My name is Kaplyn Lasthlan," he said. Lasthlan was his mother's maiden name and he hoped that Hallar would remember it. He gave Vastra a sideways glance in case he recognised the name, but he didn't seem to.

The guard nodded. "Go and tell the baron that he has guests," he said to his companion, who turned and left, giving the three men a curious backwards glance.

"In the meantime, you can go to the guest quarters," the Guard Captain continued. "If you enter through the gate and go across the courtyard, you will see a low building on your right. That's where visitors stay. Someone will meet you and take your horses to the stable."

"Thank you," Kaplyn replied, dismounting, and waiting while the others followed suit. Leading his mount by its reins he led the way through the narrow gateway. As if upon command, the rain ceased as soon as they reached the inner courtyard. Both Kaplyn and Lars laughed but it was of little consolation for they were already soaked and, to make matters worse, their feet quickly became sodden as they splashed through deep puddles that had formed on the uneven cobbled street.

A tall youth, in his early teens, came running from an open doorway within the large central building and offered to take their horses to the stables. Kaplyn was frustrated that he had no money to tip the boy, and he was angered that Vastra did not offer. The boy did not seem to mind though as he led the animals away.

The lodge comprised several large rooms, each containing three or four beds, a few chairs and best of all a fireplace. It was mean lodgings compared to what Kaplyn would have expected under normal circumstances. A servant was lighting a fire in one of the rooms and gratefully they put their belongings onto the beds. Eagerly they gathered around the flames to warm themselves.

A liveried servant entered. "Which one of you is Kaplyn?" he asked.

Kaplyn raised a hand. The servant eyed him suspiciously for a moment. "You are to accompany me," he said at length, a note of disdain clear in his voice.

Kaplyn started forward and so too did Lars.

"Just Kaplyn I was told," the servant snapped. "You'll get your turn, no doubt." The servant glared at Kaplyn. "If you have clean clothes then I suggest you change."

Kaplyn felt his cheeks flush. No one had ever spoken to him like that before. He dried himself on a towel that had been draped at the end of the bed and quickly changed. His last act as he left the room was to place his sword by his bed; it would have been considered bad manners to take the weapon into Hallar's house. His Eldric blade remained concealed within his belongings.

The entry hall was just as Kaplyn remembered. An imposing wooden staircase led up to the minstrels' gallery, which circled the lower room. On the walls hung several displays of antique weapons including pikes, swords, and axes. Kaplyn had always admired the collection, many of which dated back to the Krell Wars. Even still, Hallar would be envious of his Eldric sword.

The servant led him through a side door to one of the many audience rooms. Numerous candles brightly lit the interior and, standing by a large log fire, was his friend. Neither man spoke until the servant left. A broad smile creased the Baron's broad face as soon as the door thumped shut. He strode over to Kaplyn and gave him a mighty slap across the shoulders.

"Orlastor, old friend," he said cheerfully. "I have not seen you for far too long."

Kaplyn grinned broadly, "Don't be formal," he said. "You know I prefer my middle name, Kaplyn — and less of the old. By the looks of you, I see you are keeping well," he said.

The Baron patted his bulging waistline and looked sheepish. "I have a fine wife to look after me now," he said by way of explanation and the pair laughed. "But you are looking well. How are the King and Queen and the rest of the family?"

"Well ... everyone is well! My father is still as stubborn as ever though."

"Ah... that runs in the family."

Kaplyn frowned but couldn't deny it.

"But why are you here?" Hallar asked. "A palace messenger reported you were missing. Everyone is frantic. Look at you — you are more like a poacher than a prince. I'm surprised that the guards let you in. I can see that I'll have to speak to them later," he said with a mischievous grin. "And why are you using your mother's maiden name? It took me a while to think who it might be. I was about to tell you to be off, until I realised it was you."

"You would have received my father's displeasure if you had," Kaplyn replied laughing. "It's a long story ... if you have the time."

The baron looked serious and offered him a seat, which Kaplyn gratefully accepted. Long days on horseback and the sudden drenching had left his muscles tired and stiff.

He told Hallar about Lars and Vastra and then spoke of the Pendrat fair and even bragged about his own win. In the relaxed atmosphere and by the warmth of the fire, Kaplyn felt more at ease. The baron interrupted the story after a while for refreshments. Ringing a bell, they awaited the servant who returned promptly. It was the same man who had earlier escorted Kaplyn.

"Mulled wine for my guest," the baron requested.

The servant nodded and glanced warily at Kaplyn as if he had cast a spell over the baron. As soon as the other man had left, Kaplyn told Hallar about his adventure in the Eldric tower. The baron interrupted him on occasions and asked him to elaborate, clearly horrified that Kaplyn had endured such danger.

Strangely, Kaplyn found his memory of the events had already become vague. Talking about them now brought back the strange feelings he had experienced at the time. A knock at the door warned them the servant had returned and they fell silent as he entered, carrying a tall flagon of steaming red wine from which came a pleasant, bitter aroma.

Kaplyn gratefully accepted a wooden flagon of hot wine from the servant who turned to serve the Baron before leaving.

"The thing that amazed me most of all was that it all had to be an illusion," Kaplyn said, resuming the tale. "I kept telling myself that over and over. There was no way a lake that size could have been inside the tower but, like everything else, it seemed so real." He paused to take a sip of the wine, enjoying its flavour.

"The Eldric were mighty sorcerers," Hallar interrupted. "I could believe anything from the tales I've heard. You are fortunate to be alive. However, that does not excuse you for putting your life at risk," he admonished seriously. "You should take care, especially of this Vastra. He sounds dangerous. Are you sure that you know what you are doing? Wouldn't it be wise just to take the pendant and leave him? Then at least he cannot cause any mischief."

Kaplyn shook his head, warming his hands on the flagon. "No, I can't do that. Vastra might be right about the pendant; it could be a clue to where the Eldric went."

"Then let him take it and good riddance!" Hallar declared. His voice had lost its earlier humour and it was clear that he was genuinely concerned for his friend's safety. "After all, he freely admits that he hates your father. What would Vastra do if he knew you were his half-brother?"

Kaplyn again shook his head, swilling the warm wine in the flagon and enjoying the strong smell. "I admit that his suspicion may be aroused after my visit to see you. I told him I was a palace guard and that I saved you from a thief. I think he believes me, but I am not sure for how much longer."

He placed his flagon on the table at his side and looked at his friend seriously. "It's an unfortunate business, but there is too much at stake. According to Vastra, the pendant will reveal the whereabouts of the Eldric. Think what that could mean," Kaplyn said, his eyes sparkling with excitement.

"It sounds like a fool's errand. The Eldric disappeared long ago and may not want to be found, but if you insist on pursuing this task then let me go in your place. I would keep an eye on this wizard for you."

Kaplyn raised his eyebrows. "And leave your lovely wife?"

Hallar looked exasperated, "What do you intend then?"

Kaplyn stretched luxuriously, "Tonight, a meal, a bath and a good night's rest."

"No tomorrow, you fool!'

Kaplyn feigned surprise at Hallar's choice of words. "We are going to the Pen-Am-Pelleas Mountains and will travel through the KnAnar forest. It's a short cut and will save us a few weeks going that way."

Hallar looked perplexed.

"I will write to my father before I leave," Kaplyn suggested as if reading his friend's mind. "I will tell him what I intend and explain that you tried to talk me out of it, offering all the help that you could."

Hallar brightened suddenly, "That's it! Take some of my men! I could easily spare a hest as an escort."

Kaplyn shook his head. "I've already taken a great risk coming here. If Vastra suspects who I am then I could be in danger and an armed escort might do just that. Your offer of help is generous, but I must decline."

Hallar sagged back into his chair looking very much defeated. The pair sat in silence for a moment.

The sun suddenly broke through the clouds and a bright light, marking early evening, streamed through the thick glass.

"If you insist on going then you must take care. You might not be aware, but there have been several krell raids on our eastern borders recently. Last time we met, I spoke to your father about this, and he promised to send a patrol into the mountains to see if they could flush them out."

"That's the second time I've heard of krell raids. Yet there was no mention of them at the palace." Kaplyn rose, deep in thought and went across to the window to look out onto the courtyard. It was deserted and the light reflected brightly from the wet cobbles.

The baron nodded. "Your father must be keeping the news from the people. I fear he is mistaken in this matter. He should be more honest. There are many who would use such news to discredit him."

Kaplyn frowned. "What are you saying?"

"For one—the lack of protection annoys farmers," Hallar continued.

Kaplyn grinned. "Farmers always complain. You know that. Too much sun, too little sun—not enough rain, then floods. I think it's a farmer's lot to complain."

"That may be true, but I worry that your father is not in touch with his people. The fact that you did not know about the krell raids shows that there is a problem. The King is protecting some folk while ignoring others and that is dangerous."

The pair fell silent. Kaplyn had always thought his father to be a good king and had never considered that the people might not think so. He could not consider otherwise.

"I have to admit, this talk of krell worries me," Kaplyn said as his thoughts turned away from his father.

Hallar nodded. "Do you remember when we were young, we used to talk of the Krell Wars and the Prophecy; they were good times, but we never really gave thought to what might happen if the Prophecy came true. To live through a second Krell War would be terrible."

"That was a long time ago. We wished for war so we could be heroes. Now we are older we hope that war will never happen."

"What of Trosgarth? Is it possible their influence is growing and that is why the krell are becoming bolder?"

Kaplyn shook his head, but Hallar looked unconvinced as he stroked his chin thoughtfully.

"Trosgarth and Aldrace are no longer a threat," Kaplyn said. "The alliance of the Southern Kingdoms is more than a match for them."

"But what about the Prophecy? I agree the alliance is strong enough to counter a threat from a sizeable army, but what if Drachar's shade was summoned back to the land? Ever since the Eldric left, there has been no defence against demons."

"Do not forget there has been peace since the Krell Wars; surely we can rest assured it will last for a while longer."

Hallar grinned at his friend's determination. "I'm sorry, I was being pessimistic. You are right; another war is unlikely."

He replenished his flagon and offered Kaplyn a refill. "It's nearly time for dinner. I insist you join us. I will have fresh clothes sent down for you and your friends. You can meet Gayle. I am sure that she will be pleased to see you again."

Kaplyn readily agreed, accepting more mulled wine.

"I'm not happy with you staying in the travellers' quarters though. You should be in the main building with the rest of us. Your father would not forgive me if he knew you were not being looked after properly."

"I still need to keep my identity secret, so I'll remain with the other two, but we will attend dinner. That will keep Vastra guessing," Kaplyn replied, settling back in the comfort of the deep chair.

They spoke for a while longer, remembering less troubled times before Kaplyn returned to his room to pass on the baron's invitation. Kaplyn felt relaxed and carefree for the first time in quite some while.

Later that evening Kaplyn escorted Lars and Vastra to the dining hall, carrying his Eldric sword wrapped in his spare clothes beneath his arm. Hallar had been true to his word, and someone had brought them fresh clothes. A bath had been a real tonic and he felt very comfortable dressed in the rich garments. It was a marvellous feeling to be clean again. Lars, on the other hand, had been crestfallen when a servant had taken away his own clothes for laundering.

As Kaplyn led them up the broad flight of stairs, Lars looked about in awe of the rich surroundings. "You say that you stopped a thief from stealing the baron's purse and that is why he invited you here?"

Kaplyn nodded and Lars whistled softly. "It's a good way of getting a free meal if you ask me."

The dining room was immense, dominated by a long table whose polished surface reflected the light from numerous candles arrayed about the room. A sizeable log fire burned at one end of the hall, where a pair of large shaggy hunting hounds lay as close as the heat would allow. One raised its massive head to watch the strangers, and its tail thumped the floor half-heartedly before it lay back down to soak up the heat. Two richly dressed servants stood attentively by a door at the far end of the dining room, while another escorted them to their seats.

There were three other guests already present at the table, and they looked unfavourably at Kaplyn and the others as they went by. Kaplyn felt annoyed for if anyone deserved a second look it was these men. Their heads were shaven, and they wore ochre robes encrusted with grime as though they had travelled far. It was normal for a baron such as Hallar to allow guests to dine at his table, and Kaplyn assumed that they must have recently arrived and requested an audience.

Hallar and his wife Gayle entered, smiling broadly at their guests as they took their seats at the head of the table. To Kaplyn, Gayle looked as beautiful as ever. She was petite, much smaller than Hallar. Her dark hair cascaded over her shoulders, and she wore her fringe long, almost hiding her eyes. She smiled mischievously at Kaplyn who hoped Hallar had warned her not to give his identity away.

Kaplyn and Lars were seated next to them while Vastra was adjacent to the other three guests. Hallar introduced Kaplyn who in turn introduced Lars and Vastra. Lars was clearly in awe of the pomp and ceremony of a formal dinner. Vastra treated the baron and his wife graciously, but Kaplyn could see the resentment reflected in his eyes.

One of the strangers, a prematurely wrinkled man with heavy bags under his eyes, introduced himself as Aldor. His voice was deep and his speech slow and methodical.

Aldor indicated to the rotund, rather short man sitting next to him and introduced him as Diran. He had large shaggy eyebrows that gave him a perpetual frown. Diran nodded to the other guests as Aldor turned to his remaining companion, a tall thin youth with a hawk-like nose who he introduced as Borrin.

Servants entered carrying trays of food, which they arranged upon the table. Kaplyn and Lars relished the meal after so many days on the road. By comparison, Vastra ate sparingly, merely picking at his food.

Initially the conversation avoided the three other guests, apart from a few pleasantries. As the servants cleared the last dishes away, the baron turned to Aldor. "Now, what is it that you wish to discuss?" he asked politely.

"Sir," Aldor said, rising, and looking serious. "Ours is a religious order based on new concepts, which we are bringing to the people."

It's money, Kaplyn thought. He cast the baron a meaningful glance and his friend raised his eyebrows in reply, placing his chin on his hands.

"Our people's needs are few and we live simple lives. We believe that if the body is pure then the mind is capable of greatness. For this reason, our followers must give up false comforts and easy living. Instead, we ask that they live frugal lives and in return we promise to enrich their souls."

Kaplyn looked at the priest's empty wine goblet but refrained from comment.

"Our following increases daily and more are turning to our order to satisfy their longing for harmony, to fill their sad, dreary days with meaning, to have a purpose in life, to belong."

Aldor's voice was rising, and the words flowed freely, coming faster and faster. A fleck of spittle ran down his chin and his eyes took on a glazed distant look as though he was elsewhere. "The old gods are no more," he said dangerously, looking at the others as if challenging them to contradict. "It is now time to turn to a new god!'

Kaplyn frowned. Although he did not believe in the Kalanth he knew that many folk still did. To some people, pronouncing them "no more" was like stating that the sun would not rise in the morning. These priests were toying with fire and there had to be more to them than met the eye if they were to gain credence.

"We can offer the people a better life; they can achieve much more with our teaching. Our god, Ryoch, is strong and has promised to guide us, while those who do not will wallow and flounder in mire and dung of their own making. Ryoch offers immortality, while the Old Ones offer *nothing*. They have long since forsaken us, passing into oblivion, and leaving *nought* but the ravage of time."

Kaplyn could stand no more. "What proof is there that there is a new god?"

"Our minds are the only proof *we* need," Aldor said, pointing to his own temple and eyeing Kaplyn darkly. "This lets us talk to our god and to our brothers. We have heard his voice; he tells us to follow and great will be our order in the days to come. We shall bask in Ryoch's glory. However, he is not a tolerant god and he tells us to choose. We have chosen," he said indicating his fellows.

"Then you have no proof?" Kaplyn asked.

Aldor's smile darkened. "Write something and do not show me," he suggested.

Kaplyn frowned but asked one of the servants to fetch a quill and ink. An uncomfortable silence prevailed while the servant was away. Aldor and the others sat smugly, oozing confidence. Lars cast Kaplyn a warning look, but he chose to ignore him. Vastra leant forward attentively, a look of concern on his face. Kaplyn realised he had slipped out of his role as an ex-palace guard; a guard would not be expected to be able to read, but then he remembered that most palace guards he knew could.

The servant returned, handing Kaplyn a quill, parchment, and a pot of ink. Kaplyn dipped the quill in the ink and scratched some letters on the paper.

Aldor spoke as Kaplyn wrote. "The Kalanth live." His eyes widened and his jaw dropped as he completed the sentence, realising what he had said. The other two priests cast him dark looks as if he had meant the blasphemy.

Kaplyn frowned; the priest had read exactly what he had written.

Aldor gave Kaplyn a baleful look. His voice became low and threatening and a humourless smile touched his lips. "You are wrong, and I fear for your soul." He held his chin high, his look of contempt plain for all to see.

The baron reached for Kaplyn's parchment and read it. A frown crossed his face.

"What is it you wish from me?"

"We need money and land to build on," Aldor's voice cracked with excitement, he clearly assumed the Baron was conceding to his requests. "We will build a temple to Ryoch."

"And in return?" the Baron asked.

"You will be privileged within our ranks and the smile of Ryoch will shower you with riches."

The baron paused. "I'm sorry, I cannot offer you anything."

Aldor stiffened. "Very well, but do not say that you were not warned." He and his companions left without saying anything further.

"He's a charlatan!" Kaplyn said when they had gone.

"And dangerous," the baron added. "He's a fanatic and they are always dangerous. They convince good men to turn from everything that they hold dear, with their stories and magic tricks."

"There was no magic used tonight," Vastra interrupted softly. Having seen what Vastra was capable of, Kaplyn was inclined to believe him.

"Then how do you explain his trick?" Hallar asked.

"As you said, he is a dangerous man," Vastra replied simply.

"I did not like or trust him," Gayle said. "He is frightening. Did you see his eyes? Thank the Kalanth he is only staying the one night."

"Will you be all right sharing the same quarters with those men?" the Baron asked.

Kaplyn nodded, smiling.

Hallar shook his head, "I'm sorry now that I invited them to dinner. A friend asked me to speak with them. Had I known what they were like I wouldn't have offered."

"I have heard of these Priests of Ryoch before," Gayle said. "Apparently, they have a considerable following. I have also heard, but it is only a rumour, that they preach against the king."

Kaplyn frowned.

"It appears they are an ambitious people then," Vastra said softly, without a trace of humour.

Kaplyn glanced at him while the others either did not hear him or chose to ignore his comment.

There was a moment's silence and then Hallar spoke, clearly trying to lighten the mood. "Now Kaplyn, where's this sword you told me about?"

Kaplyn bent, retrieving the bundle by his feet. He unwrapped the Eldric blade then withdrew it from its scabbard and was shocked to find the blade shining dully with a blue radiance, but the glow faded as he looked. He was about to hand the weapon to the baron when Vastra interrupted.

"Don't touch it!" he warned icily, standing, and knocking his chair over backwards in his haste. "It's an Eldric blade! You should have warned me that you had it! A weapon like this chooses its master. In the wrong hands, it is a curse."

In the candlelight, the blade's silver runes stood out against the dull metal as if in challenge to Vastra's wrath.

"What does the lettering say?" Hallar asked, pointing to the runes.

Kaplyn shrugged and turned to Vastra who merely scowled; although he leant forward, his face flushed, he was clearly ill at ease.

"It is an Eldric script with which I am not familiar," he grumbled.

Kaplyn frowned, hearing Vastra admit to not knowing every Eldric script came as a surprise after his constant boasting.

"I know," Hallar interrupted, "I'll summon Jastin, the librarian. He is a scholar of texts both ancient and modern. If anyone can translate the letters he can." The Baron requested a servant to find Jastin and he promptly left in search of the old man.

Vastra retrieved his chair and sat down heavily, clearly angered by Kaplyn's disclosure that he had the sword.

The servant returned after a few moments, closely followed by a grey-haired old man wearing long flowing robes. He almost ran to keep up with the younger man. Jastin bowed towards the baron.

"How may I be of service, my Lord?" he asked in a voice cracked with age.

"Could you tell us what the inscription upon the blade says?" the Baron asked.

Kaplyn held the sword for the old man to see. He bent low over the weapon, peering closely at the fine lettering. His eyesight was obviously poor, and he studied the blade carefully before rising slowly with his hand on his back as though he was experiencing some pain.

"It's an Eldric script, but not one I know," he said. "However, with the aid of my books I should be able to translate it."

"You will have to write the runes down," Kaplyn said. "I will not let the sword out of my sight."

The old man nodded and from his pocket produced a parchment and a piece of charcoal. He copied the runes and then examined his work before declaring that it would suffice.

The Baron smiled as he left. "He is a good man, even if he can't see his own feet."

Kaplyn smiled, "I'm surprised he can find his books."

"Oh, he doesn't need eyesight for that. He has each one's position firmly fixed in his mind," Hallar announced.

They spoke for a short while longer until Vastra declared he was tired and excused himself, wishing everyone a good night. Gayle soon followed leaving only Lars, Kaplyn and Hallar remaining. The dogs, seeing that dinner was finished, returned from their vigil at the table (hoping for titbits) to the contentment of the warm fire where they flopped down, panting with the extreme heat, caring nought for the discussions of men.

Chapter 12
An Unwelcome Visitor

The servants replenished their goblets and stoked the fire before retiring to a discrete corner until Hallar, with a wave of his hand, dismissed them. Kaplyn and Hallar soon fell into a conversation about friends and family, but Kaplyn quickly realised Lars would soon guess they were more than casual acquaintances. Over the brief period he had known him, Kaplyn had learned to trust him, and he decided to take him into his confidence. He told him the truth that his father was the king.

"I deliberately kept my identity a secret, but when I realised Vastra might be my half-brother, I knew I could never trust him until I learnt more about him. You heard how much he hates my father. I dare not confide in him until I know what he intends doing."

"Don't worry, your secret is safe," Lars replied. "Vastra is a bitter man; he carries the seed of his own destruction within him."

Kaplyn smiled, relieved by Lars' co-operation and friendship.

All at once the flames within the hearth changed colour. A blue flame burned brightly, eerily illuminating the room with its pale radiance. The change was not natural, and the three men looked at the fire, and then each other.

The dogs stood up, their hackles rising. They both faced the end of the hall, growling menacingly. Other dogs within the castle started to bark until the castle was alive with noise.

A cry of absolute terror pierced the night, causing even the stoutest souls within earshot to cower in dread. As abruptly as it started, it ended. The three men looked at one another, eyes wide with fear.

"What was that?" Lars asked.

Kaplyn reached for his Eldric sword and drew the weapon. It gave a chilling whine as it cleared the scabbard. The blade shone with an intense blue light, causing Hallar and Lars to step back.

Kaplyn stared at the blade, but another scream distracted him. Together the three men raced to the door leading to the west tower, which Hallar threw open to reveal a white-faced servant who stared at Kaplyn's glowing sword.

"Fetch me a weapon," Hallar urged of the bewildered man who nodded and ran off. Lars called after him for an axe. Hallar led them to a small stone archway beyond which a steep winding staircase led to the upper levels of the west tower.

Two guards stood with swords drawn at the base of the stairs, looking fearfully up. Both seemed uncertain and the sight of Kaplyn's glowing blade made them step back, eyes wide with fear. At that moment, the servant returned carrying a heavy broadsword and an axe, which Hallar and Lars gratefully took, each testing their weapon for balance.

"Fetch some torches," Hallar told the servant who gladly fled.

"What has happened?" Hallar asked of the two guards.

The guards looked terrified. "We were patrolling the corridors when we heard a scream from upstairs. Tumarl and Narn went up to investigate a short while ago. Since then, we've been calling their names, but there's been no reply."

"Where does this lead?" Kaplyn asked.

"The library," Hallar replied.

"The old man?" Kaplyn asked.

The Baron nodded. "He'll be up there."

Kaplyn started for the stairs, but the baron held his arm. "Wait for the torches." Kaplyn nodded, taking a step back. Shortly the servant returned carrying three flaming brands, each burned with an unnatural blue flame and the sight caused the guards' eyes to widen.

"Demon," hissed one under his breath.

The other guard looked at the torch as if a demon was about to materialise from its fiery heart.

"You two follow me," Hallar said. "Kronar," he said to the servant, "fetch others. If we do not return soon then seal this doorway and await the dawn before sending anyone else up."

Kaplyn started up the stairs before Hallar could protest, using the light from his sword to illuminate the stone steps. He went cautiously, knowing that if it was a demon then it was already too late to aid the librarian and anyone else with him.

The guards came next. "Don't let the demon touch your heart," the older guard cautioned the other in a hushed whisper. He was referring to the old wives' tale that if a demon took a man's heart it would take his soul to eternal damnation. Kaplyn continued the twisting climb, feeling the wall for support with the back of his sword arm. He held the pendant through his shirt in his other hand; the talisman seemed to aid his courage. It was Eldric made. In the past, they had successfully fought and defeated demons.

The stairway was deliberately narrow to prevent an enemy from climbing or descending in force. It also prevented Kaplyn from seeing further ahead than the central stone column supporting the stairs. Suddenly he missed his footing and nearly fell, his heart beat wildly and the guard behind him cried out in fright.

Kaplyn continued more carefully; then all at once the blue light was no longer reflected from the stone wall beside him, and he saw a partially opened doorway ahead. An eerie green glow filtered through it. Kaplyn pushed the door wider and cautiously looked in. Row upon row of bookshelves, stacked with large dusty volumes, filled the room, making a clear view of the interior impossible.

Everything glowed with an unearthly green pallor and, as Kaplyn entered, a terrible numbing cold greeted him. In response, the hilt of his sword seemed to twist in his grasp. Behind him, the others followed equally as wary, each looking surreal in the odd light.

Kaplyn needed to know what was in the room. Crossing to the nearest bookcase, he tried toppling it. Lars, understanding his intent, helped and together they rocked it so that it slowly picked up momentum until finally, it toppled backwards. The two men leapt back. With an almighty crash, it smashed onto the one behind, causing that to fall with it. Within seconds, other bookshelves toppled, creating a fountain of dust and paper. Some did not quite fall, and these ended up wedged against each other.

Mingled with the crashing, a piercing shriek split the air. The onlookers jumped visibly as a dark shape erupted from within the mass of books and broken wood. The figure scrambled onto a precariously balanced bookshelf where it sat, looking down on them with undisguised hatred. It shielded its eyes from the glow of Kaplyn's blade, as though the light it cast was causing it pain. Behind the creature was a gaping hole in the wall; from this spewed the green light and numbing cold.

The demon, for there could be little doubt that was what they faced, was easily about eight feet in height, although its immense limbs were curled up beneath it like a giant spider. A hideous grin split its ugly face and its long-pointed tail lashed angrily like a giant cat's. Its arms ended in vicious looking talons and in one talon it grasped something that looked like it had come from a butcher's yard.

As if caught in a spell, neither side moved. Then, emitting a fearful scream, the demon leapt across the intervening bookshelves, landing with a crash and a shower of debris in front of the group. Its cry froze the watchers. With a mighty swing of its arm, the demon cut one guard in two, catching the other guard a glancing blow across his shoulder. Its speed was impossible.

Screaming battle cries, Kaplyn and the baron leapt at the monster. The demon turned, lashing out, and the attackers suddenly became the attacked. Hallar blocked a vicious stroke with his blade, but the steel barely scratched the demon's flesh. The demon struck out wildly, its talon coming under Hallar's guard.

Kaplyn stepped in the way, blocking the blow with his sword. The blade sliced deeply into the demon's flesh at the elbow, severing the arm, which flopped limply to the floor, oozing green blood that hissed angrily in contact with the stone. The demon screamed. Kaplyn's blade twisted impatiently within his grip as though endowed with a life of its own; he brought the weapon around and thrust up, under the demon's damaged limb. The blade tore eagerly into the demon's flesh, emitting a deep sonorous keening as if sensing the demon's imminent demise. With astonishing speed, the demon leapt back, screaming in both rage and pain. Before Kaplyn could complete the thrust, he slipped on a pool of blood and went down on one knee.

The demon, intent upon escape, raced for the hole, but before it reached the hole, Lars intercepted it, swinging his axe in a wide arc. The blow would have decapitated it if it had connected, but once more, the demon's speed saved it as it ducked beneath the weapon, leaping to one side. Even so, the axe caught it a glancing blow and the demon screamed in rage. It continued its wild flight, scrambling awkwardly across the stricken bookshelves, until it stood once more upon the top of a bookcase. From there, it turned to stare at the men and the look of malice froze Kaplyn's blood. Green blood oozed from its wounds, smoking when it came in contact with the bookcase.

Suddenly, with an ear-splitting cry it turned, disappearing into the hole, which continued to spew cold air and a pungent sickly smell. Kaplyn shouted and made as if to follow, but Lars grabbed him by his shoulder.

With a loud clap, the hole disappeared, cutting off the eerie glow. A rush of air doused their torches, plunging them into darkness. With trembling hands, they relit the smouldering brands while Hallar called down to the guards at the bottom of the stairs to come up and lend a hand. Kaplyn wiped the demon's blood from his blade on scattered paper.

The first guard to enter looked deathly pale and his eyes were wide with fear. At any other time, he might have appeared comical, but now, amongst the bitter stench of death, no one noticed his gaunt expression. Others timidly followed and they, too, stared in horror at the carnage.

Hallar urged them to help and the urgency in his tone broke the spell binding them. The room was abruptly a hive of activity as men cleared the books and shelves in search for wounded.

A tall man came across the body of the guard cut in two, and he could not stop trembling. The other injured guard was trying to stem the flow of blood from a gash on his arm; his jerkin was soaked red from the shoulder down. The baron attended him, applying a tourniquet. The man cried out when the baron tightened the bandage. A colleague grabbed him by his uninjured arm and helped him to remain standing.

Hallar looked worried. It was rumoured that demons carried disease and he clearly feared the wound would fester.

"Take him to the surgeon," he said. Two men helped him from the room whilst others carried the halves of the other body to the cellar to await the dawn.

Hallar then ordered the men to burn anything even remotely contaminated by the demon's blood. A man picked up the demon's arm; his face grimacing as he carefully wrapped the limb in a sheet. Others mopped up the demon's blood, gathering the soiled cloths together in a pile.

When one of the guards let out a cry of shock, others went to investigate. From beneath one of the toppled bookcases, a leg protruded. Men manhandled the bookcase out of the way, revealing the bloody remains of the missing two guards and the librarian. The demon had ripped their bodies apart. One of the corpses was missing an arm, which was the object the demon dropped earlier.

Kaplyn found the parchment the librarian was working on, but apart from the copy of the runes from his sword, there was nothing else. Whichever book he had been referencing was lost beneath the pile of other books.

Hallar and Lars joined Kaplyn as men started to remove the bodies.

"It's a bad business," Hallar said sourly, wiping his eyes. "I wouldn't have believed demons existed if not for tonight."

"I've never seen anything like that before," Lars said bewildered. The ordeal had clearly stunned him. Kaplyn realised that he, too, was shaking like a leaf. He tried to still his hands but failed. Only then did he consider that they should have sought Vastra's help, but it was too late now for recriminations.

Many present started to demand an explanation for the carnage, looking expectantly to Hallar. "Quiet!" he shouted above the hubbub and a silence descended. "A demon has attacked, killing three guards and the librarian."

Several men shouted out in fear.

"It's been driven off and there is nothing to fear now." Hallar barked above the din.

"Was it killed?" one man asked.

Hallar shook his head, and more voices raised their concern. "But be assured that it has gone. I doubt it will be back. Now please leave and return in the morning to help clear up this mess."

Sullenly the men filed out, making their way down the narrow flight of stairs. Hallar posted a guard at the tower's entrance with instructions not to allow anyone to pass unless he gave permission.

Hallar took his leave of Kaplyn and Lars. They understood, there was a lot to do that night and people were coming from their rooms to ask what had happened.

"Come!" Kaplyn said to Lars. "We'd better get some rest; there is nothing else we can do here."

"Do you think *it* will return?" Lars asked as they strode along the dim corridor.

"I hope not," Kaplyn answered, although there was no way that he could be certain. He thought about his sword and its blue light. It was evidently a powerful weapon against demons, and he was glad he had it, shuddering to think what might have happened otherwise, remembering all too clearly how Hallar's sword had barely scratched it.

When they returned to their quarters, they found Vastra asleep upon his bunk with blankets piled in disarray about him.

"Some *wizard!*" Lars spat, looking with disdain on the sleeping form.

Kaplyn shook Vastra's shoulders, angrily calling his name.

Blearily, Vastra opened his eyes, looking up bewildered at the two men standing over him. He looked ill and groaned softly as he sat up. "What is it?" he demanded.

"A demon has attacked," Kaplyn replied, noticing Lars going into the adjacent room.

Vastra looked surprised. "A demon? Are you sure?" he asked.

"Of course I'm sure," Kaplyn stormed. "We fought it and drove it off."

At that moment, Lars returned, looking worried. "What has happened to our religious friends?" he asked.

Kaplyn frowned; the priests should have been in the guest quarters for it had been late when they had left.

"They were not here when I came in," Vastra stated.

"I'd better tell Hallar," Kaplyn said wearily, knowing that his friend already had a lot to occupy him. As he stepped once more into the cold night, he heard Vastra asking Lars more questions about the demon attack, and if anyone had been killed. Kaplyn shook his head; it was going to be a long night.

Kaplyn returned sometime later. Both Lars and Vastra were asleep. Wearily he sat down on his bed and with difficulty removed his boots, noisily throwing them to the floor before remembering that the others were sleeping. Lars snorted and turned over and Kaplyn paused. The other man started snoring, causing Kaplyn to grin. He went to a desk where he found paper and a quill. Swiftly he wrote a note to his father, explaining his absence and that he would return soon.

Once satisfied with the letter, he continued to undress. The sentries at the castle's entrance had told him that the priests had left earlier that night. Kaplyn had questioned them further, but by his reckoning the priests had left before the demon had struck. He had then found and informed Hallar of his discovery. Between them, they had then spent some time reassuring people that it was safe to go to their beds. It had been a difficult task, persuading folk they were safe, when a demon could literally pop out of thin air at any moment to kill indiscriminately. With a shake of his head Kaplyn lay down, but sleep was a long while coming; his imagination kept conjuring demons from the room's dark recesses.

When Kaplyn finally dropped off, almost immediately dreams engulfed him. He dreamt about the eerie hole in the library wall and once again experienced the cold breeze and baleful green light. He shied away from the hole, comprehending a terrible danger and yet something compelled him to enter. He could not help himself. One part of his consciousness screamed not to, but in the way of dreams he stepped forward and the glowing void swallowed him up. A loud click announced that the exit had closed.

He seemed to float along a tunnel. In the frigid air, his breath plumed into white clouds and his skin tingled. Then he was within an immense cavern, larger than anything he had seen before, reaching far above his head.

In slow motion, he drifted across the cavern floor, effortlessly skirting large columns of rock that magically transformed from the gloom. A nagging fear accompanied him; he knew that he should escape rather than continue.

Lazily a demon arose from the shadows, grinning maliciously as it displayed a grizzly trophy. He could not decide what it held and then realised; it was an arm. A finger beckoned and with mounting horror he turned to flee.

The rock beneath his feet became slippery and he could not grip. Behind him the demon laughed, mocking his futile efforts. He could not help but look back and found himself involuntarily turning towards it. His mind screamed to flee, but his legs continued to slide. He grabbed at something to stop himself.

Out of the corner of his eye he saw an object and as a last resort, reached out for that. His sleeping mind seemed to come to his aid, and he realised that he held his Eldric sword; with recognition, he felt a familiar tingling sensation in his palm. Slowly the cavern and the demon dissolved into inky blackness.

With a sudden shock he awoke, trembling and bathed in sweat. The horror of the nightmare remained. Panting for breath his eyes searched the darkened room, but there was nothing present apart from the silhouette of furniture.

Calming himself, he discovered he was tangled in his bed sheets, and he realised he must have been running in his sleep; the sheets had restricted his movements, making the dream seem so vivid. As he moved to untangle himself, his palm closed about the hilt of his sword. The weapon's presence mystified him, and he was sure that he had left it by the chair at the side of the bed. The glimmer of the runes was still visible in the half-light.

Should he have taken it from the tower? He recalled Vastra's warning about a curse. He also remembered, with some trepidation, the eerie crooning the sword had made as it bit into the demon's flesh, but it was too late now and if there was a curse then he could not avoid it. Besides, he thought grinning, any weapon that could wound or even kill a demon was worth keeping.

He found the scabbard on the floor and sheathed the weapon. Lying back on the hard but comfortable bed, he soon fell asleep; this time he slept fitfully, and dreams did not bother him again that night.

Kaplyn awoke with sunlight streaming through a chink in the curtains. He listened to people moving about outside before arising stiffly from his warm bed. Vastra was sitting on the edge of his own bed, and he nodded by way of greeting.

Kaplyn bade him good morning and padded towards the window, pulling back the heavy curtain. In the daylight, Vastra looked pale as he coughed feebly onto the back of his hand. From his bed, Lars groaned and raised himself bleary-eyed onto his elbow, giving Kaplyn an accusing look for letting in the light.

"What are we doing today?" Lars asked. He sounded sullen as though hoping for a postponement of their journey.

Kaplyn, too, felt that the night's events had changed matters. He looked to Vastra for guidance. He was buttoning up his shirt, and he stopped when he realised they were awaiting a response.

"We need to continue today, towards the mountains," he said, picking up his trousers and putting them on.

Lars groaned.

Vastra flashed them an angry look. "If you don't want to accompany me, then give me the pendant and remain here."

Kaplyn smiled and started to dress. "You're not getting rid of us that easily!"

Vastra scowled but remained silent.

"We will need supplies," Lars said miserably.

"What do we need?" Kaplyn asked, looking up for an instant.

"We have some ropes, but that's about all. We are low on food, and we are not prepared for bad weather."

"It's spring!" Kaplyn said somewhat surprised, "Surely the weather will be reasonable."

Lars shook his head and rose from the bed. "There could be a cold spell still, especially on the slopes. If we go high enough there may even be snow."

"He's right," Vastra acknowledged.

"Give me some money and I'll ask the baron where to get supplies," Kaplyn suggested.

Vastra nodded and removed his purse, handing Kaplyn a handful of silver *calder* after fumbling with the small sack.

Kaplyn turned to Lars, who was busy listing the supplies they would need.

"Two pack mules, thick woollen vests and jumpers, waterproof cloaks, and plenty to eat."

"You'd better get some torches as well," Vastra suggested. "Oh, and candles as well."

Kaplyn was relieved to have an excuse to talk to his friend before they left, and he hurried off before they remembered anything else. He took with him the letter for his father, hidden in his jacket.

Hallar was sitting in the main dining hall, looking perplexed; however, he still managed a smile and greeted Kaplyn warmly.

"Any news of the priests?" Kaplyn asked, taking a seat next to his friend. He sank back, enjoying the comfort.

Hallar shook his head "No—and if they are stupid enough to go traipsing off into the wild in the dead of night then they deserve all they get."

Kaplyn could not agree more. The two men sat in silence. Kaplyn knew that Hallar would object to his leaving, especially after the night's events.

"You have decided to go with the wizard then?" Hallar asked as though on cue.

Kaplyn nodded and briefly their eyes met.

"It's a foolish quest which you would do best to forget," Hallar advised strongly. "Did the demon not make you realise how dangerous your journey might be?"

"I have considered that, and, in a way, it has made my decision easier. What if there were more demon attacks? We need the Eldric and their power to defeat them. If we can find the Eldric, then we should."

Hallar looked away and Kaplyn could see his pain.

"I'll be as safe in the mountains as you are here, possibly safer. A demon is less likely to strike in the wilderness when there are large towns and cities full of people to prey on."

"You forget the other dangers though—krell and dwarves. If you think you are safe strolling into the mountains, then you had better think again!"

Kaplyn knew that Hallar was right, but nothing was going to deter him.

"We need supplies."

Hallar nodded.

"Winter clothing, food, pack mules and other items on this list." Kaplyn continued, relieved that his friend was not going to say anything further.

Hallar arose stiffly from the comfort of his chair and called for one of the servants who promptly entered.

"Take Kaplyn's list to Ralnar and have him get the supplies ready within the hour."

The servant took the list and left.

"Before I forget," Kaplyn said, removing the coins from his pocket, "I will have to pay for the goods." He saw that Hallar was about to refuse. "It is Vastra's money, and he will be suspicious if I return with both these and the supplies."

"See Ralnar when you leave; give him the money," Hallar conceded.

Kaplyn arose. "I will be back soon," he assured his friend. "Will you deliver this letter to my father? Could you also see that he gets this?" he said handing over his old sword.

Hallar took the note and the weapon. "Take care, and good luck," he said; the look in his eyes made Kaplyn feel guilty about leaving and for a moment, he considered abandoning the search, but Vastra, and what he might do, compelled him to continue. With sadness in his heart, he returned to the others, feeling very uncertain about the future.

After only a short while Ralnar arrived at the travellers' quarters accompanied by three men who carried the supplies they had requested. Ralnar was a thickset old man who had risen through the ranks to become the quartermaster, and, like others of his trade, he did not take kindly to requests for supplies from his neatly stacked shelves. Initially he was surly, but when he saw the money, his manner changed.

Lars checked the provisions and requested a few additional bits and pieces. Ralnar hurried away and soon returned with the missing items. By mid-morning they were finally ready to leave. Lars went to get their horses and newly purchased mules, and returned, leading them by the reins shortly later. Mounting, Vastra led them through the small gateway and turned eastwards to the open fields and beyond.

Kaplyn looked back over his shoulder, knowing that Hallar would be watching from one of the upper windows. He raised his hand in farewell and turned to concentrate on their path. A terrible fear swept over him that he might not see his friend again. He was heading out into the wild on a quest leading to who knows where, following a man who hated his father. Kaplyn shuddered. He felt as though his world was collapsing about him.

Chapter 13
The KinAnar Forest

The day grew warm, and the sun's heat was welcome on their backs. They rode across lush green fields, still damp from the previous day's rains. As the castle disappeared from view, the path became narrower and more disused; brambles grew thickly along its edge making the journey more difficult. As the day wore on woods became more frequent, forcing them to ride in single file beneath heavily blossomed branches.

They continued to ride in silence as their mounts plodded along the narrow winding trail, following the course of a quick-flowing stream. In places the stream was wide and shallow, and water bubbled merrily over shingle. This close to the river, the air felt cool which was pleasant as the sun reached its zenith in a clear blue sky.

A wider track leading north intersected theirs, crossing the river over a small rickety looking bridge, stretching far into the distance. They decided to stop for lunch by the crossroads before continuing. Vastra told them the path was an ancient dwarf road, used long ago on their pilgrimages to Thandor, their ancestral home. Kaplyn looked in awe at the path, trying to imagine long ranks of heavily laden dwarves marching along it.

All too soon, they finished their meal and, after replenishing their canteens from the river, they mounted their horses, setting off along the pinched path once more. Vegetation grew thickly about them, as high as their horses' flanks. Birds and insects flittered across their path, filling the air with vibrant sounds. Occasionally they disturbed a deer or some other wild animal drinking at the water's edge. These would scurry for cover in the nearby undergrowth, spooking the horses and, more often than not, their riders.

In the late afternoon, they came across a vast curtain of trees towering high above them. The girth of each was astounding and they craned their necks to see the tops. Beneath them, Kaplyn could imagine what a mouse felt like, lost amongst a field of ripening wheat.

"These trees must have been growing for centuries," he exclaimed in awe.

"Which forest is this?" Lars asked.

"KinAnar," Kaplyn replied.

Vastra was staring into the forest, looking dreadfully afraid much to Kaplyn's surprise.

"I don't like this place," he announced, coughing into his hand; his eyes looked red and sensitive.

"It's the quickest route," Kaplyn explained.

"How long would it take to go around?" Vastra asked, fidgeting nervously with his reins.

Kaplyn thought for a moment. In truth he did not know but remembered seeing the forest marked on one of the maps in the palace libraries and made a guess.

"I think it could take a week to travel its length and then another to backtrack the ground we would lose in the detour."

Vastra scowled, turning to stare deep into the wood, his eyes searching the dark places. He did not look well; his cheeks were sunken, and his complexion was pale.

It was already late and Kaplyn came to a decision. "Let's camp here," he said, dismounting. "You two prepare a camp and I'll scout ahead and investigate a little way into the forest. I'll look for game," he added as an afterthought, removing his bow and stringing it. He was keen to try it. He threw his quiver across his shoulder and while adjusting the strap he set off along the trail, quickly entering the outskirts of the forest.

Kaplyn was relieved to be on his own. The forest was beautiful, not dark like the wood he had encountered on his way to Pendrat. The trees were very tall, and their lowest branches were high above his head. Soon the trail petered out, but that did not dismay him. The stream continued by his side, and he knew that if they followed that, it would eventually lead them to the mountains. He paused, lying down to drink, enjoying the cool clear water.

For a while longer he continued, following the recent spoor of some wild animal. The ground became gently undulating and climbing a particularly steep slope he peered over the summit. Below, a wild fowl pecked at the ground. Slowly and quietly, Kaplyn nocked an arrow and took aim.

He was unaccustomed to the strength of the bow and the arrow passed clean through the fowl killing it instantly. It took him quite some time to find the arrow, which turned out to be considerably further into the forest than he had expected. He decided then there was nothing to fear beneath the trees, which seemed so tranquil and peaceful.

By the time he arrived at the forest's edge, the sun was already low on the horizon. Lars was busy tending a fire, partially concealed within a natural hollow, while Vastra was sitting with his back to a tree reading a book. To one side, the horses and mules were tethered to trees.

Lars looked relieved to see Kaplyn and equally pleased to see he had fresh meat. Vastra had earlier supplied some herbs and tubers, so they would eat well. As soon as the meal was ready, Lars served it to them on wooden platters, while Vastra put a pan of water on the fire to boil. They ate in silence and, when they finished, Vastra made himself tea. He seemed to recover slightly as he sipped the strong-smelling brew and colour returned to his cheeks.

"Did Lars tell you more about the demon?" Kaplyn ventured, secretly hoping to learn more about them.

Vastra nodded as he poured himself another cup of tea. Lars wrinkled his nose as the pungent aroma reached him. He grinned at Kaplyn.

"Demons strike at random," Vastra said, holding his mug in cupped hands while blowing on the hot liquid. Fortunately, he had missed Lars' grin. "Last night was an unfortunate incident for the people of Kinlin, but it was probably nothing more than coincidence. You were fortunate though, from what Lars told me; it was driven away empty handed."

Kaplyn smiled at the wizard's unintended pun, having cut off the demon's arm.

"What do you mean, we were fortunate?" Lars asked.

"You disturbed it feeding, before it had time to claim a soul. I have read about the Krell Wars, and, in those days, people believed that if a demon returned to hell unaccompanied by a soul, then its power was decreased as punishment. I think Kaplyn's sword was more than it bargained for."

"I don't understand," Lars replied. "The demon had killed at least three men; why do you believe it returned without a soul?"

A smile touched Vastra's thin lips. "The demon was probably overconfident. Normally it would have time to kill and feast on human flesh before returning to its own world, and only then would it seek a soul, or souls, to accompany it on its homeward journey."

"Is it true that demons can be summoned? Kaplyn asked.

Vastra's eyes narrowed. "Yes, but not without risk. A demon will oppose its summons with all its power. Being in this world causes them pain, or so I believe. It's a very risky spell and if the sorcerer makes a mistake the demon will likely kill him and take *his* soul for his impudence."

"Is it possible that the priests summoned the demon?" Kaplyn asked.

"I don't think so. Summoning a demon requires considerable power and as far as I could tell last night, when the priest read your mind, he did not use any magic, at least none that I could detect."

Lars listened to the exchange patiently but looked confused. "You say that demons strike at random. Is it possible then that my own people are at risk?"

Vastra's barely perceptible nod caused Lars to pale.

"Demons will strike anywhere there are people. If they haven't attacked your people, then it is simply because they haven't been discovered…yet."

"What is it?" Kaplyn asked, sensing Lars' inner turmoil.

"I dreamt last night that my village was attacked by demons."

"It was only a dream," Vastra said with undisguised contempt.

Kaplyn flashed him an icy glare and was about to rebuke him when Lars spoke. His voice was angry, and it was the first time that Kaplyn had heard him speak this way. "*By Slathor!* Do not mock me! My people take dreams very seriously and consider them a portent."

"I wouldn't worry. It's unlikely that demons will ever again attack in force. It was sorcerers who summoned demons and they have long since disappeared," Kaplyn said by way of comfort. "I have only ever heard of two attacks in my lifetime."

"Fool!" Vastra pronounced coldly. "What do you know of demons? All you have heard is hearsay. I have read countless texts about them, texts which you, too, could read if you tried."

Kaplyn did not like being called a fool; he felt his face burn with anger. "I can read," he snapped.

"I do not mean the barbaric Allund language." Vastra flashed back angrily. "Eldric is the true script of a scholar."

Vastra sat back with a condescending sneer. "Demon attacks are *not* rare. At present, they are less often, but they are on the increase. Perhaps we are already seeing this happen. The werewolf and then last night the demon. Two such events in a short time span are more than coincidence. If this trend escalates, then soon this land will be plagued by demons, and *then* you will see real fear." Vastra looked at them dangerously as if daring them to contradict.

Neither did, and so Vastra continued. "In the past, there have been many periods when demons have attacked. If you read your own history books instead of idling your time away, then you would discover that only sixty years ago there were over two hundred attacks in Allund in just one year!" He fell silent, angrily holding up an index finger as though to further the point.

Kaplyn was stunned, although he realised that Vastra spoke the truth; it explained why his people were so superstitious. "Where do demons come from?"

Vastra lowered his hand. "Demons exist in another world, separated from ours by a void where nothing can live—other than elementals. There may even be other worlds as well. In certain periods in time these worlds come close together, squeezing the void until it is thin enough for those with the power to do so to cross. Presently the worlds are far enough apart that only the most powerful demons can cross. But the time is fast approaching when demons will be able to travel more freely between the worlds, and then they will come — all too often."

"When's the next time when demons can cross to our world?" Kaplyn asked.

"That is not what you should ask," Vastra replied. "The occasional attack is fearful, but the consequences are tragic for only a few. I have studied the heavens and the stars," he continued, staring into the fire. The Prophecy predicts that one-day Drachar's shade will return. Mark me, when that happens, there will be all-out war and *thousands* will perish!"

Kaplyn shrugged. "But that's not supposed to happen until two to three hundred years after the Krell Wars and surely that is still some time in the future."

Vastra looked angry. "Where does the Prophecy say that?"

Kaplyn did not know. It was clear though that Vastra was finished talking; he sat back and continued reading, ignoring the other two men.

Frustrated, Kaplyn gave up the discussion and, as the stars began to appear in the black velvety sky, he and Lars spread their blankets on the soft grass. A silvery moon sailed high in the night sky softly illuminating the ground below, casting long shadows upon the grey landscape. All about the camp, small animals sought refuge from nocturnal hunters, and the occasional high-pitched shriek of a hunter, or its prey, replaced the more familiar daytime sounds.

Kaplyn lay awake looking up at the stars as though seeking the meaning of the Prophecy from within the complicated pattern of specks. He wondered whether the demon world was somewhere out there amongst the cloak of night and the thought made him wonder whether Drachar's shade also existed. Vastra's explanation worried him more than he cared to admit, and it was a long while before sleep would come.

Kaplyn awoke early the next morning with gentle sunlight bathing his upturned face. He breathed the morning air deeply before rising to wake the others. After a hurried breakfast, for he was keen to press on, they once more endured the tedium of breaking camp. As if not to disappoint them, Vastra again refrained from helping. Kaplyn noticed how pale and gaunt he looked; his movements were slow as though he was in pain, and he stooped like an old man.

"I do not like the feel of this forest," Vastra declared once they were mounted.

"Don't fret. I've travelled some way in and it's fine. There's nothing to fear," Kaplyn said, although deep down he was enjoying the other man's discomfort.

Vastra merely scowled.

Ignoring him Kaplyn urged his mount beneath the trees. The soothing cooing of wood pigeons accompanied them as they rode, and Kaplyn was at a loss as to why Vastra objected to taking this route. He glanced around. The other man's shoulders were slumped, and he looked miserable. Kaplyn suddenly felt guilty at having forced him to ride through the forest. Still, it was too late now, and the journey seemed pleasant enough. Indeed, it was difficult to imagine anything evil living here.

Through the dappled shade, bright pools of light shone on the forest carpet, highlighting the rich greens around them. Kaplyn's spirits rose. It seemed that the world was timeless, and he could imagine this forest as it was thousands of years ago. Engrossed in his own thoughts he failed to notice the trees thickening about them and all the while Vastra become quieter as though his mood matched the changing nature of the forest.

They rode most of the day with little event. Much to their alarm, towards late afternoon, the stream they were following disappeared under ground. Without it to guide them, they might become lost. Shortly after that the wood thinned and ahead, they could see a glade. Within the clearing was a small pool of clear blue water. A rocky hill rose sharply from the water's edge, and a waterfall spilled noisily into the pool, filling the air about it with myriad specks of flashing lights. Bright coloured flowers grew in tight clusters about the pool. However, there was no sign of a stream leading away from it and Kaplyn guessed that this was the stream's source, and the water must continue underground from here.

Both Kaplyn and Lars were hot and sweaty from the long day's ride. Kaplyn eyed the pool, considering a swim. "Let's camp here," he declared. The others did not object, although Vastra looked too ill to complain. He dismounted slowly before wearily sitting down in the shade of a large tree, leaving the other two to make camp. Kaplyn led the horses and mules to the pool's edge to drink.

He and Lars then stripped, ridding themselves of their sweaty clothes before plunging naked into the pool; the water was cold, forcing them to swim vigorously.

Kaplyn swam to the edge of the waterfall where he allowed the cold jet to massage his back, enjoying the force of the water. As he swam away from the cascade, he decided to investigate the depths and swan dived, swimming down. The temperature quickly dropped, and the light faded, leaving a murky world tinged with green. The cold and the darkness made him suddenly fearful and swiftly he retraced his way to the surface, breaking through in a fountain of water. There was no doubt that the pool was deep and Kaplyn felt compelled to re-join Lars in the shallows.

When they clambered out of the water, Vastra was still sitting in the shade of the tree, looking pale. Kaplyn asked what the matter was, but Vastra replied tersely that it was a trifle. Seeing that there was nothing they could do to help, they set about preparing their evening meal. Vastra fell asleep so they decided not to disturb him. Much later, as night fell, they turned in and, feeling invigorated after their swim, soon fell into a deep dreamless sleep.

A slight ripple at the centre of the pool was the only indication of the fear to follow.

Chapter 14
The Alvalah

Prince Lomar stood by the small window, looking intently out upon the silvery forest beyond. Its beauty enchanted him, and his heart soared at the myriad of colours. The barks were sublime shades of silver and their surfaces smooth as the purest silk. Sprouting from tiny vulnerable shoots, gold and vermilion leaves unfurled to trap the little light defusing into the leafy domain.

The silver, golds and reds combined to create a scene of immense beauty. Sighing deeply Lomar turned his gaze from the forest to his reflection trapped within the windowpane—a pale, stern countenance looked sadly back.

He was an albino, as were all his people, the Alvalah. Behind him, hanging in the great hall, portraits of his ancestors hung on the walls, each with the same deathly white pallor, fierce red eyes, and hair the colour of fresh snow. The portraits were a remarkable collection. Few people could claim to know their lineage beyond two generations, and yet the collection in the hall spanned an incredible thousand-year period.

Often, he studied the paintings, reflecting on his predecessors, and wondering about their lives; his favourite, or at least the one he studied most often, was that of Dalamere II. Although he hated to admit it, there was an uncanny resemblance between them.

Regarding his own reflection, he pondered on the distant king who held such a grim fascination for him. The only difference between them was the permanent frown that Dalamere wore; he looked incapable of humour.

Lomar glanced at the other portraits—the one common aspect was that the subjects were all clean-shaven; none had a beard or moustache. This was true of all the Alvalah for they could not grow facial hair, even if they wanted to. That was also supposed to have been true of the Eldric, a fact that substantiated claims that the Eldric and Alvalah were once distantly related.

There were, however, no portraits of any Eldric among the collection and even though the Alvalah claimed kinship, there had been little love lost between the races.

Lomar frowned. Perhaps that had been the greatest difference between the races; the Eldric were forward thinkers, whereas the Alvalah seemed to dwell on the past. Long ago, his people had secluded themselves in the forest, building their homes high in the branches of the KinAnar forest.

A sudden pang caused him to frown for he knew that the forest was fading. Perhaps that is why his people preferred the past for it was so hard to bear, seeing the forest diminish.

Soft footfalls interrupted him. The intrusion annoyed him and deliberately he turned his gaze back to the forest, ignoring the newcomer.

A polite cough indicated that the person was unwilling to leave, forcing Lomar to acknowledge their presence. Garth, his retainer, at least had the decency to look sheepish for disturbing his Lord. He was old even for an Alvalan. His hair was long and gossamer thin and deep wrinkles etched his face. Like all Alvalah, his clothing was of the brightest colours and today he had surpassed himself with a scarlet tunic and vivid green breeches.

"Your highness," Garth requested timidly. "It's nearly time for dinner. It would be bad manners to keep your mother, the Queen, waiting."

Lomar frowned, but then realised that the old man did not deserve his hostility. He had served him faithfully for many years. Ashamed, Lomar turned away once more, angry with himself for his lack of tact.

"Garth," he said at last. "Something has entered the forest; I feel…" the prince paused, unsure what it actually was he felt. "I feel that something terrible is about to happen."

"The forest has its own defence," Garth offered. "If anything evil entered, then the forest would prevent it from getting very far."

Lomar shook his head and turned to face Garth. "That's not what I meant. Important events are occurring beyond our forest, and I don't think Gilfillan will be allowed to ignore them—not this time."

Without realising it his gaze inadvertently went to Dalamere's portrait.

Garth's eyes followed the direction of his look. "Dalamere was a tyrant," he said softly.

Lomar waved his hand dismissively. "He doesn't concern me. It's more the power that he is said to have possessed…."

"He was an evil man. It was not his power which corrupted him, but rather it was he who corrupted the power."

Lomar was unconvinced. "I once read he could separate his soul from his body, allowing his soul to walk the corridors. I also read that he used these powers to further his own ends, spying upon his friends and enemies alike, using this information to blackmail them."

"It's an old tale, often told by mothers to frighten their children. *Behave*, they are told—*otherwise the shade of Dalamere will get you.* It works too," Garth replied.

"Is it possible, do you think, for a person to separate their soul from their body?" Lomar asked.

Garth went to a chair and sat down, not in disrespect to the prince, but merely the actions of a tired old man.

"Your father and I asked the same question many times," he admitted. "We knew quite early on that you were different from the other children." Garth smiled at the memories the conversation provoked. "I liked your father; he was a very strong man. Unshakeable, I often thought. Even still your mother could twist him around her little finger." He paused for a moment thoughtfully.

"You were four or five years old when we first suspected something was amiss. There was not a secret anyone could keep from you, which frightened many of the courtiers and your parents, too, at first. You had a knack for knowing what was going on, far beyond the ken of a small child. Your father had a theory about this."

Lomar waited patiently for Garth to continue.

"You know about shaols?"

Lomar nodded, "Of course, a shaol is a guardian spirit which is supposed to watch over us."

"Some people believe a shaol is more than that; a guardian spirit set to guide us. They also believe that when we die, they guide our spirits to the halls of the Creator, so that we are not lost to the evil that stalks the way between the worlds."

Lomar did not understand where Garth's train of thought was leading. Garth, sensing the prince's impatience, continued.

"Your father and I believed that long ago a shaol had a much stronger influence on our lives, steering us away from harm and warning us of danger."

Lomar had heard this before and, in a way, it seemed to make sense, explaining why some people appeared to have a sixth sense. "I've heard this. But over the years we have lost the ability to communicate with our shaol and hence also our ability to sense danger."

"That is what your father believed. He also believed that our shaol is the spirit of an ancestor. That is why the link with our shaol was once stronger, because the relationship between the two was that much closer. For example, long ago, the shaol could have been the person's father or grandfather, whereas now it is more likely to be a great, great, great grandfather."

Lomar looked horrified. "And you believe Dalamere is my shaol and it is his evil spirit which enables me to see things?"

"No," Garth assured him, relieved that at least he could deny that terrible possibility.

Lomar waited for the older man to continue. Garth took a deep breath as though uncertain of what to say next.

"When your mother was pregnant with you, a seer predicted she would have twins," Garth said. Lomar's expression showed that he had not known this.

"However, when you were born there was no other. The seer was questioned but was adamant about her prediction."

"She was wrong then?"

"She had never been wrong before."

"She must have been wrong on this occasion then!"

"Consider that she was right and that in your mother's womb there had been twins. What might have happened to your twin do you think?"

Lomar shook his head.

"It could be possible that he or she was absorbed in the womb, not by your mother, but by yourself."

"You mean that it still lives within me?" Lomar asked, stepping down from the alcove to stand beside his friend.

"I do not think so, but what if that twin was now your shaol?"

Comprehension dawned on Lomar's face. "So, you think it is my brother or sister's spirit that sees things and relays them to me," he asked.

"That's possible. Alternatively, it could be your brother or sister's spirit that allows yours access to the ethereal world—in effect, you have become your own guardian?" he ventured.

"How does this idea fit in with Dalamere?" Lomar asked.

Garth shrugged his shoulders. "That was long ago, and he could have found access to the spirit world some other way. No one will ever know."

They fell silent while Lomar considered the explanation.

"How did he die?" Lomar asked.

"Dalamere? He was relatively young when he died, or so I believe. By all accounts he died in his sleep, but many believe otherwise, preferring to think that his soul became lost as it went upon some evil errand. Eventually, without a soul, his body died."

The thought bothered Lomar, and he conjured the image of a ghostly apparition doomed to wander the halls of Gilfillan, searching for its mortal host. He felt as though someone had just walked over his grave.

Chapter 15
Ghostly Spectres

The gentle tinkle of the waterfall echoed softly in the dreams of the three travellers, lulling them deeper into sleep. Gradually, the pitch changed, becoming higher and more urgent, until it was as if many voices were crying on the still night air. In his sleep, Kaplyn sensed the change and fought to regain consciousness.

He awoke at once, immediately clasping the Eldric pendant, his gaze sweeping the clearing for signs of danger, but nothing stirred. His eyes kept returning to the waterfall and his mind fastened on the soft cries that seemed intermingled with the gentle splashing. The moonlight reflected brightly from the water; sparks of silver light danced as if seeking to hypnotise his weary mind. In mounting fear, he tried to awaken the other two, but neither stirred no matter how hard he shook them. Even the horses and mules seemed to be sleeping. Other than the plaintive cry of the waterfall, no living thing could be heard, and an unnatural silence pervaded the ancient forest.

All at once his pendant felt warm against his chest. Drawing his sword, he was shocked to see the blade was glowing eerily, reminding him of the recent demon attack. Fearfully he crouched, casting around for signs of danger.

The pool seemed to be the source of the unnatural sound, and, to his horror, the water started to ripple then boil as though alive. Transfixed, he watched as a shape broke surface, clambering from the bubbling waters. Two more shapes surfaced, clambering from the pool to join their comrade standing by its bank.

Cold eyes locked on Kaplyn's, and from dead throats came hollow laughter as the spectres raised dull blades.

As he slept, an all too familiar sensation swept over Lomar, a feeling he dreaded and which at first his subconscious mind tried to fight. It was something he had not experienced for some time, and it triggered distant memories, some happy, some sad. Restlessly he turned, entwining silk sheets about his pale body.

Abruptly, his subconscious lost its fight, and he felt his spirit slipping away from its earthly shackles. All at once he was floating effortlessly and, at first, he revelled in the weightlessness, momentarily forgetting his bleak mood. Then he felt very cold; blackness engulfed him and at once, he was desperately afraid.

Forcing his eyes open, he willed himself to waken. To his amazement, he was in a forest, not the one he was accustomed to, for there were no bright colours here. This was a very drab place, and the shades of greys and blacks seemed more akin to a nightmare than reality.

He was compelled to move in a particular direction and carefully he skirted the trees, preferring to go around rather than try to pass through them, which he was sure he could do. Nocturnal forest animals scampered out of his way, either seeing him or sensing his ghostly form. As the animals fled, he realised that this was indeed his forest, but he was far from the silver trees; the magic in this part of the forest had long since faded which saddened him, and he wondered whether this was what he was supposed to see.

Abruptly he came to a glade and the sight that met him left him stunned.

Within the clearing a waterfall noisily cascaded into a pool. Its sound was peculiar and Lomar sensed magic at work. However, it was not the pool that shocked him; a lone figure crouched to one side, a blue-glowing sword in his outstretched hand. A second figure lay asleep on the ground, while horses and mules stood behind the two men; oblivious to the horror that confronted them.

Three silvery knights stood before the crouching man. Each wore ornate silver breastplates and tall conical helms reminiscent of a bygone era. In ghostly hands, they held spectral swords that surely no earthly weapon could counter.

A memory from the previous night's conversation came back to Lomar and he remembered Garth saying *the forest has its own defence*. He wondered if the two men were evil, but decided that they were not, for he felt no malice from them. He decided that he had better act swiftly as the spectres were advancing upon the crouching man who was as yet unaware of Lomar.

Lomar saw the spectres' faces and at that moment he nearly failed. Grinning skulls looked out from under ancient helms and vacant sockets, glowing eerily, stared out with deadly intent.

"Stop!" Lomar commanded.

The figures came to a halt, their faces swivelling towards him. The crouching man also turned, a look of horror on his face.

The dark-haired man gave Lomar a jolt. He had the distinct impression they had met. He had no time to think about this though, as he returned his attention back to the dead knights.

Their sightless orbs locked on his, but he could sense their uncertainty.

"Command us, Lord," said the lead knight. Its voice echoed clearly within his mind and yet he knew that the knight could not have spoken.

"Return to your resting place and leave us," he ordered. His heart was pounding with fear, and he wasn't sure that the knights would obey. However, the spectre's reference to "Lord" was encouraging.

A groan sounded nearby and Lomar turned to look in that direction but could not see anyone. Again, uncertainty assailed him. Who were these people, and why had they come to his forest?

The lead knight hesitated but held his ground. "Master we sense a great evil here and it is our duty to destroy it," he proclaimed, pointing his sword in Kaplyn's direction.

Lomar was shocked. If there was evil here, then surely it must be the knights.

"Return!" he commanded, hoping his voice carried sufficient conviction. "I shall attend to this matter."

The dead knight's sunken orbs fixed upon Lomar who could not help but shudder. Finally, and with some reluctance, the spectre lowered his blade. He motioned to his companions and together they re-entered the pool. The tone of the waterfall changed and briefly, the water within the pool boiled again. Gradually the surface became calm with only a gentle ripple marring the otherwise still surface.

At once forest noises returned. Lomar felt a familiar sensation as though someone had hooked his navel and was pulling him backward. Around him the forest became surreal, as though seen within a dream.

He turned to the man. "You must go," he urged. "The knights may yet return. Head north and I will find you."

A great weariness crept over Lomar, and he knew no more.

Kaplyn sheathed his blade that whined eerily as though in anger. He couldn't believe what he had just witnessed. The thought of fighting dead knights had been terrifying and when he saw the newcomer, he had been certain he was a demon, with his red eyes, white hair and face.

Kaplyn knelt by Lars and shook the big man. The other man groaned. "What's up?" he asked, sitting up and rubbing his eyes.

"We must leave," Kaplyn said, going over to Vastra and roughly shaking his shoulder.

"It's still night," Lars complained, arising, and struggling into his boots. Vastra remained asleep despite Kaplyn's shaking.

Lars came over and felt Vastra's brow. "He's cold and clammy," he said, looking worriedly at Kaplyn.

"Gather your things," Kaplyn urged. "We'll see to Vastra once we are away from here."

The sense of urgency in Kaplyn's voice spurred Lars into action and hurriedly they packed their gear. When they returned, Vastra was still unconscious and no matter what they did, would not stir.

"We should not have camped so near to the water," Lars said, scratching under his armpit. "There is a host of biting things around here. Perhaps he has caught a fever."

Kaplyn shook his head. "I doubt it is insects. He looked ill yesterday. Help me get him onto his horse."

Together they lifted Vastra, his lightness surprising them both. "It's a wonder he's as strong as he is. Beneath these clothes, he's all skin and bones," Lars commented.

They deposited him unceremoniously across his mount.

"We'll have to walk. I'll lead the horses. You see to it that he doesn't fall off," Kaplyn said.

He led them in the general direction the spectre had indicated, not entirely sure whether to trust the apparition or not, but he had helped them and at least they were better off moving. As they walked, Kaplyn told Lars what had occurred.

"I was awake, I can assure you, and my sword was glowing, like in the demon's presence," Kaplyn concluded.

Lars was silent although he looked about the trees fearfully. "Perhaps you should draw it now and check if we are safe," he suggested.

Kaplyn partly drew the weapon, but the blade was dull. He peered into the gloom ahead; in the daylight, the forest had seemed a friendly enough place but now, in the dead of night, it felt much more sinister. He realised that it was going to be a very long night.

Chapter 16
Recognition

Lomar awoke shortly before daybreak. His head ached and it took several moments to recollect the events of the previous night. Vaguely he remembered that disorientation was usual after his spirit had travelled on the astral plain. As a child, it had been bad enough, but now, as an adult, it seemed much worse. It was also uncanny that it had happened so soon after discussing it with Garth. It had seemed dreamlike, and yet the events during the night had been real; of that much, he was certain. But never had his mind travelled so far, and that thought alone terrified him.

The memory of the dark-haired man's face came back to him, and he suddenly remembered why he was familiar. He had seen him before in his dreams and the realisation came as a shock for, if the man truly existed, it added additional meaning to his terrible nightmares. He could see future events. He had to find out what was going on.

Arising from the comfort of his warm bed, he shivered as the cold night air caressed his naked flesh. Opening the curtain, he discovered the dawn was still some time off, but he refused to delay. Hurriedly he dressed. On the way out, he took his longbow and a quiver of arrows. His people did not hunt, nor did they eat the flesh of animals, but they still practised archery, using wooden targets for sport. He also found his sword; it was delicately wrought, slim and seemingly fragile, but the steel was strong and his arm swift.

Peering through the doorway, he was relieved to find the corridor empty. He hurried towards the stairs, momentarily considering asking Garth to accompany him, but rejected the idea. If there was danger, he did not want to subject his friend to it as well.

In the darkness, the corridor was eerie and for an instant he imagined Dalamere's shade searching for his body. The thought made him shudder as he started down the broad, winding staircase leading to the main palace halls, built within the bole of the greatest Gilfillan tree. From the lower palace level, Lomar went by way of the least frequented corridors until he reached the stairs leading to the forest floor far below. These had also been built within the massive trunk and had been exquisitely carved over long years. So not to disrupt the sap, the stair was a tight spiral and, as a result, he arrived in the stables breathless and his head spinning. He paused to let the giddiness pass. One of the horses nickered a soft welcome.

Swiftly he saddled his horse before leading it outside. Once in the open he leapt lightly into the saddle. Normally his rides were sedate as he took in the stunning scenery, but now he took little notice of his surroundings and instead turned his mount in the direction he sensed his spirit had travelled that night.

He ignored the forest creatures, which scampered up to the rider, seeking titbits that the Alvalah often carried. This time he hastened on his journey as the sun ascended in the morning sky. After his swift passage, the animals milled around uncertainly, for they had never seen one of the Alvalah in haste before; however, the pale prince was soon forgotten as they returned to their foraging.

When dawn broke, Kaplyn and Lars found themselves in a denser part of the forest. They had to force their way through the thick undergrowth and soon the humidity increased, causing the men and their mounts to sweat profusely. Kaplyn started to fear they were lost.

By midday, the trees thinned making their journey easier. Briefly, they paused to check on Vastra, but he was still unconscious and looked even paler than the night before. Whatever ailed him was a complete mystery and they decided that they had to leave urgently. They ate a hurried meal and set off, riding even though the ground was uneven. Each rode either side of Vastra to support him and, for a while, they made good time.

Sometime later Kaplyn halted them. Ahead, partially obscured by the maze of thick tree trunks he thought he could see a figure sitting astride a horse. There appeared to be only one person, although the trunks were large enough to conceal an army.

Pausing, they debated what to do, while ahead the figure remained motionless as though content to let them see that he meant no harm. His inaction made them more confident and so they urged their mounts forward. As they approached, Kaplyn became aware that the stranger's complexion and hair was deathly white and his eyes fiery red. He knew at once that it was this man's spirit he had seen the night before and again he had a terrible fear that he was a demon, but common sense prevailed, for the stranger seemed to be as afraid of them as they were of him. Kaplyn had seen an albino rabbit once and the characteristics seemed to fit this man and so he assumed that he, too, must be an albino.

The stranger was dressed richly in a bright yellow doublet partially covered by a long, pale blue silk cloak. Long riding boots reached up to his knees, covering his britches that were green and as a bright a colour as his doublet. About his waist, a broad leather belt supported a long, delicate sword and a small dagger, while about his shoulders he carried a long bow and quiver. His horse was equally garishly adorned with a rich looking saddle blanket and Kaplyn gazed in wonder at the reins that looked as though they were spun from fine gold threads. In all, the stranger seemed as out of place in the forest as they felt.

"Welcome," the stranger said when they were within a comfortable distance. "Welcome to Gilfillan."

Kaplyn was about to reply when the albino interrupted him, a look of concern on his face.

"I did not expect three of you," he said, suddenly looking at Kaplyn. "And your companion, he is ill." He urged his mount forward a few steps and bent over to examine Vastra.

"You helped us last night?" Kaplyn asked uncertainly.

The albino nodded as he continued his examination. Finally, he sat back. "I do not know what ails him," he admitted.

"How did you help us? I mean, you were a ghost," Kaplyn said.

"I will explain as we ride. Firstly though, my name is Lomar, and I am an Alvalan. Who are you and why is it that I was not aware of your companion last night?"

It was Kaplyn's turn to frown. "I'm Kaplyn and this is Lars. Our companion is Vastra. He's been ill since early last night. As to why you did not see him, I do not know. Perhaps his dark clothes concealed him?"

Lomar looked worried. "You must accompany me to my people. We have healers who will be able to help."

Lars glanced at Kaplyn who nodded. As they rode, Lomar asked them where they were going. When Kaplyn told him they were seeking a means of finding the Eldric, Lomar frowned.

"The Eldric have long since departed. How can you find them? Of course, that is if they *wish* to be found."

"Vastra has read that the Eldric travelled into the mountains, and we are following the route they took," Kaplyn explained.

Lomar's frown deepened. "That journey is madness, krell inhabit the mountains and besides, after all these years, the chance of finding anything even slightly connected with the Eldric is remote to say the least."

"We will try though," Kaplyn replied.

"Well, I wish you luck," It was clear from Lomar's tone that he thought that their quest was folly.

"What happened last night, by the pool?" Kaplyn asked.

Lomar shook his head, "I don't really know. I have a gift I cannot control, but at times it seems that my spirit leaves my body and I travel to places, seeing things that I should not normally know. I also see glimpses of the future and I am sure that I have seen you in my dreams…"

Kaplyn could tell by his tone that the experience frightened the albino. Hearing that the other man had seen him in his dreams was also scary.

"Last night was one such occasion," Lomar said, looking closely at Kaplyn. "I have no idea how or why it happened, but it was lucky for you that it did. The other oddity is no one else has ever seen my spirit before, but you could; I could tell by the way you looked at me."

"Yes, I could," Kaplyn answered. "And a shock it was too. I thought you were a demon. But what were those *things*?" Kaplyn asked referring to the ghostly knights.

"They were possibly some part of the forest's defence, but that is only a guess; possibly guardians placed there long ago, even before the Krell Wars, to secure the forest's borders."

"It was very nearly a successful defence," Lars said pointedly.

Kaplyn smiled although it was somewhat forced; Lars did not realise how close to the truth his words were.

Chapter 17
Gilfillan

By mid-afternoon Kaplyn detected small changes occurring in the forest; the leaves had started to take on autumnal shades of reds and golds, even though it was still early spring. Brightly coloured squirrels scampered lightly from branch to branch, inquisitively peering down on the group. Suddenly one ran lightly from a branch and across Kaplyn's shoulders, causing him to jump in shock. It paused on his shoulder as though studying him before hurtling off in its search for food. Kaplyn looked around at Lars who was smiling broadly at the tiny creature's impudence.

Within a few yards, a family of deer casually crossed the path in front of them; the doe even turned to watch them pass as her youngsters hurried into the surrounding bushes. Lomar seemed surprised by their astonishment at her lack of fear.

Soon the forest changed even more dramatically; the surrounding bark became delicate, translucent silver and the leaves even more beautiful shades of gold and red. Kaplyn found himself holding his breath in awe.

Shafts of sunlight stabbed through the intertwining branches, reflecting brightly from the leaves in a magnificent blaze of glory. By their side, a stream glittered as ripples in turn caught the light, its surface reflecting a myriad of colours.

"It's truly beautiful!" Kaplyn stated in wonder.

Lomar was watching his reaction and a smile touched his bloodless lips. "It does make your world seem dull."

"Why is it like this? I have never seen anything like it before in my life," Lars stated, looking up and nearly falling off his horse.

Lomar's smile broadened; to him, complimenting the forest was the same as complimenting the Alvalah. "My people believe that the entire world is like this," he said indicating the trees with a broad sweep of his arm. "I used to myself until last night when I saw what the forest was becoming. Where I saw you last night, was a very dreary place."

"Lomar, how long will it take us to reach your home?" Lars asked.

"We will not get there today," he replied. "However, it's not far and we should arrive early tomorrow, if we can go a little farther while the light lasts."

Kaplyn glanced at Vastra and hoped that whatever ailed him was not too serious. The unconscious man was bouncing about uncomfortably on the horse's broad back.

They rode for a while longer, but Vastra showed no signs of recovery and started mumbling in his fevered sleep. Slowly the sun began sinking and, as the light failed, the colour of the leaves seemed to match that of the sunset. The ground started to rise steeply, causing their weary horses to stumble on the cluttered forest floor. Lomar's mount, by comparison, seemed much fresher, floating lightly over the soft turf. Slowly but surely, they started to fall behind until Kaplyn knew they could go no further. He called softly to Lomar who turned and saw their weariness.

"Come, we will rest here this night," he said, looking guilty that he had not realised how tired they were.

They dismounted and Kaplyn removed Vastra's limp body from his horse, laying him on the soft ground before covering him with a blanket. Lars tended to the horses while Lomar went into the woods. He reappeared shortly, carrying several large, golden fruit. These he placed upon the ground and, using his knife, segmented them. Since it was warm, there was no need for a campfire; indeed, Kaplyn would have been surprised if a campfire was ever needed beneath the faintly glowing trees.

Sitting together, they ate the fruit, delighting in the succulent flavour. The only noise, apart from Vastra's occasional mumbling, was the chirping of crickets. Lomar offered them his flask to quench their thirst. It was a fiery drink and Lars coughed after he had taken a sip.

"What is this, Lomar?" he asked, holding up the flask appreciatively.

"It's a wine made from the fruit you are eating," he replied nonchalantly.

Lars' eyebrows rose appreciatively as he took another draught, this time taking time to enjoy the flavour.

Above them, the moon peeked through the branches, encapsulating the trees in a silver radiance. Kaplyn looked up and could just make out the stars shining brightly in the heavens.

"Do you know anything about the Eldric, Lomar?" he asked.

"A little. There are some who believe that our peoples are distantly related."

Kaplyn frowned, "How can that be? I though the Eldric came from across the sea."

Lomar drank a little of the fiery liquid, wincing as he did so. "Long ago my people were more adventurous, and it is said we used to live by the sea. I find that hard to imagine. I've never seen the sea; it must be very beautiful."

"It is," Lars said. "I loved sailing, but it's a treacherous business. You are at the mercy of the gods the moment you step aboard."

Lomar smiled and continued his tale. "Long ago my people supposedly built ships and travelled across the sea, seeking new lands and new wonders. It's a fanciful tale, one told before my people learned the art of keeping records, but there may be some truth in it. Anyway, it may be possible that my people left many thousands of years ago, returning later as the Eldric."

"What about the storms though?" Lars asked. "I was told that they rage almost continually and sailing far from Allund is very perilous."

"It was many years ago," Lomar conceded. "Perhaps then the great storms were less ferocious. Whatever the case, I believe the Alvalah and the Eldric are related. Many others also believe this—as no doubt many do not; it's a subject of great contention amongst my people."

"Do your people know what became of the Eldric?" Kaplyn asked, leaning forward, and taking more interest.

Lomar shook his head. "There are many theories, but at the time of the Eldric's disappearance, my people had already turned their backs on the world. We are rather reclusive now, living in the forest. Our knowledge of the outside world has been second-hand for many years."

"If your people were related to the Eldric as you believe, then why do you know so little about them?" Kaplyn continued.

"We were never close to the Eldric," Lomar admitted. "Our history books tell mainly of our own histories and even though we think there was once kinship between us, there was no love lost.

"Even at that time we preferred our forests, never venturing far. The source of our outside news arrives via the few traders who still remember us. No doubt by the time we received tales of the Eldric's departure it was some years afterwards."

"By the way, do you know roughly when the Eldric left?" Kaplyn asked, suddenly realising that Lomar might know that.

"By our reckoning, it would be close to five hundred years."

"That's not possible," Kaplyn said, truly shocked.

"My people have kept records ever since the Krell Wars and I'm certain of the date," Lomar replied.

"Why is the time so important?" Lars asked.

"It might mean the Prophecy is closer to happening than we thought," Kaplyn said, grimacing. "My people believe it was only a few hundred years ago since Drachar was defeated, not *five*."

At Drachar's mention, Lomar shuddered.

"Surely Drachar's returning is only a fairy tale," Lars said.

Lomar shook his head. "The Prophecy is of great concern to my people. We fear that one day someone will try to release his shade from its imprisonment."

"So, you believe that he did not truly die then?" Lars asked.

"No—his soul was too strongly linked to the spirit world to die. A Narlassar sorcerer's power comes from the spirit world and that binds him to that. As to the time though, that is very uncertain. The Prophecy does not mention a time when he will return; the closest clue is W*hen Tallin's Crown once more does shine*."

"Kaplyn and I discussed that. What do you think it means?" Lars asked.

"We are not sure," Lomar replied. "But it is thought that Tallin's Crown is a constellation."

This was news to Kaplyn although it made sense. "Do you know which?"

Lomar shook his head. "The Alvalah were once great astronomers, but since coming to the forest, we tend not to look towards the heavens as much as we once did."

Kaplyn considered Lomar's words for a while. The news that the Eldric left so long ago concerned him. When his thoughts came back to the present, Lars was asking Lomar about the material of his cloak and the albino was showing it to the big man who was explaining the origin of the material. Now that Lars had mentioned it, Kaplyn marvelled at the softness of the cloth and closeness of the weave.

"It is made from spiders' silk," Lomar said.

Lars laughed. "That's impossible; it would take years to collect enough silk."

"Not at all," Lomar answered." The forest has especially large spiders, high up in the trees. They are venomous and harvesting the silk is hazardous, but it's considered a great honour to do so. As you can see, the thread is very strong and elastic; it makes an excellent cloth."

Kaplyn glanced up as though expecting to see spiders on every bough. It was Lomar's turn to laugh. His laughter was as clear as a bell.

"Do not fear! The spiders rarely come to the forest floor, only once a year and that is much later in the autumn."

The conversation continued late into the night. Eventually they turned in, lying on the soft ground with a blanket over them against the chill. That night Kaplyn and Lars slept better than they had for a while and, when they awoke, even Vastra seemed slightly improved; his skin colour looked healthier, although, as yet, he had not recovered consciousness.

After breakfasting on the golden fruit, they departed with Lomar leading the way. He seemed eager now to press on. "My city is only a short journey. We should be there by mid-morning and then your friend will receive treatment."

The ride continued pleasantly and Kaplyn kept peering between the tall trees, expecting at any moment to see a clearing and a walled city. Sometime later, Lomar saw Kaplyn's look of confusion, and he briefly halted them, pointing high up into the trees ahead.

Between the thick foliage, Kaplyn could see wooden buildings constructed on broad tree limbs that were veritable giants amongst their kind. Kaplyn felt dizzy looking up at the dwellings and he feared what it must be like to look down from the Tree City.

Most of the buildings upon the broad branches were single storey. From some of these, diminutive figures looked down. Lomar waved and several waved in return.

Larger buildings were constructed around the trunks, and these were many storeys high.

Lars looked up at the buildings and shuddered. "If the gods had intended for us to live in trees, then surely he would have given us wings." He glanced nervously at Lomar who merely smiled.

"Come," Lomar said. "And meet my people."

Chapter 18
Where God's Dwell

Lomar escorted them to the base of a particularly large tree where several soldiers awaited them. Kaplyn was shocked to see that, like Lomar, the men's pallor was deathly white and their eyes fiery red. He realised that the entire race must be albino.

They were a strange people. Even their armour was outlandish and not very functional. Their breastplates looked to be made of silver with intricate patterns embossed upon them, regardless that the designs would trap a spear or an arrow point that might otherwise be deflected. Their helmets were also made of silver, sporting long coloured feathers, which Kaplyn later found out denoted the soldier's rank. Their clothes, barely visible beneath their armour, were bright colours much like Lomar's.

A tall man strode purposefully forward from between the soldiers, coming to a halt by Lomar's side. His eyes betrayed his anxiousness and he looked disapprovingly up at Lomar who promptly dismounted. Smiling, he held out the reins for one of the soldiers to take.

"My prince," the man said saluting smartly, eyeing Kaplyn and Lars warily. "The queen has requested that you attend her in her audience room immediately."

It came as a shock to hear Lomar referred to as prince, though he recognised by the messenger's tone that Lomar was in trouble.

"I shall attend her presently, after I have seen to my guests," Lomar replied quietly, but with authority.

The man looked uneasy, and his cheeks flushed. "Sire, she said that I was to request your presence *immediately* upon your return."

"Then I shall attend her directly," Lomar conceded much to the messenger's obvious relief. "Would you take these guests to Garth and ask him to entertain them in my absence. One is ill and must be taken to the healers with all haste."

The messenger nodded, stepping back to allow his prince to pass by, but before he did Lomar turned to speak with Kaplyn. "I apologise that I have to leave but I shall endeavour to return shortly. In the meantime, my retainer Garth will attend to your needs so please feel at home here."

Kaplyn thanked him and Lomar took his leave, entering a door in the base of the tree.

Two men carried Vastra away. The messenger then turned to Kaplyn and Lars and politely requested that they follow him. They entered the same tree as Lomar had moments earlier and behind them four soldiers followed.

The interior of the tree opened into large stables, against one side of which a flight of stairs spiralled upwards. Inside the stair, beautifully crafted silver lanterns softly illuminated the way. At intervals, narrow windows allowed them to judge how high they had climbed.

They finally came to a door leading to a corridor, cut deep into the heart of the ancient tree. If they had expected the forest dwelling to be frugal then they were pleasantly surprised; dazzling silks decorated the walls and a deep, rich carpet covered the floor. The furniture was exquisite, formed from branches that had grown into odd shapes. Deep shiny boughs formed fine reclining armchairs, while knotted limbs made trestles upon which ornately decorated boards were placed to make tables, some of which were so fine as to be almost translucent. Indeed, the interior was more exquisitely decorated than Dundalk's palace, and Kaplyn was reminded of the Eldric citadel of Tarel, even though he had only seen it briefly. Lomar's claim that the Alvalah and the Eldric were related seemed increasingly plausible, the more he learned.

The corridor led them inside one of the buildings built outside the trunk. Their escort led them through a door and into an audience room filled with yet more ornately carved furniture. A small man seated by the window arose, looking confused by their sudden presence. Kaplyn then realised it was probably *their* complexion that made him frown, and that came as a shock.

"Garth, prince Lomar has requested that you attend to his guests while he has been summoned to speak with the queen," the messenger said before leaving, although he remained outside with the escort.

After a brief and uncomfortable silence, Garth suddenly looked shocked, presumably because he had been staring at Kaplyn and Lars.

"I am G…Garth," he stuttered uncertainly, blinking like a great owl.

"I am Kaplyn, and this is Lars," Kaplyn said, indicating the big man by his side. Garth's eyes widened more, as he looked at the blond bearded giant who carried a broad axe strapped to his back. Lars smiled back warmly, and his eyes shone with humour at the other man's discomfort.

"I'm afraid that the prince is likely to be some time,' Garth explained. "Perhaps in the meantime I can show you around?"

"That would be interesting," Kaplyn replied, glancing over Garth's shoulder at an open doorway, leading to a balcony. "How high are we?" he asked. A cool breeze blew through the opening, carrying with it the scents of the forest beyond.

"Come and see," Garth said stepping out onto the balcony.

Kaplyn turned, grinning at Lars' obvious discomfort. The other man was clearly not happy with heights. Kaplyn went through the door, stepped forward to a rail, and peered over. It was higher than he anticipated and to make matters worse the tree was swaying, albeit gently. However, he soon forgot his fears as he looked at the city and the golden forest. It was truly breath-taking. Many aerial pathways linked the buildings and a method of intertwining broad branches with thinner ones had been used to create the bridges. People of all ages walked between the trees as though the crossing was second nature. Some were carrying heavy packs or even pulling carts.

Lars joined them, his face pale, but after a while even he seemed impressed with the view.

"There's something else you might like to see," Garth said, eager to please the newcomers.

Kaplyn nodded. Garth, with their escort faithfully following, led them through corridors and then out onto one of the walkways. As they started to cross Kaplyn's fear vanished. From above it had looked much more dangerous, but now they were upon it the sides prevented him seeing over the edge.

Above, the branches had been knitted together to form a protective roof against the rain so that the Alvalah could go about the city without fear of getting wet. Garth pointed out how tight the weave was, explaining that it took several years and constant pruning to acquire the right shape.

He then led them down a flight of stairs, circling one of the great trunks. Excitedly he spoke about the city, pointing to each building, and telling them its use, or who lived there, and they listened half-heartedly, concentrating instead on the winding stair. When they stood upon the forest floor, both Kaplyn and Lars visibly relaxed and they had to hurry to catch up with their eager guide who strode purposefully ahead. A large rocky outcrop stood like a giant tooth from the moss-covered ground. Garth led them towards this, telling them of its beauty, confusing them with the sudden rush of words.

A large gaping wound opened in the side of the rock and Kaplyn and Lars looked at each other as Garth halted before it, neither fully understanding what all the fuss was about. Garth, on seeing their puzzled looks, smiled, and gestured towards the cave.

"We believe that this was once the home of a Kalanth," he declared excitedly. "The Old One's presence is why we believe the forest still retains its beauty while all else fades."

Kaplyn frowned. There was a certain tranquillity about the mound, and he could not deny the beauty surrounding him, but he found it hard to believe that a god had chosen to live here.

"Have you heard of the Kalanth?" Garth asked Kaplyn, upon seeing his puzzled look.

"Yes, I have. My people still leave offerings at hallowed sites," he admitted.

"Is it not a little *small* for a god?" Lars asked.

Garth smiled. "Enter, and you will see."

The narrow entrance looked as though the rock had been torn open sometime in its past. Inside, Kaplyn expected the cave to be cold and damp, but it was neither; instead, it was breath-taking. Small crystals, half the size of his fist, almost completely covered the cavern walls, making the place both bright and cheerful. However, to Kaplyn it was only a cave, and he could not see what all the fuss was.

"Wait," Garth said in a hushed tone. "I hope we are not late."

They stood in silence while they could hear the escort outside conversing in low tones. Kaplyn glanced uncertainly at Garth, wondering why they were waiting and, in the meantime, decided to examine the cave once more. The upper part was nearly perfectly spherical, and, on its walls, there were literally thousands of crystals, each fitting perfectly with its neighbour. However, there were some gaps where crystals were missing. These seemed to make the cavern incomplete, more so than Kaplyn could explain.

He was about to ask Garth about them when the old man gestured towards the entrance. At that moment, the sunlight increased as the sun aligned with it and then, quite suddenly, an intense white light flared brightly all around them as the crystals caught the sun's rays, reflecting them in a dazzling display. Kaplyn covered his eyes to reduce the glare but stopped when the intensity quickly and dramatically dropped.

To his amazement, coloured lights streaked by him as the glass-like surface of the cavern refracted the sun's rays. Hundreds of tiny rainbows were hurled across the cavern in a seemingly endless game. Kaplyn found himself constantly turning to watch the patterns and he started to feel giddy. The light blazed a trail of glory, and he began to understand why people believed in gods.

Lars was also clearly in awe and the colours danced gaily on his face, enhancing the movements of his muscles as he smiled. Kaplyn grinned and Lars broke into infectious laughter. The other two men joined in, and their senses seemed heightened as if the light was purging their souls of all their worldly fatigues.

To their disappointment the display faded, leaving them feeling bereft of its beauty. Never had Kaplyn seen such splendour and his mind reeled with the memory. There were no words to describe it. By his side, Garth gestured that they should leave.

Kaplyn asked Garth about the crystals as they made their way back towards the tree houses.

"The cavern was found long ago when my people first entered the forest," the older man replied.

"The crystals are beautiful," Lars commented.

"Yes. I believe that your people call them kara-stones," Garth replied.

Kaplyn was surprised. "I've never heard of so many existing in one place before."

"Vastra mentioned kara-stones. He believed they might be the remains of a magic user when they die, but that can't be true if there are so many together in one place." Lars said.

"I'm not sure if anyone really knows what they are," Kaplyn replied. "There is one in Dundalk, although I'm not sure if it's a true kara-stone. However, it's guarded very closely; the people believe the city's fortunes are linked with it and if it is stolen or lost, then the city will fall."

Garth nodded his agreement. "My people have studied the stones and have discovered that they can be used by healers."

"Will they use one to help our companion?" Kaplyn asked.

"I did not realise that you had a companion with you," Garth answered. His tone suggested that he was shocked that no one had mentioned this earlier.

"He was taken to the healers when we arrived," Kaplyn replied.

"Then it is more than likely that the healers will use a kara-stone. We could go and see him if you like?" Garth said.

"If it wouldn't disturb them, I would like that," Kaplyn replied.

Garth smiled, gesturing for them to follow.

Chapter 19
Vastra's Demon

Garth led them into the trunk of one of the trees and, after a long climb, they entered a richly decorated building constructed on one of the broad limbs. He then led them into a large, well-aired room where Lomar and several men and women, dressed in long flowing robes, crowded around a low dais. They were in heated debate, although they quietened somewhat when the newcomers entered. Vastra was lying unmoving on the dais; his pallor was grey, and his flesh looked flaccid. Lomar looked up and, recognising Kaplyn and Lars, smiled warmly, walking towards the two men.

"My mother didn't keep me long, and it is timely that you have arrived. I was just about to send for you. We, unfortunately, are having some difficulty in determining what ails your companion. We were about to try other means, but there appears to be some discussion about how best to proceed."

"Do not let him deceive you," one of the women healers said. She was strikingly beautiful with wide almond-shaped eyes and a slim figure. "We were arguing, as no doubt you were well aware." She glared at Lomar as though daring him to contradict.

Tactfully Lomar remained silent and then he said, "This is Hannas," indicating the woman by his side. "She's our foremost healer and has studied your companion's illness, but we do not know what the problem is. However, we have discovered something that is proving an enigma. There appears to be a spell deflecting our attempts to probe his illness. The spell may have been invoked to prevent such a probe as we are now trying."

"You can remove this spell though?" Kaplyn guessed.

Lomar nodded, glancing at Hannas as if expecting another argument. She interrupted him before he could say anything further. "It's a minor spell of no consequence which we can remove," she replied tersely.

"What is stopping you then?" Kaplyn asked curiously.

"It's a moral issue," Lomar explained, balefully eyeing Hannas. "If he has chosen to hide something then we do not have the right to interfere."

Hannas looked at Lomar, angrily folding her arms. "The spell prevents us from discovering what is wrong with your companion, and *your* stubbornness, Lomar, may well result in his death." The other healers within the room looked expectantly at Kaplyn, clearly hoping that he would solve the dilemma and end the stalemate.

"He is our companion. Would you accept our guidance?" Kaplyn suggested.

Many of the healers nodded and so Kaplyn continued. "If his illness threatens his life then I think you should investigate it, whatever the cause, including anything he has chosen to hide, be it deliberate or not."

"Thank you," Hannas said, smiling broadly. "*Finally! S*ome common sense."

With that, the Alvalans turned back to their work, positioning one of the kara-stones on a table by the recumbent form.

Hannas placed a hand over the crystal and started to chant in a high singsong voice. Very quickly, the crystal started to glimmer and Kaplyn felt drawn towards the stone as small bright lights started to form deep within it. As the pitch of her chant increased, the lights started to move faster and faster, compelling Kaplyn to draw nearer.

An exclamation of surprise from one of the healers brought his attention back to Vastra's body. A similar pattern of lights had appeared several feet above his chest, and these danced in a frenzied pattern in time with those within the stone. A shocking cold penetrated the room accompanied by an uncomfortable silence, a premonition of the events to follow.

A sudden flash of light over Vastra's chest caused everyone to jump. Above him, a shape coalesced from within the whirling lights, which were moving so swiftly now that they became a blur. All at once hovering a few feet above Vastra was a creature about the size of a cat. Kaplyn initially thought that it was hairless, but as it turned baleful hate-filled eyes about the room he realised it had a long streak of hair, like a mane, hanging down its bony back. Its skin was a sickly shade of green and its limbs were long and skinny. It squatted in indignation, blinking its cat-like eyes at the hateful light. A thin tongue flickered from its mouth, revealing small, pointed teeth. An incredible stench of decay accompanied the creature's appearance.

Nobody moved and the creature remained, hovering in mid-air as if dazed.

"Bind it, Hannas!" Lomar hissed. She remained transfixed, staring at the demon, mesmerised by its presence.

Lomar moved to her side, grabbing her arm. "Bind it!" he repeated.

As he moved, the creature screamed a thin piercing wail that penetrated their very souls and leapt towards them. Instinctively, Kaplyn drew his sword, which suddenly flared brightly, casting back the gloom that had settled on the room. The blade crooned eerily as it cleared the scabbard. The creature cringed in fear, covering its eyes, and cowering from the intense glow, mewling pitifully.

Hannas shouted commands of power above the melee, holding the kara-stone aloft. A sudden shaft of light sprang forth, filling every nook and cranny of the room. The creature wailed, falling back on its haunches, hovering eerily in space, rocking in agony.

The others quickly recovered. Most of them had hurled themselves away from the small form as it had attacked and one man had fallen over a chair, cracking his skull on a table. He held his wound, grimacing with pain.

Kaplyn's sword twisted in his hand, groaning as if eager to be let loose. Lomar's eyes were wide with fear as he looked at the eldritch weapon, as though the very sight of it defiled the room. Swiftly he recovered, turning back to Hannas. "Will the light hold it?"

She nodded. The creature wailed and Kaplyn lowered his sword that seemed to resist his efforts.

"What manner of creature is it?" Lomar asked in disgust, pointing to the apparition, which squirmed uncomfortably within the blue light still flooding from the crystal.

"A demon!" Hannas snapped angrily, looking accusingly at Kaplyn as though the creature's presence was his doing.

"It is an abomination, your Highness," said another. "It should be returned from whence it came immediately; its very presence fouls the air and despoils our homes."

"Can we return it, Hannas?" Lomar asked.

"It's our incantation that keeps it here. We only have to stop the light of the kara-stone and it will disappear back to the hell that spawned it."

"Do it!" Lomar said, with a look of disgust as the creature mewled pathetically, futilely clawing the air as if seeking to erase the agony that bound it.

Hannas spoke a few words and the light within the crystal vanished. Instantly the demon disappeared, and its cries ceased, leaving an empty silence in the room. Pure sunlight streamed in as if the sun had reappeared from behind a cloud, but somehow the room felt tainted as if some terrible crime had been committed.

"Open the windows," Lomar ordered. "What happened?" he asked.

"It was an imp, I believe," Hannas said. "One of the lesser demons, but still deadly. We were fortunate."

"Kaplyn, did you know about this creature?" Lomar demanded.

"No! I knew that he was a wizard, but nothing more." Kaplyn was shocked and angry. He was also very confused for he thought that he had seen a creature like that somewhere before and then he remembered. The night when he had met Lars, he had seen something when he had awoken. Could that have been an imp? The memory was distant, and he could not be certain but shivered, nonetheless.

"Wizard!" Hannas spat, her eyes blazed with fury. "He is no such thing. He is a Narlassar sorcerer, a *necromancer*," she spat as if the very name defiled her. "That is what he was hiding – and that is why he is ill!'

"That does not necessarily mean he *is* evil," Lomar said. "After all, the Eldric were Narlassar and as far as we know, only Drachar was evil."

"You are correct, but the imp is evil and if it is at this man's beck and call then he cannot be totally free from its influence," Hannas retorted.

"I do not understand," Kaplyn said. "Is Vastra ill and what does this imp have to do with it?"

"He is ill because he is close to a holy site, once inhabited by an Old One," Lomar explained. "He has an imp at his call, and it is the forest's influence upon that which is causing his illness. Evil is not tolerated here. However, it does not necessarily mean that your companion is evil," he continued. "The Narlassar used demons to focus their powers, which they used for good."

"In any event, these strangers cannot be tolerated," Hannas stated bluntly. "They must leave Gilfillan immediately before any harm is done."

"Look after our guests and treat them well until I return," Lomar said softly. "I must speak with the queen."

Kaplyn saw a change in Lomar at that moment. His shoulders sagged and he sounded dispirited. Before he could say anything, however, Lomar left and as soon as he was gone the other healers started arguing once more, leaving Kaplyn and Lars isolated and at a loss.

Lomar was convinced that he knew what he must do. His terrible dreams seemed to make sense, but he felt more afraid than ever before. He was about to make a decision that would affect the rest of his life and that of everyone he held dear. He was dreading talking to his mother, and a great sadness overwhelmed him.

Within her chamber, the queen was sitting at a table with a quill and parchment before her, but she touched neither. Lomar stopped in the doorway and for a moment, he nearly failed. Never had he seen his mother so anguished. Her scarlet eyes brimmed with unshed tears. She raised a hand, trying to hide her face.

"Lomar," she sobbed, her shoulders shaking as silently she wept.

"What's wrong?" he asked softly.

She smiled, although it seemed forced, and tears slid down her pale cheek. "You are leaving?" she asked, sniffing softly. She rummaged through her purse, withdrawing a handkerchief, and dabbing her eyes.

Lomar nodded, unable to lie.

"Your father knew that you would. He said that your gift would be called upon, but I have prayed every day since then that he was wrong!" She looked pleadingly up at him. "Don't go," she begged.

"I must," he answered.

"Why?"

He lowered his gaze, unable to meet hers. "Our people have avoided their responsibilities for far too long. We have been complacent while others have had to fight for the freedom that we take for granted."

Her eyes widened in sudden anger. "It was the Eldric who caused this evil, not us," she retorted bitterly.

Lomar shook his head sadly. "They did not help, certainly, but evil was present before the Eldric came; they merely precipitated an inevitable war."

The queen bit her lip. "There is still time before the Prophecy comes to pass; by then it will not matter. Let it lie. It's not our concern."

"I cannot," he replied, hanging his head.

"One day, you will be king!" she countered. "You cannot leave and shirk that responsibility."

"And what sort of king would I be, knowing that I did not try to save our race. Without the Eldric another war would be our downfall."

She arose as though everything she loved was broken and they hugged for a few heartbeats before separating.

"I shall return," he said, stepping from her embrace. Somehow, though, he knew it was unlikely. He left the room with a heavy heart leaving his mother watching the door as though willing him to return. Her sobs came clearly to him as he turned into the corridor without a backward glance.

On his way to his room, he sought one of the guards and asked him to take his guests to the stables where he would join them shortly. In his room, Garth was waiting, his eyes reflecting his uncertainty over the recent events. This was yet another moment that Lomar had been dreading.

"Garth, I have to leave," he softly said.

"I know," Garth replied. "And I am coming with you."

Lomar could not help but smile, "I am so sorry, my dear friend, but I cannot take you with me."

Garth looked crestfallen. Lomar felt uncomfortable under Garth's hawk-like gaze, as he changed into clothes more suitable for a long journey. He then packed a few belongings into a stout pack. When finished, he glanced about the room one final time before turning to leave.

Garth offered to take his pack, making it clear by his look that he would not let his prince refuse this last offer of help. Lomar smiled and handed it to Garth who carried it down the long flight of stairs, muttering all the way.

Kaplyn and Lars were making final adjustments to the mules' heavy packs when Lomar and Garth entered. Lomar's people had provided a cart to carry Vastra, which they had harnessed to his horse. His face was barely visible from beneath a thick blanket.

Immediately Lomar announced his intention to accompany them.

"No!" Kaplyn replied flatly. "We do not know what lies ahead. Besides, you have your people to consider."

Lomar silently saddled his own horse leaving Kaplyn looking on bemused. Garth shuffled past, glaring at Kaplyn as though he had bewitched his prince.

Lomar mounted, looking expectantly down at the other two men. Kaplyn realised that they could not stop him from riding with them if he so chose.

Lars grinned and Kaplyn cast him a dour look.

"Very well," Kaplyn sighed. "You are more than welcome to join us. But understand that the quest is likely to be dangerous," he continued. "Also, Vastra will object and may insist that you leave."

Lomar nodded then smiled, raising a hand in farewell to Garth as they rode from the stables. Kaplyn glanced back to see Garth waving; a forlorn figure soon lost within the darkness of the great tree.

Chapter 20
Journey to the Turn Marsh

They rode down a gentle incline for a short way before Lomar requested a halt to look back one final time at the city. When at last Lomar turned his horse away, he kept his gaze stubbornly fixed upon the path as though afraid to look back.

It was already late in the day and the light filtering into the forest was fading. However, it was obvious to Kaplyn that Lomar preferred to be as far as possible from Gilfillan by nightfall.

It was Lars who finally raised the subject that was also troubling Kaplyn. "What are we going to do about Vastra and the imp?" he asked in a hushed tone, even though Vastra was still unconscious.

"There's nothing we can do until he recovers," Kaplyn said. "When he does, we should keep quiet about the imp and see what he does."

Lars nodded. "I suppose you are right. If we admit knowing about it, he will simply deny it."

They rode in darkness for several hours with only the light of the moon to guide them, until at last Lomar called for a halt. They made camp and sat around a small fire eating fruit that they had picked upon the way. It was pleasant sitting by the gentle orange glow of the fire while high above, between the gently swaying branches, stars winked against the night sky.

Lomar asked them to tell him more about themselves, clearly fascinated by the outside world. Kaplyn saw no reason to lie, given how much Lomar had forsaken in accompanying them, and he told him openly that his father was the Allund Monarch. He also told Lomar that Vastra claimed to be the King's bastard son and spoke of his fears concerning the sorcerer.

Lars, in turn, briefly spoke of his own home and being shipwrecked and cast alone onto the Allund shores. The tale horrified Lomar and he marvelled at Lars' tenacity. Lars and Kaplyn then went on to describe their meeting and journey to Tanel. When Kaplyn described the Eldric citadel, Lomar was fascinated and asked them both to describe it in detail.

Kaplyn showed Lomar the pendant, but unfortunately, he could not read Eldric, although he did say that the writing looked frustratingly like that of his own people.

In silence, they drank wine and the forest seemed to close in around them as if seeking to protect them from the surrounding gloom. A large pale moon peeked through the thick vegetation, and Lars looked wistfully up at the giant shining orb. Kaplyn saw the big man's pained look and guessed that he was feeling melancholy. He tried to think of something to distract the big man.

"These gods that you keep telling me about," he asked softly. "Does any one god rule over them, or are they all equal?"

Lars smiled. "Etu," he replied. "He created the world for the other gods to shape." He pointed up at the moon. "My people believe that he has set his eyes high in the sky so that he can watch over us. One eye is bright and that lights up the day and none can look at that without going blind, while at night he watches the world with the other eye from behind a thick cloth so that the world can sleep."

Kaplyn and Lomar smiled, although Kaplyn found it hard to believe that a god would pluck out his own eyes so that he could watch the goings-on of the world. Lomar was especially interested in Lars' homeland, and he questioned him late into the night about his people and their beliefs. Lars brightened as he spoke and when they eventually retired to their makeshift beds, they all fell quickly asleep.

For two days, they travelled through the forest. It was pleasant and the going easy. They were all disappointed when the forest changed back to drab colours; it seemed a dreary place after being in the enchanted wood.

Then the trees abruptly ended, and they found themselves on the forest's edge looking out. Lomar looked shocked. A marshland stretched for miles before them, giving way in the distance to tall mountains, bleak and forlorn in majestic glory. The mountains were still at least a day's journey away and the prospect of crossing the intervening bog was not a welcome one. The marsh looked barren and only long grass and the occasional shrub grew on the inhospitable ground.

"I never imagined the world could look so dismal," Lomar said.

"After your forest, you will find most of the land bleak," Lars answered.

Kaplyn nodded. He, too, felt depressed at the sight and especially the smell coming from the bog.

They agreed to camp at the forest's edge and immediately set about making a fire, placing the unconscious Vastra as close to it as they dared. They hid the fire as best they could, using their baggage and the cart as a screen.

Kaplyn grew more concerned that Vastra had not yet woken, his flesh was pale' and he had dark circles around his eyes. Lomar had packed a kara-stone and he used this to probe Vastra's illness and, once done, seemed positive that he was recovering now that they were out of the forest.

The evening passed unpleasantly with the constant reek from the marsh. As they sat miserably trying to warm themselves by the fire, tiny insects filled the air about them. Lars yelped as one bit him.

"Zelph," Kaplyn informed him, clasping his cloak more tightly about his throat to cover his flesh.

"They are eating me alive," Lars complained. It soon became unbearable and, judging it dark enough to hide the smoke, they decided to see if that would drive the flies away. They piled large handfuls of wet leaves on the fire and soon copious amounts of thick, acrid smoke engulfed them. To their relief, the zelph disappeared, but the leaves smothered the heat and smoke irritated their throats and eyes. It was going to be an uncomfortable night.

In the grey light of the dawn, Lomar awoke with a start to find Vastra glaring down at him. Lomar gave out a short, sharp cry of shock, causing Kaplyn and Lars to leap from their blankets while Vastra turned to glare balefully at them.

Vastra kept blinking, his eyes red from the fire's smoke, making him look uncannily like one of Lomar's people.

"Where are we?" he croaked.

"You've been ill," Kaplyn explained. "We have travelled through the forest which now lies behind us." Vastra's gaze went quizzically back to Lomar and Kaplyn realised that he had better introduce the albino. "This is Lomar, his people are the Alvalah."

Vastra sat down as though his legs could no longer support him. Kaplyn sensed that an argument would follow and was already waiting with a retort, but Vastra merely sighed.

Lars glanced in frustration at Kaplyn and without a word set about preparing a fire and hot water for breakfast.

They broke their fast in silence and no one dared speak for fear of recrimination. For a change, Vastra ate with gusto and afterwards prepared a potion from herbs he carried in a pouch. As he drank, colour returned to his cheeks.

"How long have you lived in the forest," Vastra asked, looking at Lomar as he toyed with his cup.

"My people have lived in the forest for many generations. It was a shame that you missed seeing our city."

"You bring to mind the Eldric," Vastra said, putting the cup down.

"We believe our people are related."

"Has Kaplyn shown you the pendant?" Vastra asked.

"Yes."

"Could you read it?"

"No. The script is very like ours, but I couldn't make sense of it."

Kaplyn thought he saw Vastra relax. "Pity," he said, picking up his cup and sipping its contents.

"We should go soon," Lars muttered. A cloud of zelph hovered over the big man and he looked glum as he waved his hands, trying to fend them off.

Kaplyn grinned at the sight of him itching at his thick tangled beard, but his smile swiftly vanished when one of the insects bit him and he realised that their attention was shifting towards him.

"We have to cross the marsh," Vastra declared. "The tallest peak over there is BanKildor," he said pointing to the horizon. "That is our destination."

Kaplyn nodded. Suddenly the wind increased and changed direction, blowing now from the mountains. It became much colder and hurriedly they packed their gear hoping that they would be warmer once they started to move.

When they were ready to leave Kaplyn looked out one final time over the marsh. It was a barren landscape with a few stunted trees trying to eke out an existence. White marsh-cotton was the only splash of colour, bouncing on long stalks in time to the gusting wind.

Kaplyn looked to either side of their position to see whether they could skirt the bog, but the forest swung around in a great arc, merging in the distance with the grey of the mountains.

"How do you propose we cross?" Kaplyn asked turning to Vastra.

The sorcerer mounted and looked at the marsh. "Marsh-cotton only grows on firm ground. I can see several paths—we will follow one and hope that it connects to others."

It was not a very satisfactory suggestion but would have to suffice. The others mounted and, with Vastra leading, they set off, leaving the cart at the forest's edge.

Initially the ground was soft and spongy, and their horses' hooves sank considerably as they went. However, they soon found a broad path, which rose slightly above the surrounding bog. It was sufficiently wide to allow several horses to ride abreast and the ground became firmer.

The croaking of thousands of frogs and the occasional splash from somewhere in the bog accompanied them as they rode. A large bird flapped noisily from the tall reeds close to the riders, startling their mounts as it ran across their path. It launched itself clumsily into the sky, squawking loudly as it went. The horses spooked, nearly throwing their riders, and carrying Lars off the trail and almost into the swamp. The big man threw himself off the horse, which ran a short way and then stopped as its foreleg plunged into the mire. It took them a while to calm the animal while Lars sat on the ground, grimacing with pain, and swearing never to ride again.

The fright forced them to dismount and Vastra complained bitterly at the delay. He seemed to be in a hurry and anxiously looked towards the distant mountains as if willing them closer.

Chapter 21
Betrayal in the Dark

The day passed slowly and, as the sky darkened, they appeared to have made little progress. To their chagrin, the mountains still seemed distant, although behind them, the forest no longer dominated the skyline. Bone-weary they decided to halt, and Lars spotted a hollow where they could camp. Little was said as they unpacked; their spirits were at a low ebb. A quick search revealed little wood and what they found was damp, so a fire was out of the question.

As they settled down in the hollow, wrapped in blankets, they discovered that it provided little shelter from the frigid wind. To make matters worse thousands of zelph surrounded them in a thick cloud, and Kaplyn considered asking Vastra to use magic to get rid of them. He dismissed the notion almost at once, knowing Vastra would take offence at a request to use his powers for trivia.

A sharp wind sprung up and at once the zelph disappeared leaving the group with large itching bites. Vastra plucked some leaves growing nearby and rubbed them on his bites and the others followed suit, gratefully finding that the itching became less severe.

Uncomfortably they settled down for the night, hugging their cloaks tightly about them to keep out the keen wind. Kaplyn's feet were icy cold, he debated putting on another pair of socks, but the thought of taking his boots off, and exposing his feet to the wind, was too much to bear. He looked with envy at Lars who seemed the only one unaffected by the cold.

After they had eaten a frugal meal from their rations, Vastra excused himself. Rising, he walked along the path and swiftly disappeared into the surrounding gloom.

"Where do you think he is going?" Lars whispered.

"Probably a call of nature," Kaplyn replied.

Lars' eyebrows rose perceptibly. "Can we trust him?"

"I could follow him," Kaplyn offered.

"It might be wise," Lomar said. "Especially with the imp to consider."

Kaplyn hurried after Vastra, trying to remain hidden, picking his route carefully. Vastra's tracks veered off the main path into the swamp, following a small trail probably used by animals. Here the ground was uneven with hillocks and deep troughs.

Close to a small rise, Kaplyn lowered himself to all fours and crawled to the summit. At the top, he looked through a shrub, so that Vastra would not see him.

By now, it was dark; only a faint light from the moon penetrated the thick overhead cloud cover. It took him a while to locate Vastra amongst the long tussocks of grass. He was squatting about thirty paces from Kaplyn with his back to him.

Kaplyn felt foolish but remained where he was, patiently waiting. He became damp lying on the wet ground and wanted to return to the camp. Just as he was about to give up, movement betrayed a figure close to Vastra. Straining his eyes, he tried to make it out. A faint green glow emanated from it, and he recognised the imp.

At that moment, the clouds parted, and, in the better light, he saw the imp cavorting around Vastra who seemed to be having difficulty controlling it. In the still of the night, he could hear Vastra speaking, but could not hear if the imp replied. Kaplyn felt exposed where he was, and deciding that he had seen enough, crawled out of sight. Swiftly he retraced his path.

He had only gone a few yards when the clouds once more concealed the moon and darkness enveloped him. Kaplyn paused, momentarily confused as to which way was correct. He was afraid that the imp might be close and drew his blade to see if its glow would warn him. Fortunately, the blade was dull, but he kept it drawn as he retreated farther.

Eager to find his way back to the others he quickened his pace, becoming more aware as he went that he was no longer on the original trail. He decided that he should be going more to the east, but before he could correct his mistake the ground beneath his feet heaved as something large reared up, emitting a fearful scream.

He leapt backward, but the creature threw him off-balance, and he tumbled to one side, misplacing his footing. He took a couple of strides and agony lanced through his ankle as he twisted it. The marsh creature tried to charge through him as it sought sanctuary deeper in the swamp, knocking Kaplyn to one side.

Grabbing at the tall grass he dropped his sword and, with a sickening splash, fell into the marsh.

Fearing the creature would attack, he desperately tried to reach firmer ground, but with each stride he sank deeper. After a few moments panic, he realised that it must have been as frightened of him as he had been of it. Listening to the silence he realised it was long gone.

He stopped struggling and the pain in his ankle slowly subsided. He tried to extract himself more carefully but to his horror he was stuck fast. To make matters worse, the thick cloying mud was slowly sucking him under, and it was already up to his waist.

He ceased struggling and tried to see how far he was from the bank, but the tall grass made it difficult to tell where the firm ground started, and marsh ended. He reasoned that it couldn't be far to solid ground, but there was nothing for him to push against.

"Lars! Lomar!" he cried out.

Only the quiet of the night answered and he was just about to shout again when a figure noisily entered the hollow. Initially, the sight of a rescuer relieved him, but recognising Vastra his relief instantly soured.

"Vastra, help me," he said.

Kaplyn saw a flash of anger behind Vastra's eyes and then he looked coldly at Kaplyn. Carefully he came forward, testing the ground with one foot before edging forward.

By now Kaplyn's clothes were sodden and the additional weight was pulling him under more quickly.

"Throw me one end of your cloak," Kaplyn called out.

"Throw me the pendant first," Vastra replied, his arm outstretched in expectation.

Kaplyn knew he could not trust Vastra, and he tried again to extract himself. The mud made great sucking noises and noxious fumes assailed him, causing him to gag. By now only his head and arms were above the surface.

Above him Vastra smiled. Kaplyn was furious; no doubt, if he sank, Vastra would find some means to recover the pendant. With a mighty bellow, he again called for help.

Vastra looked over his shoulder, clearly ill at ease. As Kaplyn's voice faded into the night, with relief, Kaplyn heard Lars shout back. His eyes locked on Vastra's and again he saw hatred reflected there, and then the look was gone. Vastra hurriedly tried to remove the clasp securing his cloak. Shrugging it off he threw one end to Kaplyn who grabbed it. Vastra pulled but lacked the strength to make a difference.

Kaplyn shouted again to Lars, fearing Vastra might yet take advantage. Perhaps he saw an inkling of Vastra's cowardice for he did nothing more than hang onto the cloak.

Lars' voice came back in answer, but closer this time. Again, Kaplyn shouted knowing how easily the marsh disorientated people. Almost immediately, the big man entered the hollow, swiftly followed by Lomar. Lars grabbed Vastra's cloak and with supreme effort started to haul Kaplyn from the clinging mud. Lomar, too, took a hand while Vastra stood to one side, sullenly watching.

Finally, Kaplyn felt himself moving and, with renewed hope, he kicked his feet to help propel himself from what might have been an early grave. After what seemed an eternity, they succeeded in dragging him clear. There he lay, panting and trembling with a mixture of cold and fear as the wind whistled around him.

Anger burst through his other feelings, and he leapt to his feet, starting towards Vastra with fists clenched. Vastra glanced at the other two men, his eyes imploring their aid, and Lars, seeing Kaplyn's murderous look, grabbed Kaplyn's arm.

"He was going to let me drown," Kaplyn hissed through clenched teeth. He was shaking from a mixture of cold and rage. Lars looked to Vastra for an explanation.

"I only asked for him throw me the p…pendant first. It might have been lost as we pulled him out," he stuttered, taking an involuntary step backwards.

"By *Slathor*, but you are an *evil* man!" Lars said, through gritted teeth.

He let go of Kaplyn who, with a cry, surged forward, throwing Vastra from his feet. Thinking his life was threatened Vastra muttered, tracing a rune in the air and instantly the imp materialised, scant yards in front of Kaplyn. Its forked tail lashed angrily from side to side and its eyes gleamed with anticipated pleasure.

Kaplyn reached for his sword but realised he had lost it in the bog. In desperation he clutched the pendant, raising it over his head for all to see.

"Vastra, stop or I'll throw this into the bog." Seeing the pendant, the imp hissed but did nothing more, as though waiting Vastra's command.

Vastra's hesitation allowed Lars to draw his axe and Lomar his kara-stone. Shouting words of power, a silver flame sprang forth, causing the imp to recoil.

Kaplyn sensed they had gained the upper hand. "Command the imp to return my sword," he ordered, waving his free hand in the direction of the swamp.

The imp howled causing Kaplyn to recoil and he wondered if Vastra did indeed hold mastery. Fortunately, Vastra failed to see his fear as he concentrated instead, muttering words of power, tracing a rune upon the cold night air.

Before Vastra could complete the spell, the imp lunged. Razor sharp talons opened a gaping wound across his face. Vastra screamed and recoiled.

Lomar shouted his own words of power; the light from his kara-stone flared, causing the imp to cower.

Vastra recovered and shouted a string of commands in haste and obvious fear. His spell was enough to stay the imp as it hissed and squirmed in front of him. It glared balefully, its eyes narrowed against the hated light; then, all at once and with a sudden wail, it disappeared in a flash.

The bright light temporarily blinded everyone. Kaplyn heard a dull thud by his feet and fearing attack he leapt back, holding the pendant aloft. For some moments, Kaplyn was disorientated but then Lomar shouted, "The imp has gone!"

Coloured lights flickered before Kaplyn's eyes, and an afterglow of the flash remained each time he blinked. Gradually he made out the blurred shape of his sword, buried to the hilt by his feet. With considerable effort, he drew it from the ground.

Vastra had not attempted to rise and he, too, was having difficulties with his vision. A deep scratch marred his face, from the side of his eye down to his lip.

Kaplyn stalked over, placing the point of his blade on Vastra's chest. He was tempted to end Vastra's vile existence, but Lomar interceded, laying a firm hand on his shoulder. As their eyes met, Kaplyn knew that he couldn't kill Vastra. However, he knew of a better way to punish him.

He was still holding the pendant and he held it up for Vastra to see. "Tomorrow, I *will* return to Pendrat, but before I do, I shall ask Lomar's people to melt this down." Vastra's betrayal was the final straw. To his satisfaction, he saw a look of fear in the other man's eyes. However, Vastra's fear only served to anger Kaplyn even more.

"You would have killed me! Is life so unimportant?"

Vastra glared defiantly back but remained silent.

"How many men have you sent to their deaths in your efforts to recover this?" Kaplyn asked, realising that they were not the first to go into Tanel. He remembered the strange creatures he had encountered and wondered if that had been the fate of the others Vastra had sent to the tower.

The defiance in Vastra's eyes disappeared and he looked truly afraid.

"The pendant is important," Vastra blurted out. "You must not destroy it. Without it there will be no hope and the Prophecy will fail."

"But you have killed," Kaplyn hissed. The sword remained at Vastra's throat, causing him to look fearfully down at the dark metal.

"The men went because they were greedy; that is not my fault."

The tip of Kaplyn's sword forced Vastra's head back. The blade seemed to moan eerily, like the wind in the trees. Vastra's breath came in short, sharp rasps.

"How many did you kill?" Kaplyn hissed.

"Ten. No twelve—I don't know!"

"You don't even care," shouted Kaplyn as he flung himself from Vastra in disgust. "You are a butcher and one day you'll pay for your actions." He stormed away, returning along the path back to the camp. Lars and Lomar followed, leaving Vastra trying to stem the flow of blood from his wounded cheek.

Chapter 22
Tallin's Crown

When they returned to camp, Kaplyn and the others gathered wood for a fire. As they had feared, the wood proved too damp to light. Accepting defeat Lomar took out his kara-stone, placing it between them and, uttering words of power, silver light sprang from its heart. They gathered round but the heat was not enough to warm Kaplyn who sat miserably on the ground, hugging his knees and shivering violently.

Vastra returned. Seeing the pile of wood, he muttered and waved his arm. Instantly a blaze sprang forth as he retreated to the edge of the circle of light, sitting forlornly on a rock.

The others eagerly warmed themselves, grateful for the heat. Kaplyn changed out of his wet clothes and, since they couldn't spare any water, was forced to scrape the mud off his body as best he could. He swore as he realised that he would be spending an uncomfortable night covered in the evil-smelling mire. His boots were also soaking, and he did not have a spare pair. With some effort, he pulled them off and put on fresh socks, but the cold wind easily penetrated the wool. Grimacing, he pulled the boots back on.

By his side, Lomar spoke softly. "You cannot destroy the pendant."

Kaplyn frowned. "*By the Kalanth*! I can do what I like," he retorted.

"If there is a chance of finding the Eldric, then we must," Lomar continued. "Another war is inevitable and *sooner* than you think! That is too hard to bear. In such a war, my people will be destroyed utterly."

Kaplyn's frown deepened. "What do you mean—*sooner than I think*?"

"After our last discussion, I went to the library to check. Tallin's Crown is a constellation, and it will form a crown in about sixty years. That is when Drachar will rise once more to lead the enemy."

"That *cannot* be!" Kaplyn blurted, his thoughts in turmoil. "My people couldn't be that wrong! It cannot be so soon!"

"Lomar's right," Vastra said softly. Kaplyn glared at him, but Vastra continued. "That is the first line of the Prophecy—*when Tallin's Crown once more does shine*. Tallin's Crown is a constellation of seven stars. Normally the constellation comprises only six stars, but every five hundred years another star moves slowly across the heavens to join this group, the resultant formation looks like a crown."

"How do you know that the Prophecy will happen though?" Lars asked dubiously.

"It *will* happen!" Vastra replied simply. "Demons have seen this world and, as soon as they are able, they will cross to claim souls. When Tallin's Crown is complete, their world and ours will be at their closest and the fabric separating them will be at its weakest. Trosgarth is bound to take advantage to wage war."

"*Why?*" Kaplyn asked. "They were defeated and Drachar killed. Why wait hundreds of years to resume a war that will benefit no one?"

Vastra grimaced. "Do not think that the people of Trosgarth have forgotten their defeat. Do you not realise that, over the years, there have been many skirmishes along their borders? I believe our history has been deliberately withheld so that the people will not panic," Vastra continued. "These attacks are not the actions of a defeated nation. Believe me, Trosgarth is biding its time and, as soon as it can, its people will summon Drachar's shade."

"I agree," Lomar said. "Our records show that demon activity peaks in about five hundred-year cycles."

They fell silent while all about them frogs croaked loudly, and an occasional splash heralded a fish or a marsh creature feeding. Kaplyn listened to the abundant wildlife, his thoughts too confused to warrant a decision. Vastra was dangerous and he doubted if they could ever trust him.

"A short while ago I had a dream," Lars said softly interrupting his thoughts; all eyes turned to the big man. "In it, my people were butchered by demons while I was forced to watch. They murdered both my wife and my son. *By Slathor*, I *will not* allow that to happen. If demons win here, then they will seek prey elsewhere, and my people may be next. The gods rescued me for a purpose, and I think it is to prevent demons entering this world. I, too, believe the quest must continue."

Kaplyn rocked gently back and forth, clutching his knees to keep warm. He did not know what to do.

"If we continue, Vastra, what will we find?" he asked eventually. His tone suggested his anger had subsided, although his eyes warned Vastra to reply truthfully.

The sorcerer came closer to the fire, warming his hands. He kept his eyes on the flames. "I believe the Eldric have left our world," he said softly.

"What makes you think that?" Kaplyn asked.

"After the war the Eldric were devastated that one of their own kind lay waste to the land, using Narlassar magic for evil. The Eldric couldn't accept that the blame was theirs, or perhaps they did—in any event the truth forced them to forsake this world and they fled, seeking alternative lands where, possibly, magic doesn't exist." Vastra hugged his cloak tightly about his bony frame.

"We are following a path the Eldric took long ago." He looked up at Kaplyn, but could not meet his eyes, so looked back into the flames. "They went to the mountains, to BanKildor where they found a cavern, inside which they discovered a power so immense that it will keep a passage open between the worlds indefinitely, enabling all of their people to cross from this world to another."

"How do you know all this?" Kaplyn asked.

Vastra looked up, his eyes sparkling with excitement. "I learned some of it through the imp. He obtained Eldric books, and I have guessed the rest. The pendant and the description of the route confirm my views though. However, we will never know unless we look. We have the pendent and that's the key to finding out what happened."

"Vastra's correct," Lomar said softly. "If another war happens then, without the Eldric and their magic, we will surely fail. That fear has driven me from my homeland for, if a full-scale war occurs in six years or sixty, my people will be destroyed, and that would be a terrible burden upon my soul."

"How could this have happened?" Kaplyn asked, shaking his head. "Why are my people convinced that so few years have passed since the Krell Wars?"

Vastra poked the fire with a stick, it had already burned low and there was no more wood. He looked up at Kaplyn, "No one wants to know when the next war will occur. The people are too afraid it might happen in their lifetime, and they gladly believe it will be somebody else's problem. What chance do we have against the forces of evil without the Eldric?" he said throwing the stick into the fire.

"I've studied the Krell Wars, and what I've read leaves me cold. Besides krell, there were grakyn, fell creatures that fly. Both krell and grakyn are born of this world and, unlike demons, they do not simply disappear in the middle of a fight. Then there are the demons themselves. Some are as tall as a building while others are so fast, they can move in the blink of an eye."

Kaplyn shivered as he remembered the attack in the library and the demon's lightning response.

"We have witnessed increased demon activity. Think. The wolf attack at the farm was not normal and you saw, yourself, a demon at Kinlin castle. We have no defence against demons! It's imperative we find the Eldric," Vastra concluded looking at Kaplyn.

Kaplyn had heard enough. His eyes locked on Vastra's. "We will continue! But *mark me*, if you do *anything*, even *remotely* underhand, I *will not* hesitate to kill you."

Vastra remained silent and all Kaplyn could hear was the pounding of the blood in his ears.

In the morning, Kaplyn awoke feeling both tired and weary. He had slept poorly, and the cold had penetrated through to the very marrow of his being. The others were awakening, and he was surprised to see that Vastra was still with them. He had expected him to leave during the night. His tenacity amazed him; in his place, Kaplyn would have been too ashamed to carry on.

After eating a hurried breakfast, they broke camp and this time even Vastra helped, as though keen to show he was reformed.

They set off early, with Vastra taking the lead. The ground was firm but dipped steeply to either side of the path. The bog stank, reminding Kaplyn of his plight the night before; slowly sinking in the mud and the feeling of utter helplessness. To lighten his mood, he turned his mind to thoughts of family and friends but failed. It was with a heavy heart that he rode across the bleak terrain.

Chapter 23
In the Mountains

By the end of the second day, the forest had become nothing more than a green smudge against the distant skyline, while ahead, the mountains were much more prominent. It was late in the day, and they decided to camp. Vastra announced he needed to scout the path while the light held.

"I'll go with you!" Kaplyn declared coldly, making it clear that Vastra could not dissuade him.

"The path forks ahead, I need to determine which one to take," Vastra explained. The wound on his face looked inflamed and was still bleeding. Clearly, the imp had done more than just cut him.

Lars and Lomar remained to prepare a hot meal while Kaplyn and Vastra rode ahead. After the previous day's escapade, they had collected wood along the way so at least they could have a fire.

When they had gone far enough, Vastra halted them and then dismounted. He rummaged through his saddlebags, finally producing a slither of metal and twine. He held one end of the twine with the metal suspended below it. The metal spun erratically before settling down to point the way ahead.

"Stand on your horse and see which direction the paths go," Vastra said.

Kaplyn complied and, ahead, he could see that their path split into two. He pointed out the direction of each to Vastra, who seemed lost in thought for a while before deciding which way they should go.

"The right path is the one we want, although I dare not risk summoning the imp today to verify it," he gestured at his face. "As you can see, yesterday I lost control."

"You are playing a dangerous game with that demon," Kaplyn warned.

"And without him I would be nothing," Vastra replied.

"The imp is evil. It will seek to destroy you."

Vastra laughed. "I have mastery over it, and it does what I command." His manner during the day had been pleasant for a change, his laughter was honest, and he even smiled for a while. Kaplyn felt it was a pity that he couldn't be like this all the time, and he wondered whether the sudden change in his mood would last, but deep down doubted it.

"It does what it wants, I suspect," Kaplyn replied mounting his horse.

Together they rode back to re-join the others. Lars had opened a flagon of Lomar's wine, which they were warming over a fire. Lomar had added herbs and a strong aroma greeted them. Wearily they dismounted and unsaddled the horses and unpacked the mules just as Lomar announced the wine was ready.

Kaplyn and Vastra joined them, crouching by the fire. The hot liquid warmed them and after a moment, they felt somewhat recovered. Lars started telling them humorous tales about his village and soon had them all laughing.

The evening was bearable until it started to rain. The company thought they were in for a wet night; however, retrieving his kara-stone, Lomar positioned it within the middle of the group. As he recounted arcane words of power, the rain falling on them ceased although the cold wind continued. Kaplyn looked up; it was as though the rain was bouncing off an invisible cover, running in rivulets down the sides.

"Where did you get that stone?" Vastra asked.

"There is a cave in our city with hundreds of these."

"*Hundreds*!" Vastra exclaimed.

"Yes, we saw them," Kaplyn interrupted. "It was magnificent, especially when the sun shines inside the cave."

"I've never heard of so many kara-stones occurring in one place before," Vastra said.

"My people believe it was once the site of an Old One," Lomar replied.

Vastra sniffed, as though rejecting that idea.

They soon turned in for the night, covering themselves with blankets and falling asleep to the gentle rhythm of rain pattering off the invisible barrier.

The next morning was dreary; the ground was soft and uneven, forcing them to walk. Continuous drizzle soaked them thoroughly. However, just when they were starting to think they could go no further, the ground rose perceptibly and at last they found themselves on drier, firmer footing. Eagerly they mounted and made better progress as the foothills gave way to steeper slopes.

A single pass led high between the arms of two large peaks, framed between which they could see the awe-inspiring shape of BanKildor. This peak was taller than its neighbours were and snow-capped, explaining why the wind was biting cold.

It became too steep for the horses, so they dismounted and set about unsaddling them. There was plenty of grass and the animals would not wander far for there was nowhere else for them to go, besides the marsh. The only concern was that of wolves and possibly krell. Vastra said that he could cast a spell that would mask the horses' scent.

Soon they were ready, and the pack mules were even more heavily laden with additional burdens taken from the horses. Lomar spoke to his mount, stroking its soft nose. When they left the animals, he explained to Kaplyn that he had charged his horse with looking after the others and, if danger threatened, he would lead them back to Gilfillan. Kaplyn smiled but realised Lomar was being serious.

By their side a stream swiftly flowed through a narrow gorge, the rush of water drowned out other sounds, adding a sense of urgency to their quest. The banks were initially wide and flat, helping their progress. At times, the gorge became deep and with the start of spring, its waters were already showing signs of increased fury.

Lars informed them that the river they were following originated from a glacier, judging by its colour, which frothed a dirty white as the water tumbled over small rocky waterfalls. None of the men had heard of glaciers before and so Lars described the immense lakes of frozen water that flowed inexorably down the steep valleys of his mountain homeland.

For the remainder of that evening they ascended, taking advantage while the light of a grey dismal day lasted. The stream twisted and turned, and occasionally huge rocks blocked the path, forcing them to climb around these. It would have been quicker without the mules, but then they would have had to leave most of their provisions behind. They endured the animals' frequent stubbornness and, more than once, practically dragged one animal by brute force before it would continue.

They managed to climb for some time longer before Kaplyn suggested they stop due to the failing light. They were fortunate to find their first real shelter in days, beneath an overhang of rock where a deep hollow afforded some protection from the wind. Kaplyn took advantage of the stream to wash the mud from his body. He had to grit his teeth for the water was freezing, making his skin burn. However, it was well worth it to be rid of the uncomfortable grime. He also washed his clothes, beating them on the rocks to shake loose the dirt. Wrapping himself in a blanket, feeling greatly refreshed, he re-joined the others.

Wood was more plentiful here and they built a fire, taking care to conceal the flames, using only dry wood to reduce the smoke. Kaplyn laid his clothes close to the fire and sat back watching the steam rising from the wet garments, as Lomar mulled some wine.

Lars sang songs from his homeland and started to teach the others the words of the sillier rhymes. They were in high spirits and Kaplyn suggested they take a day off to recover. Unfortunately, however, Vastra was adamant they should continue.

"We have little time left. There is only one day every five hundred years when it is safe to enter the cavern described on the pendant. Tonight, it's important that I see the stars so I can decide when it is safe to enter."

"Why have you not mentioned this before?" Kaplyn demanded.

Vastra shrugged. "It's only important now we are getting near our destination. We do have some time to spare, I think."

"My people don't like going underground," Lars announced, squatting by the fire, and holding a mug of hot wine in his fist. "We do not bury our dead as you do but build funeral pyres."

"Why do you not bury your dead?" Kaplyn asked curiously.

"Long ago the gods captured Baldor, the cruellest and most cunning of the giants, luring him deep within the bowels of the earth. Some say he is trapped in a cavern made of gold so he cannot use his magical powers. It is he whom the gods fear most and it is said that one day man, in his folly, will release him and that day will herald the end of the world."

Lars sipped his wine before continuing. "On occasions, you can hear Baldor shaking his prison walls and that is when the ground trembles. Once free he will release the other giants and together, they will destroy the world. Then the giants will lead the assault on Fallor-Ell and all the fell creatures will unite with them."

"That's not a very cheerful tale," Lomar commented, refilling their flagons with more hot wine. "Talking of which, will we be safe with such a large fire? Krell inhabit the mountains and we don't want them knowing we are here."

"We should be all right. The rock is grey and it's masking the smoke. We'll let the fire die down before it is dark," Kaplyn answered.

"I could cast a spell to alert us if anyone approaches," Vastra offered. The others agreed and they watched as he scribed the necessary runes in the air, muttering words of power.

"Why is it that you need to summon the imp on occasions and at other times you simply say a word or write a rune?" Kaplyn asked when he had finished.

"It depends on the complexity of the spell," Vastra replied. "Some spells are relatively simple, and I only need an elemental to cast these."

Kaplyn was surprised that Vastra was being more talkative. Perhaps he was coming to accept them. He hoped that he was changing for the better. Indeed, because of their long journey, he was starting to feel different himself; certainly, he felt healthier. Even though it was hard work, living in the wild was doing him some good. Lars had lost weight and now that his muscles had hardened, Kaplyn doubted anyone in Allund could stand against him in a wrestling match.

From somewhere high in the mountain a lone wolf howled, reminding Kaplyn of the dangers, and his thoughts strayed to his home and family. He was looking forward to returning. He smiled as he thought about taking Lars with him back to the palace at Dundalk to meet his family and friends. Perhaps he might be able to persuade Lomar, and even Vastra, to come back with him as well. That would be worth seeing, he thought, especially the look on Vastra's face when he introduced him to his father.

In the middle of the night Kaplyn awoke to find Vastra watching the sky, clearly hoping for a break in the thick clouds. Kaplyn turned over. Pulling his blankets tightly about his neck, he quickly fell asleep. The prospect of the underground journey troubled his dreams and he heard Baldor's voice booming aloud in his rage as he sought to escape his imprisonment. After a while he realised it was not Baldor's voice he could hear, but his own. A tomb surrounded him deep within the humid depths of the earth and, with mounting fear he realised that he was trapped for all eternity.

When morning came, Vastra had not slept. His eyes were red rimmed, and, for all his efforts, he had not even seen the stars. He urged them to hasten as they broke camp.

Later that day they arrived at the edge of the snow line. It was a spectacular view. Small ripples of wind-blown snow cast long blue shadows while, in contrast, sunlight reflected whitely from the ridge tops. To Vastra's relief the clouds finally cleared, leaving an unblemished sky as far as the horizon, and promising at least that he might finally see the stars that night.

They decided to leave the mules farther back down the slope and so they piled their supplies on the ground before retracing their steps, leading the mules. They found a relatively sheltered spot in a crevice where they left the animals and their food. Then they started back up the slope to their supplies.

Once burdened, they continued and, although the snow was deep, the going was still relatively easy, but soon the pass became narrower and steeper. A short way farther and the stream they were following became frozen and only a trickle of water remained. They hacked a step in the ice to fill their canteens before it became completely frozen.

By mid-morning their path diverged from the stream and Vastra led them through a narrow defile. They struggled through the opening, slipping on the ice-coated rocks and then up a steep slope. Finally, they gained the top of a small ridge and from there they looked out over a wide-open valley, set between two almost vertical ridges, sweeping down from the peak of BanKildor. Stretching across the valley was a wall of ice that dominated the valley.

"That's a glacier," Lars stated, panting heavily. His breath plumed before him, hanging in small clouds until banished by the soft breeze. The group stared in wonder at the broad sheet of ice; no one had expected it to be so immense.

Vastra took off his pack and rummaged through the contents to retrieve the thin sliver of metal and twine that Kaplyn had seen before. He looked perplexed as the metal stubbornly continued to oscillate, refusing to come to rest. Frustrated, he put the device away and decided that the party should split up into two groups to search the ice wall, looking for a cave or an opening, no matter how small.

Kaplyn went with Vastra while Lars and Lomar went in the opposite direction. After several hours of searching, they had combed the entire surface without success. Clearly annoyed, Vastra sat down on a rock.

"It's here somewhere, I know it is," he stated angrily, more to himself than to the others.

"Are you sure this is the right place?" Kaplyn asked.

Vastra nodded.

With a mixture of feelings, the others sat down glaring at the stubborn ice wall. They had to find the way forward soon or they would freeze to death waiting.

Chapter 24
BanKildor

An eagle flying high in the clear sky caught Kaplyn's attention and he watched it glide; its huge wings splayed out into tiny fingers. The bird descended until, with shock, he realised that it was going to collide with the ice wall. He held his breath, willing it to rise.

At the last instant, it flapped its wings and, to Kaplyn's astonishment, disappeared. He had to blink several times to convince himself that he was not mistaken. A large rock protruded from the ice close to the spot where the eagle had disappeared. Rising he proceeded to investigate, leaving the others behind.

Baffled, he stood facing the ice wall with no clear view as to where the eagle had gone. Abruptly, a loud flurry of wings made him jump as the eagle materialised right in front of him. With a screech of outrage, the great bird soared skyward, forcing Kaplyn to duck beneath its flapping wings. There had been no warning and the bird's abrupt appearance unnerved him.

The noise had attracted the others' attention, and Vastra was watching him with renewed hope. Kaplyn ran a hand along the ice and all at once, his hand came away from the surface. He had discovered a step that due to the white glare from the ice was difficult to see. Exploring further, he found an opening sufficiently wide enough to allow a man to squeeze through.

Vastra came over and was overjoyed. He beamed happily and even slapped Kaplyn on the back.

"Well done," he said several times.

His excitement was contagious, and the others grinned back, relieved at last to find a way forward.

Was this the correct path though? Kaplyn was not certain, so he decided to explore a short way ahead.

Stepping through the opening, a narrow tunnel continued for a short way before abruptly changing direction, doubling back on itself but penetrating deeper into the ice. It continued in a similar vein for some while and the further he went, the quieter and warmer it became. Satisfied that the tunnel went some way ahead, he retraced his steps to report his findings. Vastra was ecstatic with the news and again slapped Kaplyn on the back.

"This has to be the correct path," he said beaming broadly.

"We need to find shelter so we can tell when it's safe to continue," Kaplyn suggested.

They spent the remainder of that day looking for somewhere out of the wind and large enough to accommodate them all. Gradually they made their way back down the slope.

In the end, they climbed up the steep sides of the narrow pass to where a few large boulders offered some shelter from the frigid wind. Huddled together for warmth they prepared their packs for the journey, taking only the essentials and leaving all the spare supplies. Amongst their equipment, they had oil for torches, and they diligently set about making these, soaking strips of cloth and wrapping these about stout branches.

"I hope the sky remains clear tonight," Vastra said, looking at the blue heavens.

"How long might we have to wait?" Lars asked.

"I'm not sure," Vastra admitted. "I checked the stars before we entered the forest, but I cannot be certain if my last judgement was accurate or not."

Anxious that they might have a long stay ahead of them, they tried to improve their shelter, pushing their packs into the gaps between the boulders and stretching their oiled blankets above them forming a roof. Night came swiftly now that they were on the mountainside. Outside the shelter, Vastra watched the sky and slowly, one by one, the stars became visible.

"There it is! Tallin's Crown," Vastra said pointing to the constellation. "That star to the right is moving towards the others and in about sixty years the crown will be whole once again." Vastra continued to look at the other constellations, silently considered their position within the sky.

"We are early," he declared at last with a smile, turning to face the others, his eyes shining. "We have three days wait before we can proceed. That will leave two days to follow the Eldric trail and find the cavern described on the pendant."

They re-entered the shelter. The wind whistled through gaps their packs didn't quite block and Lars suggested piling snow about the outside to fill these. Almost immediately, after they had done this, the temperature in the shelter improved, making their wait seem more bearable.

As the days slipped by, they spent their time telling stories to keep themselves amused. It was too cold to go far from the shelter and a thick crust of ice on the rocks made travelling dangerous anyway. Eventually the time passed uneventfully and on their last night, each of the company was lost in his own thoughts. They retired early with the rising of the moon in a cloudless sky, eager to be on their way the following day. The cold was intense and although they wrapped themselves in all their spare blankets, it was difficult to sleep. In discomfort, they lay huddled together to await the dawn.

In the middle of the night Vastra went to each of the company in turn, cautioning them to silence. Although they could only see his outline, they could tell he was anxious.

For a while they sat listening to the howl of the wind, wondering what had alarmed him and then they became aware of voices, coming from the narrow path below. The voices were guttural and harsh and Kaplyn realised they might be krell. Partly drawing his sword, he revealed that the blade was glowing. He swiftly re-sheathed it, hiding the tell-tale light.

Lomar crawled to the edge of the shelter, trying to peer between the boulders, but they had done too good a job in filling these. Carefully Lars picked up his axe and Lomar drew his own blade. Vastra remained hunched like a great owl, but Kaplyn could tell that he was ready to trace a rune and summon power if the need arose.

After a while, the voices faded until they could only hear the wind whistling through the pass.

"A krell patrol?" Vastra asked in a whisper.

It had been fortunate in that they had piled snow about their shelter. Kaplyn pulled aside one of the packs and crawled outside. Large white snowflakes filled the sky, standing out in stark contrast to the black backdrop of night. He couldn't see a thing and snow, freezing on his cheeks, forced him to retreat inside. There was no way that he could tell if the krell were still about and it would be too dangerous to follow them. There was nothing else to do other than try to sleep. Lying down, with their weapons by their sides, they listened to the howl of the wind, trying hard to decide whether they could hear voices within the eerie banshee wail.

By morning, they had slept little and were eager to be moving; fearful that the krell patrol might still be in the area. They checked their provisions, leaving the remaining supplies beneath the lee of a boulder for their return. Kaplyn left the shelter first to search for tracks to see what he might learn. However, with the fresh layer of snow no footprints remained.

Together they hurried towards the glacier and the tunnel. Kaplyn led them through the narrow gap. Repeatedly, the passage changed direction but at least he could see; a faint blue light filtered through the thick ice.

All at once Kaplyn emerged into a much wider corridor of ice at the end of which he could see a cave entrance leading into the mountainside. He searched the ground for signs that krell might have come this way, but it looked undisturbed. The others joined him, relieved to be free of the twisting maze.

"If the glacier is moving, as Lars suggested, then this cave will eventually be covered," Lomar said, indicating the tunnel ahead.

"Perhaps the maze of passages in the ice was deliberately made so that over the years only a narrow entrance is exposed to the outside world," Vastra suggested.

Lars was paying particular attention to the tunnel wall as if he had seen something inside it. Kaplyn joined him to see what he had found. Lars rubbed the surface, trying to get a better view.

"There's something behind the ice," he commented; his face pressed against the cold translucent surface.

"It's probably a rock or something," Vastra said.

Lars was staring open mouthed with disbelief. "*By Slathor!* It's a dragon!" he stated breathlessly.

Kaplyn glanced at Lars to see if he was joking, but he looked serious and so Kaplyn peered inside. There was something there, a large indistinct shape. As he peered from different angles, he *could* make out more. He smiled when he saw what might be a head and wings. It could indeed be a dragon! The ice blurred his view, but of one thing he was certain; this was no rock!

"He's right, it has to be!" Kaplyn exclaimed. It looked as if it was in mid-flight and then he decided it looked more as though it had fallen and was trying to right itself. Perhaps it had crashed into the freezing water or ice and died trying to escape.

Even Vastra was amazed. He told them that he had read about dragons but had never believed that he would see one. He wanted to explore further, but they did not have the time. Reluctantly they decided to continue.

The ground in the cave sloped gently downwards, aiming directly at the heart of BanKildor. As they went, the light swiftly faded. Behind them they could see the cave entrance and the ice, but ahead the darkness was complete.

Lomar took out his kara-stone and ran a hand lightly over its surface. It glowed dimly as he spoke, but the light swiftly failed. He tried again with little success.

"What is it, Lomar? Why won't the stone work?" Vastra asked.

"I don't know," he answered.

Vastra muttered archaic words, but nothing happened, although the others did not know what to expect.

"We'll have to use the torches," Vastra concluded. "For some reason the mountain is blocking our use of magic. I do not know how, although I had heard that it was possible."

They lit several torches. Even in the light, they could not tell from the rock walls why magic was blocked. It was a conundrum and without the kara-stone and Vastra's magic, they were severely disadvantaged.

Chapter 25
Journey in the Dark

Black smoke from their torches formed wraith-like clouds that lingered within the tunnel before being banished upon the subterranean winds. The acrid smoke accumulated around them, fouling the air.

Removing his pack, Vastra rummaged through its contents.

"I've planned for this eventuality. Since we won't know the time of day in the tunnel, I've made some candles that will burn at a constant rate," he said, taking out a long white candle, marked at intervals with regular stripes. "Each stripe is half a day and I have numbered them so we will know how long we've been down here."

Using Lomar's torch he lit the candle and then looked at Kaplyn. "We need to reach our destination tomorrow, otherwise we will fail and our chance to discover what became of the Eldric will be lost."

"We could always return later?" Lars suggested nervously not liking the sounds of the deadline that Vastra had imposed.

Vastra shook his head "As I have already said, there is only one day when it will be safe to enter the great cavern described on the pendant. If we miss that opportunity, then we will have to wait another five hundred years."

Lars shrugged; he looked as though he would have been happy to wait forever rather than continue.

"Are you certain that tomorrow is the actual day when we can enter the cavern?" Lomar questioned.

Vastra glared at the albino. "I'm sure! I consulted with the imp, and it confirmed this." he declared, shouldering his pack and adjusting the straps.

"You believe a demon? And what happens if you're wrong?" Lars asked anxiously.

Vastra frowned but remained silent, leaving their imagination to conclude on what might transpire.

"We had better proceed," Kaplyn urged, looking ahead. He could see little other than a wall of darkness. It was eerie and every instinct told him to return to the surface. However, the possibility of finding what became of the Eldric was too great a lure.

As they walked, Lars kept casting longing looks behind him at the spot of light marking the exit, until he finally announced that he could no longer see it. His voice sounded nervous, and the declaration seemed final as if there was now no turning back.

Before them, the gloom peeled slowly back as though reluctant to disclose its secrets. Their torches revealed rough craggy walls dotted with sharp rocky outcrops; shadows jumped about the tunnel eerily as their torches flickered uncertainly in the subterranean winds.

After walking for several hours, the tunnel suddenly dipped sharply down, and they continued along the steep descent for a while longer before Kaplyn called for a halt. They sat down on the cold stone floor and started to eat. Momentarily, at least, their flagging spirits were revived.

"Are we likely to find anything living down here?" Lars whispered.

Vastra shook his head. "If krell discovered these passages then they might also discover what became of the Eldric, and that in itself would be a disaster."

"What about demons though?" Lars persisted.

"Demons inhabit another world, as I've already explained," Vastra snapped. "Besides, the mountain seems to block the use of magic. It would almost certainly prohibit a tunnel opening between the worlds."

Lars remained unconvinced and he chewed slowly on a piece of dried meat as he considered Vastra's words.

When they continued, they found that walking into the blackness was almost hypnotic. The torchlight illuminated a short way in front, but beyond that, the tunnel remained inky black. In a way, it seemed as though they were standing still, while the tunnel slid slowly by.

After a short while they reached a slightly broader part of the tunnel where they decided to rest again. Apart from Lomar, who preferred to stand, they gratefully sat down.

Lomar was watching the darkness ahead. Something at the perimeter of the light caught his attention and he left the group to investigate. Holding his torch before him he stooped down. Softly he called back to the others to come and see.

Wearily they arose and went to join him. They found a deep recess cut into the rock wall and upon the floor lay a skeleton. A metal breastplate partially hid the bony chest, while a tall conical helm rested at a jaunty angle on the grinning skull's brow. On top of the corpse someone had reverently laid a sword and bony fingers clasped the pommel. Any other garments the warrior had worn had long since crumbled to dust and had been banished by the subterranean winds.

"He is Eldric," Vastra declared.

The corpse's sword did not have any runes. Indeed, Kaplyn was disappointed to see the quality was nowhere near that of his sword, and he assumed the soldier must have been of a lowly rank.

"This proves that the Eldric came this way then?" Kaplyn asked.

Vastra nodded. His attention remained fixed on the body and Kaplyn feared that he was going to search the corpse. Kaplyn caught Vastra's arm and gave him a warning look. He remembered Lars' tale about his people's fear of being underground. There was no point in provoking his superstitions further.

"Let him lie," he whispered.

Vastra cast him a dangerous look. However, he conceded, backing away from the grave with a mocking bow.

Lars missed the exchange; the darkness beyond the edge of the light held him captivated. The flickering flame of the torches caused the shadows to bob about, and he watched as if he expected something to step from them.

Suddenly a low rumbling echoed from deep within the mountain and the ground vibrated ominously. They strained their ears, holding their breath as the disturbance continued to echo beneath their feet. It sounded distant and the volume was low but coming so soon after they discovered the soldier's remains it seemed like an ominous portent. Gradually the rumbling faded, leaving the group in silence.

"An earth tremor?" Lomar suggested.

"More like Baldor," Lars muttered, his hand involuntarily making a warding gesture against evil.

Vastra was the only one who seemed unafraid. His dark form seemed well suited to the tunnels.

"It's just a few rocks falling deep within the earth," he declared. "It's gone now. We need to continue for we do not have much time remaining."

"A *few* rocks?" Lars questioned.

"Sound travels a long way in rock," Vastra continued in a condescending manner, much like a teacher berating a child. "Shall we go?" Vastra repeated impatiently, gesturing to Kaplyn to lead the way, almost as if daring him.

As a precaution Kaplyn drew his sword but it remained dull. "I'll lead. Vastra; you bring up the rear."

The sorcerer gave a mocking bow, and a smile touched his lips. Kaplyn started to wonder at Vastra's apparent newfound confidence or was it merely that he was contemptuous of their fear.

Once more they continued, and the blackness seemed to peel back eagerly, snapping shut behind them. They had walked for only a short way when ahead, in the half-light, Kaplyn saw a change in the reflected torchlight. He slowed. They were entering a large cave and he peered cautiously into it before daring to enter.

It was immense and he could see much farther than his torch should allow. He looked closely at the rock wall to his left and saw that it was glowing with an orange light. Reassuringly the cave appeared to be empty.

"I have heard that the dwarves use a special rock to light their caverns," Lomar whispered by Kaplyn's side, glancing over his shoulder into the cave.

He entered, running a finger along the wall. "Look," he said holding up a glowing finger. "There are algae or something covering the surface. Perhaps it is feeding on the minerals carried in the water and emits light in the process."

Lars entered the cave, holding his heavy axe protectively in front of him like an icon against evil. The fierceness of his grip made his knuckles white.

Kaplyn understood the other man's fear. He, too, felt as though they were unwanted intruders. It was as if invisible eyes were watching them.

Vastra overtook Kaplyn in his eagerness to see ahead.

"Is this cavern described on the pendant?" Kaplyn asked.

"Yes, but the main cavern is further on."

"Look there, a fissure!" Lars declared. His voice echoed from rock to rock as if unseen hands had grabbed it and were bouncing it from wall to wall. As the echoes continued, he looked fearfully at the others.

As if in response to Lars' outburst, Kaplyn's blade flickered brightly but then became dull once more.

They advanced to the chasm's edge and peered down into its depths. The darkness eagerly devoured the light from their torches, as though guarding its secrets. To either side of their position the chasm stretched into the distance, disappearing within the funeral gloom.

Kaplyn shook his head, "We have to cross. I can sense that is the direction we need to go."

"Let's follow the chasm on this side and see if the gap narrows," Vastra suggested.

To their dismay the fissure remained too wide to cross. "Over there is something," Kaplyn announced, leading the way.

"I don't see anything," Vastra grumbled.

"Nor I," said Lomar quietly, glancing after Kaplyn.

Kaplyn led them to the edge of the fissure where he paused. The others joined him.

"We can cross this bridge," Kaplyn said. However, he was unsure how to proceed; the first few feet of the span either had broken or had never existed.

"Is this some sort of joke?" Vastra snapped.

Kaplyn looked bewildered as he turned to face the others. "What do you mean?"

Vastra snorted and turned to continue his way, "Come, we need to find a way to cross."

"Wait! There is a bridge here!" Kaplyn insisted.

"There isn't a crossing here," Vastra said, glaring at him.

Kaplyn looked at the others, but they shook their heads. He frowned, confused by their reaction, but then he realised how to prove to them (and himself) that the bridge existed. Stooping down he picked up a pebble and rising he tossed it into the air.

The others watched as the stone sailed in an arc before clattering off an unseen obstacle. The noise reverberated about the cavern, but there was no further sound of the stone reaching the bottom.

"There! Now do you believe me?" Kaplyn asked.

Vastra stood dumbfounded and then his eyes widened. "The pendant," he said.

Kaplyn regarded him coldly.

Vastra looked as though he should have remained silent. "Remember, it nulls magic. The Eldric have been this way and must have cast a spell, making the way across invisible. The person with the pendant sees the bridge, because to them, the magic is void."

"That is why you should give me the pendant," Vastra continued, trying to take advantage. "You might not recognise a trap even if you saw it, whereas I would." He looked sincere, which left Kaplyn in a quandary. He accepted

Vastra's logic, but did not trust him, remembering all too clearly his earlier betrayal.

"You fool, you would get us all killed, and you would not even know it," Vastra snapped.

"And you would kill us all, knowingly," Lomar interrupted, his eyes flaring. "Your actions in the swamp prove that you do not value our lives. You are nothing more than a petty dealer in the black arts and, by the very nature of your evil magic, you consider us unimportant. I, for one, prefer Kaplyn overseeing the pendant."

"That goes for me too," Lars said grinning, unable to hide his pleasure at seeing Vastra put in his place.

Kaplyn tried to suppress a smile, grateful that a difficult decision had been made for him.

Vastra looked like thunder. Had the others known how close he was to losing control they would have been less quick to goad him. "Let's continue. Time is short and already I fear we have delayed over-long," he declared, shouldering his pack and gesturing sarcastically for Kaplyn to lead the way.

Kaplyn shook his head, "The crossing doesn't span the full width. There is about a six-foot gap in front of us and then the bridge starts. Beneath the edge of the bridge there is a solid column supporting it. It looks safe enough though..."

"We could try throwing something onto it so we can see where it starts," Lars suggested.

"Good idea, but I can already see several stones which you obviously cannot," Kaplyn replied.

Vastra shook his head; with a problem to solve his anger seemed to fade. "It would make sense for the spell to extend by a short distance; otherwise, a layer of dust would eventually reveal the crossing."

"It seems a great deal of effort just to hide it," Lomar questioned. "But why is it incomplete do you think?"

"Perhaps to prevent anyone from finding it by accident," Kaplyn suggested.

"That makes sense," Vastra agreed. "The Eldric clearly didn't want anyone following this route unless they possessed the pendant. Their magic must have been very powerful to make the bridge invisible, for these caverns block magic as we have already discovered."

Kaplyn took off his pack and tied a rope to it. Swinging the heavy weight back and forth he threw it across the gap. It landed with a clatter. They could still see the sack, although the sight of it suspended in mid-air was bizarre.

"The spell must take time to work on a new object, or it only affects small things," Vastra said, thinking aloud.

With the pack on the bridge, the next step was for someone to cross. The natural choice was Kaplyn. They attached a rope around his waist and the others took the loose end, bracing themselves. Backing a few feet, Kaplyn ran, leaping into the air at the chasm's edge. To the others the attempt looked suicidal, but to their relief he landed close to his pack where he remained upright, eerily hovering in the air. Lars grimaced, turning away, clearly unable to watch.

Kaplyn took up his pack and placed this closer to the edge as a marker.

"You must jump over this to be safe. Lars, it would be best if you were to go first."

Lars grimaced. It was no great distance but the sight of the blackness below was too much. Colour drained from his face and his mouth went dry. "I'm not confident I can make it," he croaked.

"You can do it," Kaplyn reassured him. "Look how well you did in the wrestling, and you have lost a lot of weight since then."

Lars rolled his eyes as Lomar tied the rope about his waist. Then Lomar and Vastra braced themselves. Lars took a couple of steps back where he paused, judging the distance. Then he ran and jumped, sailing over the gap and easily clearing the marker, but he landed badly and toppled to one side. Kaplyn grabbed his shirt and pulled him down onto the bridge.

"Close your eyes."

Lars did not need telling twice. Beneath Kaplyn's hand he was rigid with fear.

"Now stand slowly and let me guide you across," Kaplyn said.

By the time they had crossed, Lars was shaking. Away from the edge, he sat down as if his legs would no longer support him and he simply sat there, sucking in lungfuls of air, trying to calm himself.

Once Kaplyn was sure that Lars was all right, he returned for the others. First, they threw their equipment across. Kaplyn ferried these to Lars and then gave him one end of the safety rope to help the others to cross. Both Lomar and Vastra crossed without incident, although the experience clearly shook them.

As soon as Vastra's nerves settled, he re-lit the candle that he had been forced to extinguish before the crossing. He judged that they had been walking now for half a day.

Nobody wanted to stop for a rest; their fear of the dark pit was too great. Setting off, Lars glanced back, hoping there would be an easier exit upon their return.

Chapter 26
Onward and Downward

It took only a short while to reach the opposite cavern wall where they discovered another tunnel leading down. They continued, letting the slope carry them forwards.

Once more they found themselves mesmerised by the constant drudgery of walking within the confined space and there seemed to be no end to the tunnel. Walking became mechanical; tiredness dogged their every step until they longed for a change in their surroundings. The farther they went the greater became their fear. However, just when they felt that they could go no further, the tunnel opened into a small cavern with several tunnels branching from it.

"Which tunnel is the way forward?" Lomar groaned. He looked weary and constantly adjusted the weight of his pack on his back, trying to find a more comfortable position.

Kaplyn looked uncertainly at each tunnel in turn, but none of the five tunnels that the others could see caught his attention. Above them was a sixth passageway, considerably smaller than the others and, like the bridge, the chances of stumbling upon this one was remote. It was at least eight feet above the ground. However, something about this passageway held his attention; it looked darker than the others did.

"That one up there," he said finally. "I feel strongly that's the one, but..." he did not complete the sentence.

"It must be the right one," Vastra interrupted. "There is no tunnel there—I mean we can't see one," he corrected.

Lars and Lomar confirmed that they too could not see it and, once again, it seemed as if the true path had been deliberately hidden from anyone without the pendant.

Lars saw Kaplyn's look of concern. "Is something wrong?" he asked.

"Something's not quite right," Kaplyn told them truthfully. "But I'm not sure what."

"Give me the pendant," Vastra insisted once more. "I will recognise if there is a trap."

Vastra's persistence annoyed Kaplyn, but a nagging doubt remained.

"If there was a spell I would see it, wouldn't I?" he asked.

Vastra's reluctance to speak was answer enough.

"No—there isn't a trap," Kaplyn stated flatly. He sensed that the danger was down the tunnel rather than at the entrance. In the quiet that followed, the torches hissed and crackled.

"There's only one thing for it," he decided, removing his pack. "I'll explore a short way." He discarded his pack and climbed to the tunnel's entrance, using protruding rocks for handholds. At the entrance he paused, searching its depths. He held a torch aloft and looked inside. The tunnel walls were bare, but he was certain that this was the correct passageway for he was experiencing a faint pull that urged him to enter.

With a firm resolve he thrust the flaming brand into the hole, causing shadows to leap back as if scorched. The tunnel was empty as far as he could see, but in the distance, the darkness waited as if daring him to enter. Cautiously he pulled himself in and it was so small he had to crawl. After only a short distance, he felt his muscles stiffen as though he were crawling through thick treacle. He could not easily go back for he could not turn; he was irrevocably committed to going on. Pushing harder, he continued, fearing all the while that he had triggered a trap. He was about to give up and call for help when all at once he felt as though a great weight had been removed from his shoulders, and he was through whatever had constrained him.

He paused, panting hard. His eyes were wide as he stared expectantly into the gloom, but nothing happened, and he collected his wits. It had been a barrier and nothing more and, upon reflection, it had felt similar to the one he had encountered outside Tanel, the Eldric city.

He could no longer hear the others, even though they were only a short distance away. He suddenly felt afraid. The tunnel was very narrow, and he had to continue to find a place to turn around. As he went, the foul reeking smoke from his torch billowed about him.

Soon the tunnel abruptly widened, allowing him to stand. He could see little ahead, and it appeared that this tunnel went on for some distance. Being alone was eerie and he dreaded the return, knowing that as he crawled back, he would not be able to see anything behind him. Shuddering, he quickly re-entered the tunnel knowing that if he delayed, his courage might fail.

As swiftly as he could, he retraced his way until he could see the others once more. They appeared to be standing still, as if frozen in comic pantomime. He crawled the final few feet, experiencing once more the resistance and the sudden snap as he reached the larger chamber.

To his relief, as soon as he left the invisible barrier, he could hear the others speaking clearly. "There is nothing up here, Vastra," he said climbing down. "However, there is a barrier of some sort ahead. Like the one we experienced, Lars, entering Tanel."

"We must be close," Vastra decided. His candle showed that about one quarter of the day remained of their first day underground. "We need to remain here for a while."

The others were none too pleased with the prospect and, with reluctance, they removed their packs and sat down. Vastra informed them that they had to remain there for approximately half a day to be certain they were safe. They decided to use the time to rest while taking turns to stand guard.

They were too afraid to sleep, and wearily they waited for the allotted time to pass, speaking in low tones and keeping a watchful eye on the candle that seemed to take an age to burn down to Vastra's mark. When it was finally time to go, it suddenly seemed too soon. With a mixture of feelings, they arose, tired and stiff. Shouldering their packs, they looked to Kaplyn to lead the way.

He climbed the short way to the tunnel and pushed his pack into the opening. To the others, it looked strange to see the pack then Kaplyn disappear into solid rock. As Kaplyn crawled along the tunnel, something again restrained him, but this time he was ready, and he made quick progress to the wider part of the tunnel. Soon the others joined him, relief that they were through evident upon their weary faces.

"I'll be glad when we are out of this place," Lars said, brushing himself down. A fine layer of grey dust covered them all.

"What was the significance of the barrier?" Lomar asked.

"Possibly this part of the tunnel exists within other worlds as well as our own," Vastra replied quietly. Impatient to be off, he hoisted his pack onto his skinny frame as he spoke. "This is a place of great peril and now more than ever we must hurry. There is not much time left and we must be back through the barrier before this day is over."

A resonant booming echoed once more from deep within the mountain. The suddenness of the sound caused them to jump, and they looked about fearfully, drawing their weapons. It was much louder than before, as if the barrier had somehow muffled it. An echo rolled like thunder beneath their feet.

"And what does the barrier keep in?" Lars questioned.

Lars' tale of Baldor, the giant imprisoned by the gods, came unbidden to Kaplyn's mind. Silence returned, but this was an uncomfortable quiet, which seemed to be waiting to be broken.

Lacking enthusiasm, they collected their belongings and proceeded down the tunnel, plunging steeply into the mountain's heart. The dark within this passageway somehow seemed more sinister as it hungrily devoured the light from their torches, withdrawing only slowly as they approached, as if toying with them.

For some time, they walked until Kaplyn halted them. Ahead he could see another opening and he wanted to check it out, knowing that he was in some way protected by the pendant. He glanced at his sword; it was shining with an intense blue hue. Somewhere ahead, danger threatened.

Warily he advanced to stand before the entrance, peering within without allowing too much light through, but he could not see anything. Slowly he brought the torch forward and the view that met him was overpowering. He was standing on a ledge, running across their path and below his feet the ground simply disappeared into gloom, marking the edge of a vast cavern; the like of which he doubted any man had seen or dreamt of before. The floor was a long way below him.

Gigantic multi-coloured stalactites, as large as the tallest building, dominated his view. Many of these joined with equally large stalagmites, creating uneven warped columns as if this was truly a temple in the dreams of a forgotten god. Crystals trapped within these ancient rocks glittered in his torchlight hinting at a vast wealth in gems, hidden since the dawn of time.

Summoning courage, he leant forward trying to see the ground far below. Shadows raced across his view, and he slowed his arm to see any sudden movements.

When he raised the flaming torch further aloft, he gasped in awe. The others had become impatient and, one by one, they joined him on the ledge.

"What is it?" Lars hissed uncertainly. He held his axe in readiness before him.

Kaplyn did not reply. Instead, he moved the torch once more. As if by command the shadows retreated, scolded by the encroaching light. Before them, phantoms leapt about the cave like long lost creatures from the distant past. It seemed that a prehistoric battle was being re-enacted as shadows and light competed for dominance. Huge shambling shapes formed, while smaller shadows darted from column to column. Larger shadows fell on smaller ones, devouring them, only to flicker and disappear as the torchlight trapped them into oblivion and, as the light marched triumphantly onwards, the darkness slowly reappeared in patches, growing into huge dark masses once more. Every so often they half-fancied that they recognised a shape, but when they looked back it seemed to dissolve in front of their eyes.

Vastra snorted derisively, "We must press on; there is no time for games."

As though in response to the sorcerer's outburst, a rumbling again resounded through the giant cave and the ground beneath their feet shook. In the distance, a white flash lit the cave, causing the shadows to retreat. The light lingered before dimming, releasing the shadows that quickly became master of their domain once more.

They stood before the immense hall in silence, too afraid to speak. Eventually in a low tone, Kaplyn broke the spell binding them. "What in Allund was that, Vastra?" he asked.

Vastra shook his head, continuing to stare.

"There's only one way we will find out," Lomar announced, gesturing that they should proceed, and they followed the narrow ledge, which led to a steep stair.

As they descended the light erupted twice more, each time followed by a sonorous boom. It was difficult to see anything, and the sudden light made their vision poor. Each time they waited until their eyes became accustomed to the gloom, severely hindering their progress.

It took them quite some time to reach the cavern floor where Kaplyn paused, uncertain which way to continue. At that moment another tremor started, deep within the bowels of the earth and again the men froze in fear.

Chapter 27
Nemesis in the Dark

The tremor built in intensity and Kaplyn glanced at the others. He caught Lars' gaze and saw fear flash across his face. Before Kaplyn could say anything to put the other man at ease, a subterranean breeze gusted, causing their torches to flicker. An eerie moan followed on its heels, causing a shiver to run down his spine.

"That tremor felt stronger," Lars declared, gripping his torch so tightly that his knuckles showed white.

Kaplyn shook his head. "It just felt stronger now we are on the cavern floor," though he couldn't help but glance over his shoulder at the steep stairs.

As before, a light erupted from the cave's heart, causing him to squint against the sudden glare.

By his side, Lomar raised an arm, shielding his eyes.

"Are you all right?" Kaplyn asked softly.

Lomar nodded, lowering his arm as darkness returned.

Vastra strode up, his mere presence demanding as always. "Which way is it?"

A shiver ran down Kaplyn's spine and a memory of a half-forgotten dream surfaced, but then was gone.

Kaplyn recovered. "We must be close," he answered.

"You fool. You have no idea what lies ahead. Give me the pendant before you kill us all," Vastra snapped, thrusting out a hand.

At the venom in Vastra's voice, Kaplyn's heart raced but, remaining calm, he regarded the outstretched hand with contempt.

"We've said Kaplyn will keep the pendant, Vastra, so don't push us on this matter," Lars interrupted through gritted teeth.

Vastra muttered and walked to the rear of the group.

"Thanks," Kaplyn smiled at the other man, truly appreciative of his support. Lars nodded by way of return.

Kaplyn turned his attention to finding the path. The light from their torches was feeble, and ahead he could barely make out the outline of a few scattered boulders and a tall column of rock. The air smelt damp and oppressive, as though being deep within the mountain's heart the very weight of the rock above was forcing the darkness upon them.

"We need to go that way," Kaplyn decided.

Lomar squinted, looking in the direction Kaplyn was pointing. "How do you know?"

"I feel that the pendant's guiding me," Kaplyn replied.

"You could be mistaken," Vastra responded sourly. Kaplyn held back a retort, as the other man continued. "The pendant's no trifle. Only a sorcerer would know its true intent."

"And that would be you of course?" Lars said, a dangerous glint in his eye.

Vastra snorted, raising his hands in mock submission, stepping back from the big man, a lopsided smile on his thin face. "So be it, but when things go wrong, you remember my council." At that moment, the ground rocked again, closely followed by an ominous rumbling.

The men glanced at each other and Vastra's mouth opened but closed again when Kaplyn glared at him. The tremor seemed threatening so soon after Vastra's warning.

Kaplyn led the way. After only a short while, he stumbled on a rock and had to take a couple of extra steps to regain his balance. Raising his torch, he saw a jagged channel, intercepting their path from his right. Almost in front of him it changed course, pointing roughly the way they were going.

Kaplyn followed this, picking his way amongst the clutter of rock and pebbles. Vastra kicked a pebble and a loud clatter reverberated around the cave.

"Don't do that," Lars cautioned.

Vastra flashed him an icy look.

Kaplyn sighed. Looking across the channel, his eyes sought anything that might help him decide the correct route, but the light failed to reach the other side. The channel was not deep, but he could have injured himself if he had stumbled into it in the dark.

A short while later something else appeared ahead, slowly materialising from the gloom. Kaplyn slowed, allowing his eyes time to decipher its shape.

Lomar was the first to realise what it was. "A *tree*? *Here*, but that's impossible."

Kaplyn closed the distance, reaching out his hand.

"Don't touch it," Lars cautioned, grabbing Kaplyn's shoulder.

"Don't worry," Kaplyn said, shrugging his arm away. "It's a fossil, that's all."

His fingers caressed the bark. It felt smooth as glass, and it shone like ebony.

"A tree couldn't grow so deep underground—could it?" Lars asked.

"Perhaps, at one time, there was an opening in the mountain above." Kaplyn looked up but could see nothing. "Also, this channel we've been following could have been a river."

"My people have a legend concerning the origins of life," Lars said. "In the beginning of time the world was bare, except for a single tree. Its roots grew deep, feeding on the earth's life force so the tree became endowed with power and its fruit blessed with life."

Stepping forward he touched the old bark, his fingers trembling. "From the first fruit came the gods. They looked upon the world and to them it must have been like a blank page, waiting to be written upon. They marvelled at the tree, wishing to make life of their own. As the fruit grew, they moulded plants and animals, making all the living creatures we see today. If this is that tree then we are blessed this day," He trailed off into silence.

"Look at the ends of the branches," Lomar said.

Kaplyn looked where he was pointing. Several gnarled shapes, hung from slender twigs. At one time, they could have been fruit, but now they were shrivelled and petrified like the rest of the tree. Lomar reached up, trying to pull one away, but it defied him, clinging stubbornly to the branch.

All at once he leapt back as though scalded. A cry tore from his lips as a light erupted from deep within the trunk, swiftly spreading through the tree.

They shielded their eyes, falling back. Then the light dimmed as darkness spread from the trunk's centre, devouring the light until they were plunged into night.

They looked at each other dumbfounded; none dared to venture an explanation. Deep within the ground, Kaplyn felt rumbling that swiftly built to a terrifying crescendo. Then the rumbling faded, leaving a deathly silence.

All at once whispering started and its suddenness made Kaplyn jump. He spun around, seeking its source, but it was all around them. It grew in volume, becoming more terrifying until all around him voices shrieked and wailed. He half fancied he felt warm breath on his face and neck, and he cringed in terror.

"What is it?" Lars wailed by his side. He stumbled and almost fell as another tremor shook the ground. Kaplyn reached out to steady the other man.

"Hush," Vastra said, holding up a hand.

As though upon his command, the voices subsided to a gentle whisper.

"What's happening?" Lars snapped. "This place is not meant for mortals."

Kaplyn felt frozen to the spot, with the memory of the voices continuing to haunt him.

"We should go," Lomar agreed, looking about for the quickest way out. "This place is guarded by the dead!"

"Nonsense," Vastra hissed. "We must wait. The time is nearly right and the dead, if it is the dead we hear, cannot harm us."

Kaplyn was just about to agree that they should leave when a glow drew his eyes back to the tree. Within the trunk light blossomed, slowly unfurling along its length. The intensity was less than before and he stood transfixed, spellbound by its beauty.

With night as its backdrop, the tree stood out alone, as if cast from silver and ablaze in glory. By comparison, everything else that he had ever seen paled to insignificance.

"Look!" Lars declared, drawing Kaplyn's gaze to where he pointed. Above Lomar's head a delicate bud appeared, glowing in its own light. Slowly it unfurled, revealing a myriad of tiny petals, and the scent of spring filled the air.

Kaplyn stepped closer. Within the blossom a fruit was developing, swiftly swelling to maturity, holding captive in its heart the silver radiance from the tree. Glancing over his shoulder Kaplyn saw a similar bud growing further away. His curiosity aroused he went to investigate. It, too, radiated a silver glow.

Gradually, the light in the tree began to fade, leaving the fruit shining brightly upon slender branches, like tiny lanterns.

With trepidation, Kaplyn reached out to pluck the fruit, which fell easily into his outstretched palms. It was light and warmed his hand. About him, the light dimmed further, and he looked to see the black patch appear at the tree's heart, slowly spreading outwards, tracing the white light's route until the tree was plunged into night. Within the blackness, Kaplyn's fruit continued to glow softly.

Eager to show his prize, Kaplyn returned to the others, only to find that Vastra also held a fruit, which he quickly concealed within his jerkin, blotting out its radiance. To Kaplyn's mind, Vastra's eyes smouldered but then abruptly the look was gone.

Kaplyn sensed a change occurring and instinctively knew it was too late to return the way they had come. He searched for another exit but all he could see, beyond the faint pool of light from their torches, was a wall of shadow.

Just then the whispering started again. Its suddenness made him jump and his heart lurched.

Crying, "Follow me," he leapt away from the tree. Glancing over his shoulder he confirmed that the others were indeed following. The faint pull from the pendant guided him and he hoped beyond hope that he was right to trust it. They were running in the opposite direction to the way they had come, and he did not know where the pendant was leading them.

His fear drove him on, adding impetus to his weary limbs, whilst all about him the whispering grew in volume until he could hear tormented souls gibbering and shrieking, as though the world was ending. Unlike before, the voices did not fade, and instead the clamour increased, swiftly becoming unbearable—so much so that Kaplyn feared invisible demons might set upon them. Cries of anguish sounded to his right and he flinched, yelping in terror as the echoes disorientated him.

To his relief, a cavern wall materialised from the dark and he could make out the silhouette of a tunnel. Instinctively he headed towards it, hoping they would make it in time.

Glancing back, he saw Lars labouring at the rear of the group. He suddenly yelped, flinging his torch away.

"*Karlam! Aid me*," he yelled. His legs and arms pounded as he sprinted to catch up. Drawing his axe from its harness across his back, he desperately flayed the air as though fighting an invisible foe.

Kaplyn, not looking where he was going, stumbled on a rock and nearly fell. His ankle screamed in pain, but it recovered as he hobbled on. Abruptly he was within the tunnel, and he turned to await the others.

"Keep going," came Lars' scream. "Keep going!"

Kaplyn turned and fled. Almost immediately he thumped into something invisible and was held trapped like a fly in a web. He forced himself on, driving his arms and pumping his legs; ever so slowly, his limbs responded.

Then he was free, and he staggered forward. Someone tumbled into him and together they fell, landing in a sprawl, driving the air from Kaplyn's lungs, and cracking his knees on the stone floor. Wincing, he hurried to his feet. Lomar had fallen over him, and he helped the albino up just as Vastra appeared by their side, panting heavily, closely followed by Lars.

Kaplyn looked back the way they had come. Lars' torch lay spluttering on the ground, the flame refusing to die. All at once, it rose uncannily and danced about the cavern, as if held aloft by ghostly hands. Abruptly, it was flung at them, and, with a loud resounding crack, it struck the sidewall of the cavern, causing them to recoil, crying aloud in terror.

"We are safe!" Kaplyn shouted. "We are through the barrier."

"Something cut me," Lars complained. "Look!" He showed them the back of his leg. Through a tear in his trousers, blood welled up and trickled down his calf. Lomar knelt and, using a cloth from his pouch, dabbed the wound. It was deep but clean, and Lomar tied the cloth in a makeshift bandage.

"We should keep going," Kaplyn said. Although he had told them they were safe he didn't yet feel it. Behind him the tunnel continued, but to where he did not know.

He led them on with Lars hobbling to keep up. Finally, Kaplyn could go no further. He sat upon the ground and the others flopped down beside him.

Lars was trying to re-tie his bandage that had partly unravelled. Lomar brushed his hand away and set to helping. The big man kept looking nervously at Vastra's face and the livid red scar across his cheek. Kaplyn remembered all too clearly the imp inflicting the wound several days ago. It looked infected and still painful.

"You needn't worry," Vastra sneered. "Your wound is clean and will heal in time."

Lars looked away and Kaplyn sensed that he felt ashamed of having revealed his fear.

"Where are we? I thought we would be leaving the same way we came," Lomar asked, looking about. Kaplyn was relieved that he had spoken for it broke the tension.

Kaplyn shook his head. "We didn't have time to escape that way. The climb up the stair would have taken ages. I sensed though this was the right direction, and at least there was a barrier. That seems to mark the entrance or exit."

"I hope this tunnel leads to a way out," Lomar replied, sounding glum.

It was a point that was also worrying Kaplyn, but there was no going back.

"We were lucky!" Vastra exclaimed.

"If this is your idea of luck, I think it is time we parted company," Lars growled.

Vastra ignored him. "The candle must have burned more slowly than I'd expected. We probably entered the great cavern later than anticipated."

"You mean we've been walking for nearly two days!" Lars exclaimed.

Kaplyn was still holding his fruit that had crystallised and was now firm to the touch.

"Can I see it?" Lomar asked.

"Of course. We all helped to get it," Kaplyn answered.

"It's warm," Lomar said, cupping it in his hand.

"Can I see it?" Lars asked, holding out his hand.

Lomar handed it to him, and Lars held it up. Its radiance softly illuminated his face.

He gave it back to Kaplyn who placed it in his breast tunic pocket. If Vastra still had his crystal he could not tell, but it was unlikely he had lost it after all their efforts.

"What's the significance of the crystal, and how will it help to find the Eldric?" Lomar asked.

Kaplyn expected Vastra to remain silent and was surprised when he spoke.

"Lars' legend may contain an element of truth," he conceded. "The tree's roots had grown deep into the ground, tapping the earth's lifeblood. The crystal contains magic in its purest form. In a way, it is like a kara-stone, but instead of being an empty vessel for magic, it is full."

"Can the magic be used?" Lars asked, massaging his leg.

Vastra shook his head. "I don't think so, not at least in any way that I know."

"Then how will it help to find the Eldric?" Kaplyn asked.

"I can open a gateway between the worlds," Vastra admitted. "But I cannot hold it open for long, and certainly not long enough to search that world for the Eldric. The crystal contains pure magic. If it was placed in a gateway between worlds then the gateway would not be able to collapse, for if it did it would destroy the magic in the crystal, and that is not possible."

"Searching worlds could take years," Kaplyn said, feeling disappointed. After all their effort, he had hoped finding the Eldric would be easier.

"And we may *never* find them," Lomar stated.

Vastra merely shrugged.

After a brief rest, Kaplyn decided it was time to press on. Wearily they rose and set off. Almost immediately, the tunnel started to slope gently upwards.

"At last," Kaplyn grinned. "If it's going up then it must be the way out."

For hours, they continued. The passageway became a maze of tunnels, and, without Kaplyn's guidance, they would have very quickly become hopelessly lost. If they had tried to remember the way back it would have been impossible, for each twist and turn looked like the last and the farther they went, the more frequently the tunnels branched.

Their earlier hope that the tunnel was going up was soon dashed though as it dipped down. This trend continued so that the tunnel in one instance led hopefully up while at the next it plunged alarmingly down. Eventually they could go no further and sat or lay exhausted, very quickly falling asleep, too tired to eat or set a watch.

Some short while later Kaplyn partly awoke. His mind was fog-filled, and he thought he saw Vastra tracing a rune in the air as though in practice. Abruptly, there was a faint light, but it swiftly faded. Kaplyn was far too tired to question Vastra and promptly fell asleep, but a nagging fear haunted his dreams. He did not trust Vastra.

Chapter 28
Escape

Footfalls caused Kaplyn to awaken. He felt exhausted. Vastra knelt by his side, a torch held aloft.

"We should be going," he said.

Kaplyn had a headache and could barely think. Putting his hands beneath him he climbed to his feet.

"Get the others up," he said. He could not fathom why Vastra seemed so awake and refreshed when he felt so groggy. He listened for a moment to Lars' complaining as he, too, was awakened.

Kaplyn rummaged in his bag and found some hardtack biscuits and dried meat. His canteen was about a third full; the water was cool on his palate and helped him to swallow the rations. The others ate in silence while Vastra paced about them, eager to leave.

"Which way is it?" Lars asked. Kaplyn looked around, uncertain. He had never thought to mark the tunnel before sleeping and one end looked the same as the other. He felt a faint pull from the pendant.

"That way," he said.

Lars looked to where he was pointing. "Are you sure?"

Kaplyn nodded.

Once they had eaten, Kaplyn led the way. They came across a sequence of forks in the path and at each one Kaplyn felt the guidance from the pendant grow less and it was becoming increasingly hard to decide which way to go.

After walking for some time, Lomar announced he could hear something ahead. Kaplyn listened and became aware of a distant roaring.

"It sounds like water," Lars offered.

"Probably a subterranean river," Vastra agreed.

As they continued, the sound became louder. Ahead, Kaplyn could see a change in the tunnel and then it opened into a cavern. Before him was a small pool and a waterfall cascaded noisily into this. What worried him most though, was that apart from the way in, there was no other obvious exit.

They had come to a dead end.

"Which way do we go now?" Vastra demanded.

Kaplyn ignored him; instead, his gaze kept going back to the waterfall. He was afraid to admit it to the others, but he was no longer sure of the direction. For some time now he had felt nothing from the pendant, and to add to his frustration the waterfall's constant thunder was making his headache worse. Uncertainly, he approached the pool to study the area better and as he came alongside it, to his relief, he discovered the way.

"The path is here," he exclaimed excitedly, pointing at the side of the waterfall. The others crowded around to get a better view, relief evident upon their faces. On the other side of the pool, by the side of the waterfall and cut into the rock face, were stone steps, worn smooth by years of constant erosion. The steps led upwards but disappeared into the waterfall.

"How do we get up there?" Lars asked eyeing the curtain of water.

"You could always go back," Vastra snapped. Kaplyn knew that to do so would mean death. "We will wait here for you," Vastra continued, glaring at the other man.

Lars shuddered and looked toward Kaplyn for guidance.

"Pass me a rope," Kaplyn said. "I'll climb the steps. If I can get up there, then I can help to pull the rest of you up."

Lomar took a coil of rope from a bag but slung it over his shoulder rather than offering it to Kaplyn. "Let me try," he offered. "I frequently climbed in the forest, so I should be able to master this."

Lomar undressed, while Kaplyn helped the others to pile their packs against the rock wall. Without further ado, he sat on the edge of the pool and lowered himself into the water.

"That's unbelievably cold," he gasped.

The pool was evidently deep, and, as soon as he entered, he was forced to swim. Kaplyn watched as he hauled himself out on the other side, flopping wetly onto the first step.

As soon as he stepped within the full force of the water, he lost his grip. His feet were washed out from under him, and he fell into the water, nearly cracking his head on the lower steps as he fell.

Surfacing seconds later, coughing and spluttering, he pulled himself out. He was game to try again but after several attempts he sat on the side of the pool shivering, his chest heaving. "It's impossible," he gasped, wiping his eyes with the palm of his hand.

"There's a rock sticking out higher up," Lars declared, pointing. Above the waterfall, Kaplyn could see the rock, mainly by the shadow it cast. There was a deep V in its front face where it had cracked sometime in the past.

"If we can get a rope over it, we would at least have something to help us climb," Lars continued.

Kaplyn fetched the rope, while Lomar dried himself before putting on his clothes. He was shivering uncontrollably.

"Light a fire," Kaplyn suggested. "Use some of the torches; we should have enough."

"I'll do that," Vastra offered and borrowing Lars' axe he splintered one of the brands for kindling.

While Vastra was occupied, Lars took the rope and tied a rock to one end. Once finished he stood by the pool's edge and started to swing the rope in an arc. He let it swing a couple of times before heaving it into the air. Immediately the rock fell out of the makeshift knot, clattering noisily against the far cavern wall while the rope simply fell into the pool.

Shivering, Lomar asked for the rope. He took one end and started tying a large knot.

"This would be easier if my fingers weren't frozen," he complained. As he wound the knot, he tested it for weight and once satisfied handed it back to Lars.

Kaplyn watched as the big man threw the rope several times and each time it came a little closer to hitting its mark, but annoyingly it missed and dropped into the pool below. Being wet helped and, all at once, Lars managed to cast it over the protrusion. Carefully he drew in the slack; fortune was with them, and the knot held fast.

"I'll try this time," Kaplyn offered.

"Keep it taut or it might come away," Lars cautioned, handing the rope to Kaplyn.

Kaplyn nodded. He stripped and, taking the rope in one hand, entered the pool. The cold took his breath away and he gasped out loud. Quickly he swam to the other side where he clambered out, grazing his knee on the rock. He didn't want to stop and think about it so immediately started to climb. To his embarrassment, his foot slipped off the very first step and he banged his already sore knee. Swearing, he swayed on the spot, but the tension of the rope held him.

Climbing, he soon had to move directly into the waterfall and the torrent hit him like a sledgehammer. Desperately he clung on to the rope with water buffeting him mercilessly and, for grim moments, he could not move, and his fingers started to slip. Summoning all his strength he reached up and, slowly, hand over hand, started to climb.

Just when he felt that he could endure no more, the force of water slackened, and he looked up to see that he was beneath a slight overhang. Above him was the lip of a tunnel and gratefully he pulled himself in.

He was alone but did not feel afraid. The air felt fresh and with mounting hope he realised they must be nearly out of the terrible tunnels. Immediately his spirits soared. He called excitedly down for one of the others to come up before sitting down with the rope looped across his shoulders, bracing his heels as best he could on the rough floor.

A mumbled reply, barely audible above the constant roar of the waterfall, was the signal that someone was ready. The rope became taut as whoever it was, entered the pool and then briefly went slack. Kaplyn felt the rope tighten and he helped the climber, pulling up on the rope. Its coarseness stung his hands, but he ignored it.

Eventually Lars' drenched head and shoulders appeared in the tunnel entrance. With eyes screwed shut he spat out water, spluttering for breath. Kaplyn helped him into the tunnel where the other man sat shivering, hugging his chest for warmth. Next, they hoisted the packs, and then it was Lomar and then Vastra's turn to climb.

By the time they were all together, they were exhausted. Hurriedly they dressed and then Kaplyn lay on the ground, using his pack as a pillow. His belly growled angrily.

"I'm famished," he declared.

"Me too," Lars answered.

"Let's see what food is left," Kaplyn suggested, sitting up and looking into his pack. The others emptied their packs, but the pile of food was pitiful.

"We should share what's left," Kaplyn suggested. "It will do for one final meal."

When they had dished it out, each looked despondently at their allotted portion.

"I think we are nearly out of the caves," Kaplyn announced, trying to lift their spirits. "Smell the air; it's fresher."

Lomar breathed deeply. "I think he's right." He immediately dug deep into his pack, retrieving his kara-stone. Passing a hand over it, he spoke words of power. It flared brightly and they laughed with pleasure as warmth engulfed them. The heat helped to partially dry them while they ate.

"Where does this tunnel come out?" Lomar asked.

"Thrace, I think," Kaplyn replied excitedly. "That's assuming we've travelled right through the mountain and come out the other side." It was difficult to believe but no one expressed any doubts.

"Will we be welcome in Thrace?" Lars asked.

"Of course. There is trade between Allund and Thrace so we should be welcome," Kaplyn offered. However, he failed to mention his own concerns; his father had often threatened his marriage to one of Thrace's princesses.

"A clean, warm bed, that's all I want—and perhaps a flagon of beer!" Lars replied, grinning broadly.

Kaplyn smiled back. They were lucky to escape with their lives and for that he was more than thankful. He removed the crystal from his breast pocket and looked at it, still glowing with a pale, silver light.

"We've done it," he declared triumphantly, looking at the others in turn. They smiled back at him, their eyes shining with pleasure. "Let's press on and get out of here."

They soon left the sounds of the waterfall behind them and the comparative silence, apart from their footfalls, was a relief. After a while Lomar extinguished the kara-stone to conserve his energy while they still had some torches.

With the prospect of leaving, Kaplyn quickened their pace. However, to his frustration, Vastra hung back, forcing them to stop for him. Calling ahead to Lars and Lomar to wait, he turned to retrace his steps to look for him. All at once, he saw the light from Vastra's torch bobbing up and down, coming towards them.

Kaplyn felt a premonition of fear as Vastra appeared around a corner; he seemed to ooze confidence with every step. All at once, the imp was beside him, floating eerily in the air. Their torches flared blue, warning him too late of the demon's presence. Kaplyn drew his sword, which glowed brightly, and behind him, he heard Lars and Lomar drawing their weapons as they started to return towards him. He waved them away.

"Go! Run down the tunnel, the exit must be near by now," he said backing slowly away from Vastra and the imp.

Lars paused uncertainly, "I will not leave."

Vastra and the imp halted a few yards from Kaplyn. The imp's tongue flickered in and out, its eyes fixed on Kaplyn's blade.

"Go!" Kaplyn said. "They cannot harm me. I have the pendant and that negates his magic."

Vastra smiled maliciously and started to chant a spell. Kaplyn heard Lars and Lomar turn to leave.

"We will wait for you at the exit," Lars called back.

Kaplyn needed to distract Vastra; he lunged at the imp, which leapt back shrieking angrily. To Kaplyn's surprise, the sorcerer stopped chanting and started to laugh, "You fool," he said. "You have walked right into my trap."

Suddenly, from behind Kaplyn, a scream rent the air. He recognised Lomar's cry followed by terrified shouts from Lars.

Kaplyn turned, leaping down the tunnel, silently cursing himself for trusting Vastra. As he ran, his torch spluttered and the flame threatened to expire, making it difficult to see. Turning a corner, the first thing he saw were his friends' torches. The tunnel had opened into a small cavern. Framed within it were the two men. He risked glancing back over his shoulder, but Vastra was some way back, walking towards them as though he had no need to hurry.

As Kaplyn approached Lars and Lomar, he realised that they were struggling to escape, as though unseen hands held them fast.

"Stay back," Lomar screamed.

Kaplyn paused scant yards away, uncertain what to do. Agony contorted their faces and their eyes blazed. Kaplyn looked on helplessly. Lars was clearly terrified and Lomar cried out in anguish. Kaplyn turned—at last determined to kill Vastra, who had quietly come up behind him and was watching his friends' agony as if it did not concern him.

Seeing Kaplyn's expression the sorcerer guessed his intent. "Killing me would do no good," he said raising his hands in a gesture of submission. "The spell is his, not mine."

Kaplyn was desperate to do something but felt completely powerless. He shrugged off his pack, throwing it down. "Let them go!" he screamed, raising his sword.

Vastra did not reply and Kaplyn advanced, realising with mounting frustration the futility of the situation. If it was the imp's spell and he attacked, then it would simply retreat down the tunnel. On the other hand, if he threatened Vastra, then he would simply make the imp vanish.

Without warning he lunged at the sorcerer choosing that as the lesser of the two evils. The imp intervened, appearing many times larger than it actually was. Sharp talons raked the air scant inches before Kaplyn's face, forcing him to duck while behind the imp, Vastra backed cautiously away.

Kaplyn attacked the imp, but as he had suspected it simply retreated, hissing as it went.

A cry from behind reminded him of his friends' plight. He risked glancing around. To his horror, they had stopped moving and their exposed flesh was turning grey.

A desperate thought came to him, the pendent stopped magic from working. Perhaps he could use it to save them.

With an exasperated cry, he threw his torch at Vastra and leapt back towards Lars and Lomar. Still holding his sword, he placed a hand on each of their shoulders, realising that his back was now vulnerable.

The instant his hands touched them, Kaplyn felt a cold chill run through his body and the icy touch of fear stopped his heart.

In anguish, he screamed.

Agony lanced through the very fibre of his being. The pendant's chain seared his skin. He could not move. Gritting his teeth, his feet felt as though they were being crushed. He was being turned to stone and the pendant was not preventing it.

The crystal in his pocket flared and he felt a brief respite but then that was gone. Already his legs had been transformed to stone. His mind retreated to its farthest corner and then Kaplyn knew no more.

Chapter 29
A Sour Victory

Vastra walked around the three men, looking into Kaplyn's eyes. He was struggling against the spell's effect, but Vastra knew that it was pointless. The spell was very powerful and not easily defeated. Looking at Lars and Lomar he saw that their skin was already grey and even at a distance, he knew their flesh would be cold to touch; gradually they were being transformed into stone. A spell blocked the exit to the cavern. This was the secret he had kept ever since Kaplyn had returned with the pendant, for it was clearly described on that.

He had won, but it had been close. For a long time, he had feared Kaplyn would somehow read the script on the pendant, revealing the final trap laid by the Eldric so long ago. The pendant would destroy the spell after it had run its course, but sadly it, too, would be destroyed in the process. The spell was to trap anyone who accidentally came this way, and the pendant was the key to unlocking it.

Vastra walked around the tableau and then a scream from Kaplyn rent the air. The sound was inhuman and Vastra covered his ears. Abruptly the crystal in Kaplyn's breast pocket flared. Vastra cried out, shielding his eyes. By his side, the imp also screamed as the light engulfed it. With a terrifying wail, it disappeared into nothingness, its screech echoing back and forth along the tunnel.

Vastra cried out in terror. Blinded by the light he had no way of knowing what was happening. *Not again! Was he to be robbed of his victory when he could almost taste it?*

He fell to the floor, too afraid to breathe while power raged all around him like a torrent. Desperately he tried to press his body into the ground. At any moment, he expected to feel Kaplyn's blade pierce his flesh. He cried out for mercy; knowing that he did not deserve it.

Long moments passed as he lay whimpering on the cold floor. Gradually realisation dawned that the clash of powers had subsided When he dared to look, his sobs turned to whimpers of relief. The transformation was complete and only statues, carved as if from the very granite of the mountain, remained.

Rising, his victory suddenly seemed sour. The clash of powers had been fearful, and he wondered what had happened. Perhaps Kaplyn's crystal had fought the Eldric spell, but what then had become of it?

Removing his dagger, he tried to dislodge enough stone from what had become of Kaplyn's breast pocket to see the crystal. The knife slipped and to his shock, pierced the statue by a thumb's depth. Snatching back the blade, silver sap from the crystal and deep red blood oozed from the wound, dripping down the statue and onto the floor. Vastra stepped back. The dripping slowed as the mixture congealed, leaving a pink scar upon Kaplyn's chest.

All at once he felt as though ghostly eyes were watching him and with a cry of terror he turned and fled, seeking the sanctuary of an open sky and the company of the living. For some while the slap of his feet upon the rock persisted, and the flickering light cast by his torch marked his erratic flight. Then, with finality, the light disappeared, and the noise faded, leaving only silence.

A cold wind gusted, helping to congeal the pool of blood as a single, final droplet, fell like a teardrop to the floor. In the darkness, the statues continued to stare into the night, their faces reflecting their final moments of fear and pain. All except Kaplyn who looked strangely resolute, as though in the transformation's final moments, he had accepted his fate.

Epilogue

As the cold light from the crystal in Kaplyn's pocket filled the chamber, the power from the Eldric spell, protecting the tunnel's exit, collided with that of the crystal. For a moment, the two forces opposed each other in a titanic clash.

The sudden surge of power sent shock waves racing through the very foundations of the universe, the repercussions of which could be felt within many worlds. At that instant, the very fabric of space and time was rent; dark tears appeared suddenly within the already weakened interval between the worlds.

In one such world, a lone spirit watched over a dying land that had once been his home. He still felt, and would always feel, the blast of dragon breath that had killed him, and knew that the memory would haunt him throughout all eternity.

Shastlan. Murderer of your people!

Forbidden the full release death should bring, he was forever doomed to walk the burnt lands of his homeland; a sad ghostly spectre whom none could ever hear, if any remained alive that is.

High overhead, in a clear blue sky, a dragon flew by. Its shadow sent a thrill of fear coursing through Shastlan's ghostly veins, prompting a thousand dreadful memories; he wailed aloud in anguish. Briefly, he wondered whether the dragons knew he was there and he looked up to see a speck disappearing over the horizon. The mere sight caused him absolute terror.

Suddenly a strange sensation swept through him. He looked about in fear, suspecting at first that the dragon had returned. Behind him, he saw a gaping void from which a cold wind blew, chilling even his spectral form. Slowly the tear opened and in a fit of self-pity, he felt the urge to step within it—to throw himself upon whatever providence awaited. He glanced back on the hell that was his home, the lush green fields, and the clean blue sky. Angrily he looked back at the jagged tear and carelessly he stepped into the darkness, disappearing inside.

Then the void was gone.

The shadow of a dragon streaked over the grass where the tear had been. For some while, the dragon continued to search for the power that it had felt and then its cry of rage and despair split the air.

Beyond the hole a world waited for its destiny to unfold; a destiny which fate had already set in motion.

In complete darkness, a being awoke.

For long moments, he pondered the darkness trying to recall distant memories. Nothing came. Only vagueness, a nagging doubt—and fear.

All at once, strange thoughts tumbled through his mind and he grabbed at the half-formed images, weeping at scenes of long-lost glory. Then came a complete memory. One that he held onto, feeding his hatred. It was the memory of being cast out from his own world, banished to this realm, a realm of hopelessness and stagnant death.

A name came to mind and with the name came more hatred.

Eldric!

All at once he remembered. Long ago, the Eldric had exiled him to this place. For eons, his tormented soul had patiently waited for a sign that he had not been forgotten. Abruptly memories coalesced and he knew who and where he was.

He was Drachar, and this was hell.

Angrily he glanced around, expecting only to see the hated and blessed night. Yet, in the distance, a tiny star blazed in glory. The lure of the star was strong, and he felt an urgency to reach it. Slowly, on unseen limbs, he felt himself moving, but to his frustration, the light failed to come closer. He continued with more haste and greater speed, willing himself towards his salvation.

Panicking, he urged himself on, knowing that here at last was a chance to escape, a scream of glee erupting from unseen lips as he raced onwards.

Then the star was gone.

He wailed aloud in abject misery, spinning around, searching for the light in vain, but only a terrible blackness remained. A forlorn feeling of loneliness stole over him, and he cursed whatever gods there were for his fate and prayed to them for release.

Sleepiness overcame him—sleep, yes sleep. Wait, his turn would come again. Then, he would be ready.

Sleep.

Drachar.

He would wait.

His time was not yet ripe but when it was, he would be ready and once more the world would know evil.

Thus, ends Legacy of the Eldric. The story continues in Dragon Rider.

The three volumes in the Prophecy of the Kings are:

Book 1 - Legacy of the Eldric
Book 2 - Dragon Rider
Book 3 - Shadow of the Demon

Visit David's Website for more information, sample chapters and reviews
http://Davidburrows.org.uk/

ENJOYED THIS BOOK?

Please post a review. Your comments are greatly appreciated. Feel free to contact me.

Facebook.com/authordavidburrows/
Twitter @davidjburrows
email: Legacyoftheeldric@blueyonder.co.uk

Also, by the same author

Drachar's Demons

Set many years before the events in the Prophecy of the Kings. A tale of the Eldric, how Drachar came to power and the Krell Wars.

Drachar, banished by his own people the Eldric, forges an unholy alliance with the demons by offering them ten thousand souls, but the demons demand one hundred thousand and without quibbling Drachar accepts. Only all-out war will deliver so many souls and the Old Enemy, Trosgarth, is his only potential ally. He must cross a land in turmoil to confront their king and persuade him to his cause. The Eldric, recognising Drachar's lust for power, must learn to battle demons and a race is on, but demons are not easily controlled and fight their summons, sending souls to Hell for eternal damnation. A conflict is brewing, and the only winner in this fight for survival is likely to be the demon hordes.

Lightning Source UK Ltd.
Milton Keynes UK
UKHW011823010223
416320UK00001B/80